IN
AN
INSTANT

ALSO BY SUZANNE REDFEARN

Hush Little Baby

No Ordinary Life

IN AN INSTANT

SUZANNE REDFEARN

LAKE UNION
PUBLISHING

Text copyright © 2020 by Suzanne Redfearn
All rights reserved.

Published by Lake Union Publishing, Seattle

www.apub.com

Amazon, the Amazon logo, and Lake Union Publishing are trademarks of Amazon. com, Inc., or its affiliates.

ISBN-13: 9781542006583
ISBN-10: 1542006589

Cover design by David Drummond

Printed in the United States of America

For Halle

PROLOGUE

Mrs. Kaminski knew.

Before it happened.

Until that day, we thought she was a psycho mom, neurotic and paranoid. Behind her back, we called her *the warden* and felt bad for Mo for having to deal with such a phobic, obsessive mother. *Sheltered* was an understatement for the way Mrs. Kaminski guarded her daughter. Birthday parties at the beach or pool were off limits unless a lifeguard was present and Mrs. Kaminski was allowed to be there as well—a fortysomething shadow lurking on the sand or at the water's edge, hovering watchfully beside the reveling twelve-year-olds. Disneyland was out of the question. Though she was a small, quiet woman, barely five feet tall with a kind smile and exceeding politeness, it was hard to believe how unyielding she was about watching over Mo.

Secretly we wondered if something traumatic had happened to Mrs. Kaminski when she was young that had made her so protective, but Mo said that wasn't it. She said her mom just believed that nobody looked after your children the way you looked after your own. It was a generous view for Mo to take, her patience far greater than any of the rest of us would have had for our moms interfering in our lives the way Mrs. Kaminski did in Mo's.

Sixth-grade science camp was when her resolve finally softened from granite to steel: slightly more malleable but not by much. Every sixth grader except Mo was going on the trip. The teacher called Mrs. Kaminski, then the principal, then my mom. It was my mom who convinced her. My dad was going as a chaperone, and he would personally watch after Mo. Perhaps it was because she believed my mom, or maybe it was because she trusted my dad, or perhaps it was because she realized she couldn't hold her iron grip forever, or maybe it was because the camp was so important to that year's curriculum. Whatever the reason, for the first time in Mo's twelve years, she was allowed to leave the nest without her mom at her side.

Since then Mrs. Kaminski has repeatedly entrusted us with her daughter, each sacred trust prefaced with assurances from my parents of "We'll take good care of her," "She's in good hands," "Mo is like a daughter to us"—throwaway platitudes I wonder about endlessly these days, questioning whether those clichéd, careless words influenced what happened or whether they were meaningless and that things would have happened the way they did regardless of what had been thoughtlessly promised beforehand.

Over the years I was entrusted to Mrs. Kaminski as well, but my parents never asked for guarantees of my safekeeping. Mo is an only child, so I was taken along as company on all the Kaminski vacations. I've been to Africa and Spain and Thailand and Alaska. My parents eagerly agreed to each invitation without the slightest hesitation or demand of reciprocal pledges of protection like those given when we took Mo. Perhaps it was assumed it went both ways. Or maybe, deep down, my parents knew the promise wouldn't be granted, which would have made the decision to allow me to join them awkward. I imagine my parents understood that Mrs. Kaminski's fears were based on deep-seated self-reflection, that she had considered the possibility of a fault rupturing or a volcano erupting or a ship sinking and knew, faced with the dire choice, she would take care of her own, and though Mo and I were close as sisters, I didn't qualify.

From my earliest memories, I can remember my sisters, my friends, and me rolling our eyes whenever Mrs. Kaminski was mentioned, how we thought she was crazy.

No one calls her crazy anymore.

She knew. Before it happened. And I wonder, How? Was it because she was a prophet, a visionary gifted with preternatural premonition? Or was it exactly as Mo said—a rational, well-considered protective stance based on the simple understanding that no one watches over yours the way you watch out for your own, knowing hers would be saved second if a choice needed to be made?

These are the things I wonder, now. After.

1

One more discussion about pink ribbon or gold and I swear I'm going to lose it! WHO CARES! Just elope. Get it over with. I'M DYING!!!

Mo's text response is nearly instant: So ur having fun?

A tooth extraction would be less painful. For five months I've endured this torture. Since the announcement of my sister's engagement, the minutiae of her nuptials have been dissected and regurgitated ad nauseam, and the big day is still three months away. *Ad nauseam*. Now there's a great word that doesn't get nearly enough use (or is it two words?), and it's very appropriate—this whole outing is more than I can stomach.

It's Friday, a gorgeous blue-sky afternoon and the perfect opportunity to be at the beach, skimming or surfing or hanging out with my friends. But instead, here I am, sitting on the floor of the dressing room of a bridal salon, my back against the wall so my sister can model her dress to my mom, my aunt, and me, her reluctant maid of honor. My other sister, Chloe, isn't here. A week into the engagement, she made some comment about the institution of marriage being an antiquated patriarchal construct that oppresses women, causing her to be immediately fired from the whole affair and for me to be promoted.

I wonder where she is right now. Probably hanging out with Vance, the two of them lip locked or walking hand in hand downtown, enjoying the incredible day. I nearly groan in envy and wonder, not for the first time, if the comment was made intentionally. Chloe's brilliant that way. She knows how to make things happen, and working side by side with my mom for eight months is definitely something she would have been very determined to make unhappen.

I sneer at the pure genius of it: my sister managing to liberate herself without actually quitting and successfully shuffling the responsibility of being Aubrey's right-hand woman off to me. I imagine Chloe smirking as she schemed, knowing how much I hate this kind of stuff and knowing that eight months of talking about it while wearing a perky, supportive smile would put a real crimp in my normally sunny, never-shop-unless-in-dire-need-of-clean-underwear disposition.

"Finn, what do you think?" Aubrey says, causing me to lift my head from my phone, which is currently showing a slideshow of the world's funniest animal memes. On the screen is a cat riding a husky with its paw raised and the caption *Follow that mouse!*

I blink, and my grin drops as a surprising lump lodges in my throat. Despite my dislike of all things lacy, wedding, and girly, a well of very girly emotions balloons in my chest. For two weeks, Aubrey has been gushing about her dress, going on and on about how perfect it is. Mostly I've tuned it out—satin this, silk that, rivulets of pearls, something about ribbing, something else about a jewel neckline. But now, here she is, standing in front of me—towering, actually, in her very tall heels—billows of ivory satin, smooth as liquid, spilling from her impossibly small waist, the rivulets of tiny pearls swirling and streaming from what I assume is a jewel neckline, and she looks like a fairy princess, the fairest queen in all the land, and I'm stunned by how pretty she is and maybe even the tiniest bit jealous.

Behind Aubrey, my mom clasps her hands in front of her, and Aunt Karen has her arm wrapped around my mom's shoulders. The two of them lean in to each other as they admire my sister, their matching ash-blonde heads nearly touching.

"Nice," I say, like it's no big deal, then look back at my phone. A black dog squints, a dripping yellow Popsicle in front of him: *Brain Freeze*. I smile and continue to scroll through the images as my mom and Aunt Karen gush and circle, looking at the dress from every angle as Aubrey swishes back and forth.

Aunt Karen stops beside me. "Take a picture," she squeals. "With Finn. The two of them." And I cringe at the thought of being posted all over Aunt Karen's Facebook with some ridiculous tag like *Gorgeous bride-to-be and future runaway bride Aubrey and Finn Miller*.

"Nope," my mom says, saving me. "Not until the big day. Bad luck to take a photo of the bride in her dress before the wedding."

I sigh in relief and shift a little farther from Aubrey, worried that even my proximity will soil her. She smiles down at me and mouths the words *Thank you*, then pivots to return to the clucking hens, who have now moved past their admiration and are on to fretting and fussing about the alterations.

I feel the heat in my cheeks and tell myself to cool it. Aubrey has already thanked me like a billion times, and it really wasn't that big a deal. The conversation I had with her future mother-in-law took less than five minutes, and Mrs. Kinsell was super chill about it.

I wouldn't even have made the call except Aubrey was so upset. I thought Mrs. Kinsell's wedding dress sounded fine and that it was sort of cool that Aubrey was going to be the fourth generation to wear it— "classic lines, vintage beading, a Victorian lace collar, and satin buttons down the back." But Aubrey practically cried as she recited the words, and since I sort of suck at all the other maid of honor duties, I figured this was the one thing I could do. Mo says my way of dealing with these sorts of things is a gift, a bluntness that mystically never seems to offend. I think it's more that other people overcomplicate things. If you simply say things the way they are, there's really no right or wrong about it. After Mrs. Kinsell got over her initial surprise, she was fine with it. She even confessed that she had also wanted to buy her own dress for her wedding.

She must have called Aubrey the moment we hung up because Aubrey called half an hour later thanking and thanking and thanking me. And now, here she is, five months later, twirling and admiring herself and smiling, and I'm very glad I decided to make that call.

In front of me, Aunt Karen pushes her ample double-D breasts up with her hands and says "Va va voom" in encouragement of a little more cleavage, and my mom shakes her head as Aubrey nods, saying something about how Ben would approve, and that's when I snap the picture, their laughter concealing the tiny click of my phone.

I look at the small screen, the three of them laughing, their expressions blurred in delight, the dress reflected in the mirror, Aubrey's smile filling her face, and my mom and Aunt Karen beaming beside her. I forward the picture to Mo with the message, She looks amazing! followed by lots of hearts and smiley faces.

The screen scrolls up to reveal Mo's response: Admit it ur a closet romantic. Speaking of which have u decided?

My mouth swishes back and forth as I stare at the question, perhaps hoping the glowing pixels will offer some sort of enlightenment—the answer or the nerve I've lacked since confessing to Mo I was considering inviting Charlie McCoy to formal. It's a girl-asks-boy dance, and last year I went dateless with a bunch of other girls who were either too shy, too proud, or too ugly to ask a boy. We wore Converse sneakers with our dresses; tore up the dance floor with outrageous, never-before-seen moves; and devoured the chocolate bar while making fun of all the girls teetering in their painful heels, smiling awkwardly at their dates, and looking longingly at the forbidden calories displayed like a torture table.

I'd been certain this year I would be opting for an encore, but that was before Charlie had appeared. It was as if I'd conjured him from thin air. *Dear God, please send me one tall, gorgeous, slightly goofy, soccer-playing boy with green eyes.* And kazam, there he was on the first day of school in my first-period class.

"Earth to Finn." Aubrey throws my sweatshirt at me, and I realize she has re-dressed in her street clothes and that we are moving out of the dressing room.

I follow her into the store. My mom and Aunt Karen have stopped at the register to talk with the shop owner, and Aubrey and I continue outside. Aubrey immediately pulls out her phone to call Ben. She titters and giggles with excitement about her dress and then about what she should wear to meet his parents. This weekend she and Ben are flying to Ohio so she can bond with her future in-laws.

She says "I love you" and hangs up.

Her manicured hand goes to her mouth, and she gnaws at a cuticle.

"You okay?" I ask.

"Nervous."

I pull her fingers from her mouth before she draws blood. "Yeah, they're going to hate you. You're completely intolerable." I roll my eyes, and she crinkles her nose at me.

"At least Ben and I have an excuse for not joining you for Dad's family-bonding experiment."

"You mean you and Ben aren't totally bummed not to be spending three days in a remote cabin in the woods with no television or radio or internet, only the delightful company of our family for entertainment?"

"I can't believe he really thinks this is a good idea."

"You know Dad; he's an optimist."

"He's delusional. This isn't going to fix things."

I shrug and look away, hoping she's wrong while thinking she's probably right. Rocky waters have reached squall levels at home. Between my parents' constant fighting; the growing problems with my brother, Oz; Chloe's frequent acts of rebellion that seem specifically targeted at pissing off my mom; and my own recent screwups, I think I spend more time at Mo's house these days than my own. Like an active volcano, five minutes together inevitably triggers some sort of eruption, and three days together is going to be like tempting Mount Vesuvius to blow.

"Well, at least Mo will be there," Aubrey says. My sister loves Mo almost as much as I do.

"And Natalie," I counter.

"What?" Aubrey says, her expression turning to sympathy.

My mom's passive-aggressive retaliation to my dad's cockamamy plan was to invite Aunt Karen, Uncle Bob, and their annoying daughter, Natalie, to join us, which means Mo and I will now be required to include her in everything we do.

"And Chloe's bringing Vance," I say, putting the cherry on top of the whole harebrained scheme. The only reason Chloe agreed to join us was because Vance loves to snowboard and he's broke. The free room and board and lift tickets were too enticing an offer to pass up, even if it meant putting up with my family for the weekend. There's almost nothing else in the world that would have convinced Chloe to spend even a minute with my mom, let alone three days, except her devotion to Vance—devotion the rest of us don't share. The guy is a grade A sloth with a dose of cocky thrown in because he's ace on a tennis court and thinks he's going to turn pro.

"Wow, sounds like a rip-roaring good time," Aubrey says, her in-law weekend looking better by the minute.

Aunt Karen and my mom walk from the shop, and my mom clicks open the locks to her new Mercedes, a white SUV she bought herself a month ago for her birthday.

"Let Finn drive," Aunt Karen says innocently, though there's nothing innocent about the comment at all. Aunt Karen is what my dad calls a pot stirrer. Like a leprechaun, she loves to stir up trouble: a mischievous little imp full of devilishness, which makes her tons of fun, except at moments like this when the fun is directed at you. Her finely teased brows lift. "You got your permit, didn't you, Finn?"

I watch as my mom tenses, her whole body stiffening at the idea of someone else driving her beautiful new car.

"I'd like to be alive for my wedding," Aubrey weighs in.

"I'm sure Finn is a fine driver," Aunt Karen says, snatching the key fob from my mom's hand.

"Perhaps another time," my mom says, reaching to take it back.

"Nonsense," Aunt Karen says, pulling it out of reach as she threads her arm through mine and leads me away. "No time like the present." She gives me a conspiratorial wink and smile.

Normally, I would love this. There's almost nothing I enjoy more than watching my mom squirm, and I totally pride myself on my daring and my athletic prowess, so the idea of jumping behind the wheel and tearing through the streets like Danica Patrick while terrifying the bejeebers out of my mom and Aubrey and delighting Aunt Karen is right up my alley.

If not for one teeny-weeny little problem.

"In you go," Aunt Karen says, holding open the driver's door.

I swallow. My driving instructor, a bald man with severe halitosis and nerves of steel, labeled the impediment "pedal dyslexia," a slight major problem I have of mixing up the gas and the brake, an issue I haven't been able to correct despite how simple it seems.

"I haven't really driven a car this big," I say. "So maybe it would be better if—"

Aunt Karen cuts me off. "Nonsense. Easy peasy. Mercedes practically drive themselves. Upsy-daisy," she says with a Cheshire cat grin, clearly determined to have her fun.

Aubrey has already climbed into the back seat, and my mom is buckling herself into the passenger seat. My mom knows nothing about my affliction. When my parents have asked how my lessons are going, I've offered a noncommittal "Fine."

"I remember when I did this with you," my mom says, looking back at Aubrey. "You were such a nervous Nellie. It took you weeks before you'd even consider leaving the neighborhood."

"I was being cautious," Aubrey says, sticking her tongue out at her. "A good thing. I still have a perfect record: no accidents and no tickets. More than you can say."

My mom is notorious for getting speeding tickets—at least two a year, and that's not counting the ones she's talked her way out of.

"Chloe, of course, was brilliant," my mom goes on. "It was like she'd been driving her whole life. One lesson, and she was ready to drive across the country."

My competitive bone vibrates. That's the thing about having two older sisters: they've always done it first, which means I feel like I have to do it better.

I look down at the pedals on the floor. The right is narrow and vertical; the left is wide and horizontal. *Right, gas. Left, brake.* It's not brain surgery. One is go. The other is stop. Anyone can do it. I mean, really, half the kids in my class have their licenses, and most of them are idiots.

"Finn?" Aunt Karen says, her head tilting, puzzled by my reticence.

I smile and climb on board, and Aunt Karen claps her hands with delight, then closes the door after me.

"Plenty of room back here," she says, and I slide the seat back to accommodate my long legs.

I fiddle with the mirrors and the steering wheel, adjusting and readjusting them until they are perfect, my mind spinning. *Right, gas. Left, brake. Right, go. Left, stop. Seriously, get over yourself. You've got this. Right. Left. Go. Stop.*

"Of course I might just die of old age," Aubrey says.

I sneer over my shoulder, then turn back. Carefully I set my foot on the brake, then push the button for the ignition, and the engine rumbles to life. I check the mirrors one more time to be sure nothing is behind us and then, to be extra sure, pivot my head in every direction.

"Really?" Aubrey says. "My plane leaves at dawn. Do you think I'm going to make it?"

My mom laughs.

"You're doing fine, Finn," Aunt Karen encourages, perhaps a tinge of guilt in her voice. Mischief-maker that she is, Aunt Karen is also softhearted, the sort who coos over babies and nurses fallen birds back to life. She wouldn't have suggested this if she'd thought it would cause me any real distress.

After shifting into reverse, I back haltingly from the parking spot.

"Good job," Aunt Karen says.

"And the Millers and Aunt Karen are leaving the parking lot," Aubrey announces.

My mom chuckles again.

I pull onto the Coast Highway, and we start toward home, one block, then another, no one saying a word, and I know, despite my efforts to appear confident, they feel my stress.

The first signal comes into view, the light red, and with great deliberateness—*left, left, left*—I shift my foot from the gas to the brake.

We stop smoothly, and I exhale through my nose as I give myself an invisible pat on the back.

The light changes to green, and I shift my foot back to the gas, and on we go.

After several more blocks and two more uneventful stops, my white-knuckle grip lightens, and I start to relax. I'm totally figuring this out. I just have to focus. Think it and do it, just like in sports.

The others relax as well. Aubrey reaches forward to turn on the radio, and my mom turns in her seat to comment on some forgotten detail she needs to tell the florist.

And that's when it happens. She is saying something about lilies and how they don't have pollen when the car behind us honks, a startling blare that sends a jolt to my heart and then ricochets to my foot, causing it to leap sideways and stamp down so hard on the brake that my mom needs to catch herself with her hand on the dash.

Her face snaps sideways, and my skin flames. I don't dare look at her, guilt radiating from my Irish-freckled face, and I know she knows. That's the thing about my mom: she always knows.

Aubrey and Aunt Karen are oblivious. The honker swerves past, and Aubrey flips him off as Aunt Karen says, "Asshole. Some people are in such a damn rush. You're doing fine, Finn. Just fine."

My whole body trembles as we start again, my attention focused like a laser on getting us the remainder of the way home without further incident or incrimination, my eyes fixed on the road as I try not to think about my mom beside me or her judgment.

My promise was given less than a week ago, and her forgiveness was incredibly generous, especially considering my latest mishap landed me at the police station. A dare gone awry: the boulder I launched off the seesaw flew much farther than I expected, nearly taking out one of my friends and breaking the park's sign. My mom did a brilliant job in her smooth lawyer way of talking me out of the trouble I was in, laughing and joking with the arresting officer until he no longer saw it as a crime but rather as a curious young mind testing the laws of physics. And when we got home, all she said was, "You know, Finn, an apology is only worth something if a person means it." The words cut deep. I'd been apologizing a lot lately.

I crossed my heart and pinky swore that I really did mean it, that from then on I would make sure to look before I leaped, which actually made her smile, considering my seesaw-leaping crime.

She's not smiling now. Stone still, she sits like a statue staring out the windshield, and I feel worse than terrible. Five days. That's how long it took for me to break my promise and to let her down again.

Finally the last traffic light comes into view, and I nearly give a cheer. One more block, a right and then a left, and we'll be home. When it turns yellow, determined not to jolt us again, I tap the brake the way the instructor told me to so the deceleration will be smooth.

We are nearly stopped, the tires barely moving and my eyes on the bumper of the car in front of us, when my phone buzzes. A text message coming through. Two sharp vibrations that start in my back pocket before traveling down my leg to my foot, and the car unexpectedly lurches forward.

"Brake!" my mom yelps, the word combining with the awful crunch of metal as we ram into the car in front of us. "Brake!" she says again, which I am desperately trying to do, but inexplicably we continue to plow forward, smashing the little car into the truck in front of it.

"Other pedal," she says, and my foot leaps sideways.

My mom is out of the car before I manage to put it in park.

"Shit," Aubrey says behind me.

"Oops," Aunt Karen says.

I stumble from the driver's seat, my whole body on fire.

Already my mom is talking to the driver of the car we hit, her body bent toward the open window. The woman is the only passenger—dark, shoulder-length hair, a red sweater. A cross with beads dangles from the rearview mirror. She nods to something my mom says; then her head reverses direction, and I can't be certain, but I think by the way her shoulders hiccup that she might be crying.

I step toward them, then step back, my muscles clenching and unclenching, unsure what to do.

The driver of the truck joins them, an older man dressed in a plaid shirt and loose jeans. He looks like a contractor or a tradesman. He asks if everyone's okay, glances back at me, and then, reassured no one's hurt, waves off my mom's offer of insurance, climbs back in his truck, and drives away.

I study his bumper as he goes. It's dinged and dented but firmly in place, and it's hard to tell if the damage is from a few minutes or a few decades ago.

The woman's car did not fare as well. An old Honda, it looks as if it's been folded in two, the hood and trunk bent toward each other and the middle sagging. The woman has her phone out, and so does my mom. I stand watching.

"Finn, honey, why don't you get back in the car?" Aunt Karen says from her open window.

I reach for the door.

"Perhaps it's better if your mom drives the rest of the way."

I walk around and slide into the passenger seat.

Twenty minutes later a tow truck arrives. My mom stays with the woman as her car is hitched to the back. The woman is no longer upset, and I am incredibly grateful. My mom is brilliant that way. It's what makes her a great lawyer: the way she is able to handle any situation with complete calm and to charm anyone into believing she is their friend. When the woman climbs into the tow truck, she actually pauses to thank my mom, as if, by crashing into her car, we've done her some sort of favor.

A moment later my mom's back in the car and driving us the remaining two blocks to our home.

2

We pull in front of the house, and I slink from the passenger seat. I watch as my mom storms toward the door without a word, barely glancing at my dad or my brother, Oz, who are in the driveway washing the Miller Mobile, a camper that my dad bought when he was nineteen and that has serviced all his adventures since, from tornado chasing in the Midwest to his many surfing, fishing, and mountain excursions.

Bingo, our golden Lab, bounds over to her, his tail wagging, then skulks away when she ignores him, closing the door and leaving him behind with the rest of us. If nothing else, this proves how upset she is. The one member of our family my mom's at peace with these days other than Aubrey is Bingo, and often I find the two of them together, her sitting on the lawn with a glass of wine in one hand and the other buried in Bingo's fur.

Aunt Karen gives my shoulder a squeeze and kisses the side of my head. "Hang in there, kiddo. Accidents are part of life."

I manage a halfhearted nod, and she walks away toward her own house two doors down. Aubrey looks from me to the dented front end of the Mercedes, shakes her head like I'm an idiot, then bounds over to my dad to regale him with the story of my monolithic blunder.

Accidents might be part of most people's lives, but they are not part of my mom's. As far as I know, my mom's never even been in an accident, and now, thanks to me, her perfect car, which she finally bought after years of talking about it, is ruined.

A few feet away from Aubrey and my dad, Oz sprays the Miller Mobile with the hose, the water going everywhere. He's soaked head to toe, and despite the awfulness of the moment, I smile as I always do when I see my brother enjoying the simple little nothings of life, impervious to the concerns about achievement or appearances that seem to constantly plague the rest of us. Though he's thirteen, my brother's intellectual abilities are half that, and his emotions are even simpler: straightforward as a toddler's.

My dad howls with laughter as Aubrey tells him I have a talent for making instruments, the Accord I smashed now an "accordion," her hands moving together and apart like she's playing the instrument as she imitates the sound of crunching metal. Unlike my mom, my dad is a go-with-the-flow sort of guy, and a ding or a dent in his book is no big deal. His truck is living proof—older than I am, it's marked with at least a hundred scars.

Oz says, "Dad, come wash the M&M," but my dad doesn't hear him. He's enjoying Aubrey's story too much, his grin spread wide as she grinds, "Whrhrhr," her hands continuing to play the accordion. "And Mom's screaming, 'Brake,' which causes Finn to slam the accelerator again—whrhrhr . . ."

I want to leave, but I don't know where to go. Joining my mom in the house is out of the question, and Mo's not home because she's shopping for ski clothes for our trip. So I stand mortified and seething, wishing Aubrey would finish already and leave.

Oz is feeling the same way. He wants my dad to come back and wash the camper with him. His brow is slashed low over his eyes as the hose sprays a puddle on the lawn.

I watch as his impatience grows, his hand tightening around the nozzle and his face growing dark.

And I could stop it.

"Whrhrhr," Aubrey says again.

But I don't.

"And Mom screams, 'Other pedal . . . '"

The water hits Aubrey's hair first, then travels quickly down her silk tank top to her designer jeans before reaching her new leather boots. Quick as a rattler, my dad spins to get between her and the spray, but already it's too late: my sister's drenched head to toe, her flat-ironed hair plastered to her face, her shirt stuck to her skin. Like a dog, she grunts and shakes the water from her arms and then, without a word, spins to storm off to her car on the street.

"Oz, stop," my dad says, his hands held in front of him to block the spray and his head craned over his shoulder to look at Aubrey as she drives away.

"Christ," my dad barks. "Jesus effing Christ. Five minutes with my daughter, is that too much to ask?" He glares through the deluge of water at the closed door of the house, where my mom had escaped minutes before. "Oz! Enough!" he barks, and the smile drops from my face, my blood freezing. With my dad's harshness, Oz's face darkens to a dangerous shade that stops the humor instantly and prickles the hair on my neck. In the past year, my brother has grown to nearly my dad's height, a smidge under six feet, and he has passed him in weight by at least thirty pounds. Unlike my dad, who is built like an athlete, Oz looks fat, but mostly he is strong. Combine that with a severe lack of impulse control and the temper of a silverback gorilla, and what you have is a highly combustible bomb with a hair trigger that needs to be handled with great care.

My dad notices the shift as well and forces the anger from his face and levity into his voice as he says, "Okay, big boy, let's get this baby washed."

Oz's expression softens, and my dad and I breathe.

The water is still trained on my dad, the spray washing back and forth across his T-shirt, and just like my dad always does with Oz, he takes it, as if the ice-cold spray blasting him in the chest and soaking him all over is not annoying in the least.

"Water fight," Oz says, grinning.

"No. No more water fight," my dad answers, a sigh of weariness in his voice.

I creep forward, making my way carefully around Oz to the Miller Mobile.

"Water fight," Oz demands.

"I'm done with the water fight," my dad says, clearly done with more than just that.

From the bucket beside the camper, I pick up the sponge and scrub the spray-painted peace symbol over the wheel well, scouring extra hard to create a lather of foam. As I work, I whistle, and the tune draws Oz's attention, along with the nozzle, away from my dad. When I have a healthy froth, I sweep the suds onto the sponge, then blow the bubbles in the air, and Bingo charges from the grass to leap and bite at them, his tail whipping wildly as he tries to catch the floating clouds, a game we've played since he was a pup.

Oz drops the hose and races to join in the fun. Snatching the sponge, he sweeps up another scoop of bubbles and blows them in the air like I did for Bingo to chase.

Thanks, my dad mouths.

I shrug and turn to leave.

"Hey, Finn," he says, stopping me, "when we get back from the mountains, I'll take you driving. We'll figure it out."

I give a weak smile. The intention is there, but it will never happen. Oz doesn't allow for things like driving lessons. Maybe Aubrey or Chloe will take me.

3

The afternoon's as bleak as the mood of half of us, thick clouds obscuring the sun. The other half, who I refer to as the glass-half-full fools, include Aunt Karen, Uncle Bob, Oz, Mo, and my dad.

Even Bingo is unsure of the idea of the ten of us traveling together. His tail swishes at half mast as he wanders from person to person looking for confirmation as to whether he should feel excitement or dread.

Last night my parents fought like hyenas—growling and barking at each other over everything from the brand of pretzels my dad bought to the standard fight of how little time my mom spends with Oz. Chloe ignored it, her headphones glued to her ears, a magazine on her lap. Every now and then she would look up and make a funny face to try and distract me. If anyone understands how bad it feels to be on the wrong side of my mom, it's Chloe.

At one point she even threw me the last of her Toblerone, a gift given to her by Vance when he returned from a tennis tournament in Washington a week ago. It didn't work. I couldn't be distracted, and I couldn't ignore it. I had started it: me and my dyslexic foot. Things had already been fragile, and I'd tipped them over the edge. The final thing my mom had yelled before storming up the stairs was, "I'll make it to the wedding, Jack, for Aubrey, but then that's it. We're through!"

It wasn't the first time divorce had come up, but it was the first time I'd believed it.

My mom stands beside Aunt Karen on the lawn, her arms crossed as she watches my dad and Uncle Bob load our ski gear into the Miller Mobile. She hasn't spoken a word to me since the accident. She won't even look at me.

I feel so bad it hurts to breathe. I don't get it. I'm not stupid. I get okay grades. But it's like there's this great disconnect when it comes to common sense. I knew I shouldn't have driven her car, or at least I should have known, but then I went right ahead and did it anyways. I glance again at the smashed front end of the Mercedes—the bumper cracked, the paint damaged, the headlight broken.

Shaking my head, I let out a heavy sigh, then return to watching the preparations. Oz is helping. Kind of. My dad carries our stuff into the camper, and Oz places it where he thinks it should go—on the seats, in the aisle, on the steering wheel. Before we leave, he will be distracted, and we will fix it.

Beside me, Mo is so excited she nearly bounces. She's never been skiing. Her father's idea of adventure is chartering a yacht with a crew to sail his family around various ports of Greece or touring ancient ruins with a private docent in Bangladesh or tasting wine in the underground cellars of Bordeaux.

I smile at her excitement and at her outfit. She's decked out in beautiful brand-new mountain attire—black leggings, fur-lined boots, a baby-blue cashmere sweater, and an infinity scarf that looks like it was handwoven in Morocco, which it very well might have been, since her dad travels all the time and is always bringing her exotic gifts. The weather is around sixty degrees—cool for Orange County but too warm for her outfit—and a sheen of sweat has formed on her upper lip and forehead.

Mo's mom waits with us, her eyes skittering over the scene, and I wonder what she makes of our odd tribe. Chloe and Vance (Chlance, as Mo and I call them, since their bodies are always attached, creating a single morphed being impossible to distinguish as two separate people) huddle on the porch, whispering and kissing, undoubtedly conspiring about when they'll be able to sneak off to get stoned. My parents don't have a clue. Just like they have no idea my sister is having sex or that she drinks on a regular, fairly frequent basis.

I watch as my sister whispers something into Vance's ear; he smiles down at her, then kisses her softly, their identical black hair touching. Both turned eighteen a month ago, their birthdays less than a week apart, and to celebrate they decided to get matching haircuts. Chloe chopped off her long copper locks, and Vance buzzed his gold hair to within an inch of his scalp. They dyed what was left indigo black. Despite the self-sabotage, they are good looking. He is tall. She is petite. And both have flawless skin and pretty pearly whites.

A few feet away, my mom laughs at something Aunt Karen says, and I turn. Aunt Karen's not actually my aunt, but she's been "Aunt Karen" since Natalie and I were babies. Over the years, she and my mom have formed a near-mythical friendship, so close they've even grown to look alike. My mom's an inch taller and twenty pounds thinner, and Aunt Karen has wider lips and a narrower nose, but they look like sisters, my mom definitely the older sibling, though they're the same age.

Aunt Karen says something else that's funny, and Uncle Bob says from the driveway, "Hey, what's going on over there? Break it up, you two."

Aunt Karen sticks her tongue out at him, causing Uncle Bob to reach into the bag of groceries he's holding to pull out a bag of marshmallows and hurl it at her. Aunt Karen curls from the attack as my mom lunges for the bag, snatching the puffy missile from the air.

Sometimes I forget that my mom used to be an athlete. It's easy to do, since she pretty much looks like your average mom. She's certainly not in great shape like she was when she ran track for USC, but she still has lightning-quick reflexes.

Uncle Bob gives my mom a wink, and my mom blushes as Aunt Karen pretends not to notice. I always think it must be kind of hard for Aunt Karen to know how well Uncle Bob and my mom get along. It's not like anything weird is going on, but they have this way with each other, the two of them always challenging each other and going toe to toe, something Aunt Karen just can't do. My mom works real hard to keep it in check. Like right now, I know her instinct is to hurl the marshmallows back at him, but she doesn't. Instead she carries them to where he is and plops them in the bag.

"Can't make the shot," he taunts.

"If I recall, you still owe me seventeen Snickers from the last time we played lightning," she offers back, a glint of the competitor in her sparking, which leaves Uncle Bob smirking after her as she returns to Aunt Karen.

Natalie walks up to stand beside Mo, Mrs. Kaminski, and me. "My mom says you're going to have to pay for the damage to your mom's car," she says, her smile sympathetic, though the tone is tinged with glee.

Despite Natalie and me growing up together, most of that time was spent hating each other. The first five years, we fought. The next five, we ignored each other. And for the past six, we've tolerated each other, but just barely.

"Is that true?" Mo says, looking sincerely concerned.

I swallow. My mom hasn't said anything, but if that's what Aunt Karen told Natalie, it's probably true. I have no idea what the damage from the accident is going to cost, but my guess is it will be more than I've saved for buying my own car. My stomach clenches in a knot at the thought of all those hours of babysitting and dog walking gone in a blink, or in my case, gone in the buzz of my phone in my back pocket.

"Wow, that's, like, hardcore," Natalie says. "Do you know what my parents are buying me as soon as I get my license?"

Neither Mo nor I answer.

"A MINI Cooper. I'm trying to decide what color, yellow or red? There's this really cute red one I see all over town. It has a white roof with this Great Britain flag painted on it."

"You're not from England," Mo says.

"So?" Natalie says, clearly not happy we're not gushing over her choice.

I'd like to say Natalie isn't pretty, but that would be a lie. She's very pretty—gold hair, gray eyes, big boobs. It's only when she opens her mouth that she turns ugly.

We return to silence.

My mom yells over to Chloe, "Chloe, grab one more set of sheets."

Chloe ignores her and continues canoodling with Vance, only acknowledging having heard my mom by turning slightly so the small black swallow tattoo on her left shoulder that my mother railed against so violently can be seen.

"I'll get them," Oz volunteers, dropping the ski bag he's carrying and leaping toward the house, desperate, as always, to win my mom's approval.

I shake my head. Someone's going to end up with SpongeBob sheets, or knowing Oz, he'll bring down fifty top sheets and not a single pillowcase.

"Oz, no," my mom says, stopping him, exasperation in her voice as her eyes skewer Chloe. "Forget the sheets; just keep helping your dad."

With a sigh, my mom pivots and walks toward us. Aunt Karen follows. Painting on a smile for Mrs. Kaminski and avoiding looking at me, my mom says, "Good morning, Joyce."

"Good morning, Ann. Karen. Thank you for including Maureen. It's all she's been talking about for weeks."

"You know we love having her along."

There's a slightly awkward pause, Mrs. Kaminski's eyes sliding to the Miller Mobile before sliding to the ground. She doesn't say anything, but I feel her concern. The Miller Mobile looks a bit like a tin can on wheels. Originally it was a sleeping camper with a small kitchenette and a bed, but the artist my dad bought it from had removed all that to transform it into a studio, leaving only the small built-in dinette—a table with booth seating around it. After we kids came along, my dad added additional seating—a pair of Greyhound bus seats and a red leather bench he got from a scrapped Bentley, creating this awesome, strange blend of striped blue velour, plush red leather, and sparkly green vinyl.

Unable to help herself, Mrs. Kaminski says, "There are seat belts?"

Mo tenses. Over the last year, Mo's frustration with her mom's overprotectiveness has grown, and I know lately they've been arguing about it.

My mom nods. "Would you like to take a look inside?"

Mrs. Kaminski's eyes slide sideways toward Mo, and she shakes her head. "No. That's fine. I trust you."

The last three words hold a hint of challenge. One my mom accepts. "I'll look after her."

Aunt Karen chimes in, "We all will. Mo's like a daughter to us. She's in good hands."

With a thin smile and muttered thanks, Mrs. Kaminski gives Mo a peck on the cheek, tells her to have fun, and hurries away to worry in private.

Beside me, Mo sighs in relief, and I nudge her shoulder. "That wasn't so bad. Not too long ago, she wouldn't have let you do this at all. Did you promise to call her every hour?"

"Actually, I told her I wouldn't be calling at all," she says. "It's better that way. When I call, she works herself into a frenzy, asking me about every little detail, then obsessing on what I told her and how it can go wrong. The less she knows, the less she has to worry about. It's three days. She can survive three days without hearing from me. Besides, it's good practice. In two years I'm off to college, and there will be times when she'll hardly hear from me at all."

I believe it. Mo is itching to spread her wings, to soar into the world as far from the nest as possible. While I'm thinking of going to UCLA or UCSD so I can come home on the weekends, Mo dreams of living on the other side of the country or maybe even the other side of the globe. She wants to hike Patagonia, travel across the Sahara, scale Everest. Since she was a little girl, she has sat wide eyed as my dad regaled us with his adventures from when he was young, and he has always said, "That Mo, she's a pirate at heart."

"Let's go," my dad bellows from the driver's seat, his face radiating such optimism it almost makes me believe this wasn't such a bad idea after all and that it might actually be fun.

Mo claps her hands and skips toward the camper. Vance pulls Chloe from the porch, and they shuffle forward. My mom sighs and walks with Aunt Karen, her chin jutted as if bravely taking the dead man's walk to the electric chair. Uncle Bob pretend boxes with Oz, dancing him toward the door while his eyes slide to my mom to see if she is watching.

"Come on, Finn," my dad says.

I trot toward him, and he high-fives me through the window as I walk past.

"Seat belt," my mom says when I climb aboard, but she's not talking to me. She's talking to Mo.

Mo groans, then buckles in.

I laugh and plop beside her, beltless and free.

Uncle Bob rides shotgun, and he and my dad immediately fall into a discussion about this year's Super Bowl. Normally I would listen in and participate, since I love football and know more about the players than either of them, but I won't abandon Mo with Natalie. So instead I break out a deck of cards and deal hands to the three of us girls along with Chloe and Vance for a marathon game of bullshit that will hopefully last the entire three hours it takes to get to Big Bear. The winner gets dibs on sleeping arrangements when we get to the cabin—a prize worth playing for since sleeping beside Oz is something to avoid if possible.

Oz, sedated with a healthy dose of Benadryl my dad spiked his juice with moments earlier, snores heavily against the window, Bingo curled at his feet. In the back, on the Bentley bench, my mom works, her laptop on her thighs. She has a big trial in a few weeks she's stressed about. Aunt Karen reads a magazine.

We are on our way.

4

The clouds close ranks as we begin our climb up the mountain, the color and light draining until the world is reduced to matte gray with no sense of time or depth. It's only late afternoon yet dark enough to be dusk. Our game ended because Natalie was caught cheating and Chloe wouldn't back down when the rest of us said it didn't matter. All bets are off, and it will be a free-for-all for claiming beds when we get to the cabin.

Oz still snores, my mom still works, and Aunt Karen paints Natalie's toenails as her daughter pouts because none of us are being nice to her.

Mo and I are still at the table, our heads huddled close over my phone.

"I can't," I say, my cheeks flooded with warmth as I stare at the letters Mo typed for me on my phone. Hi Charlie Plans for formal? If not I was thinking we could go together??? Finn

The message took over twenty minutes to compose—simple and to the point. My finger hovers over the send button, until Mo, tired of waiting, swoops in and presses it for me, causing my heart to jump.

"Done," she says, a satisfied grin on her face.

My stomach lurches around nervously as I stare expectantly at the screen for an instant reply, praying for and dreading his answer in equal measure; and time suddenly slows, each second taking at least twice as long as it did before the message was sent.

"What's done?" Chloe asks, untangling herself from Vance and pulling her right earbud from her ear. Noxious music squawks from the tiny speaker, the kind of booming thrum and cacophonous screech that makes you think of tortured cats, industrial vents, and garbage cans.

"Nothing," I say, amazed how Chloe always does that: ignores you when there's something you want her to hear and listens when you don't want her to.

She snatches my phone off the table before I can react. "Who's Charlie?"

"No one."

Mo smirks.

"Not that soccer guy with the big belt buckles and boots?"

"He's from Texas," I defend.

"I think it's cute," Mo says.

Chloe rolls her eyes as she tosses my phone to the table. "Hard to believe we're sisters."

I can't argue—the room we've shared my entire life, our love of stupendous words like *stupendous*, our copper hair, and our green eyes about the only things Chloe and I have in common. She plugs the bud back in her ear, a smile on her face, and I know she's happy for me. She's been rooting for me in the romance department for some time, always telling me I'm pretty even though I pretend not to care. She's the only one who says it, but she says it often enough and with such sincerity that sometimes I actually believe her.

∼

By the time we reach the cabin, I've bitten off all my nails and checked my phone at least two hundred times. The Miller Mobile rolls to a stop, and all of us stretch and stand. Snow has started to fall, and though it isn't even five o'clock, the world is dark.

I squint at the "cabin" through the gauzy veil, and my heart fills. Some of my best childhood memories were made here. The cabin, which is more like a small mountain chalet, was built by my mother's father when he retired, his dream to live among the pines lasting two short years before he died. But his vision still stands, a regal log-and-glass A-frame accessed by a private fire road, making it the only house for miles.

I step from the camper and momentarily forget about Charlie and my phone, the cold smacking me as the winter wonderland steals my breath. Most of the time, with my long limbs and bright hair, I feel tall and conspicuous, but here, surrounded by such rugged vastness, suddenly I am small and astoundingly aware of my own insignificance.

Mo twirls around me, caught up in the moment as well, her tongue out to catch the sprinkling of snow.

"You know the snow is dirty," Natalie says.

Mo leaves her tongue extended as she turns to face Natalie, who then huffs away. Mo and I giggle.

My dad wrestles a soda-laden cooler down the steps of the camper and asks Oz to do the same with the second cooler, which Oz does, effortlessly carrying the chest behind my dad, Bingo on his heels.

"Thanks, buddy," my dad says over his shoulder, causing Oz to grin.

I carry my duffel and two bags of groceries and follow Vance, who carries nothing but his own bag. He shuffles forward, shoulders slumped as he walks in the slow, irritating way he has that manages to be both lazy and arrogant at the same time.

My phone buzzes in my jacket pocket, and I jump like I've been poked with a cattle prod.

Chloe, who is behind me, swings the bag of groceries she's carrying into my butt. "Is that your *boyfriend*?"

I glance over my shoulder to sneer but then see her excited face and blush instead.

I desperately want to look at my phone and reveal my prize, but Charlie will have to wait, because we have now crossed the threshold to the cabin, and it's a mad dash to claim your bed. I drop the groceries on the counter and leap past Vance, who obviously has no idea how important this is. Oz is already on the stairs that lead to the loft, lumbering up the steps. When he wants something, he can be fiercely determined, and I know he wants the top bunk.

This is a good thing. If he goes left, I will go right. Whichever bunk he claims, I'll stake the other for Mo and me. Natalie is hot on my heels, obviously out to sabotage us. Whichever bunk I choose, she'll claim the second for herself in order to separate me from Mo.

My mind spins with strategy, and I decide to go for the cots in the back instead. I'll claim the middle one so I end up with Mo beside me regardless of what Natalie does.

Oz turns left, and I charge forward, throwing my bag on the middle cot, then rip off my jacket and throw it on the cot to the left.

Natalie bites. "That's my cot," she says. "No saving." She tosses my jacket to the floor and throws her bag on the least desirable cot, the one beneath the heater and closest to Oz.

I pick up my jacket and toss it onto the cot to the right, the one I actually wanted.

Vance and Chloe will sleep in the second set of bunk beds. My parents will sleep on the sofa couch in the living room. Aunt Karen and Uncle Bob will get the master bedroom.

"Unpack—then we're off to dinner," my dad yells.

I plop on my cot and pull my phone from my pocket. Mo flops beside me and looks over my shoulder.

Sounds good. I'm glad you asked me. Charlie

We bounce so hard I'm afraid the small cot might break.

"He's glad you asked him," Mo squeals.

Across the room, Chloe's face spreads into a wide grin, and she gives a thumbs-up.

"You think he'll wear cowboy boots?" Natalie sneers.

I ignore her. Last I heard she was going to formal with her cousin.

"Girls, get a move on," my dad says from below. "Grizzly Manor awaits."

My mom's voice cuts in. "Jack, maybe we should stay in tonight. It looks like it's really starting to come down."

"And miss Grizzly pancakes and links for dinner? No way," my dad says, his voice full of enthusiasm.

Oz hollers out with excitement, "Grizzly pancakes for dinner."

And I know that settles it. We'll never hear the end of it if Oz doesn't get his pancakes.

"Girls, I'm going to finish emptying the trailer. You've got ten minutes."

He's talking primarily to Mo, Ms. Fashionista, who is already rummaging through her extremely large suitcase for the perfect ensemble to wear to Grizzly Manor, a diner with checkered plastic tablecloths and sawdust on the floor.

Natalie, not one to be outdone, unzips her also extremely large bag and does the same. I sit cross-legged on the cot in my sweats and UGGs and stare at my message from Charlie.

"Red or black?" Mo asks, holding up two equally gorgeous sweaters.

"Red."

"Holes or no holes?" She is asking about her jeans.

"It's freezing outside," I say.

"But the holey ones look better with the red sweater." She throws her not-ripped jeans back in the suitcase, and I roll my eyes. "I only need to make it from the car to the restaurant and back again."

She hustles into the bathroom to change, and when she emerges, she looks like a New York runway model headed to a five-star restaurant rather than a teenager in Big Bear off to the local diner to have breakfast for dinner.

"Ready?" my dad yells. "The bus is leaving."

I grab my parka, and Mo grabs a cute herringbone blazer and pulls on a pair of heeled leather boots. Natalie, seeing Mo's choice, rummages through her bag and pulls out a similar pair, then throws on a cream-colored, knee-length down coat.

"I like your coat," Mo says.

"I got it in Italy. It cost over seven hundred dollars," Natalie says.

Mo does an amazing job not reacting. I, on the other hand, shake my head and blurt, "Well, I got my coat in Paris, and it cost eight hundred dollars."

Natalie sneers at me, storms down the stairs, and stomps out the door.

Mo turns to me, and we laugh, then imitate Natalie's haughty walk.

"Girls," my mom snaps, stopping our rude behavior.

We walk into the night, and the cold steals our breath.

5

The world transformed while we were inside, the snow lacing together into a veil that drapes endlessly from the sky, the wind causing the flakes to dance and swirl before they settle into a blanket of white. I shiver through my parka. The temperature has transformed as well, the warmth of the day a memory.

"Let's go," my dad says, holding open the door to the Miller Mobile.

Mo, Natalie, and I shuffle toward it, Mo slipping and sliding in her boots.

"Finn, ride shotgun," my dad says. "I'll teach you about driving in the snow."

I jump into the front seat.

Behind me, my mom says, "Mo, seat belt."

I strap myself in as well.

We drive slowly, the chains crunching solidly as we roll cautiously down the snow-laden road. The wipers swish, and the high beams provide vision barely a yard in front of us, snow falling thick through their light.

The road is empty. Other than us, the only traffic that uses the access road is the fire department and the occasional trespasser cutting through from Cedar Lake to the slopes.

My dad doesn't instruct me as he promised, his attention tight on the road, and I occupy myself with thoughts of Charlie and the upcoming dance.

"What's that?" I point at a glint of color in front of us.

My dad slows so we're barely moving, and we crawl to what we can now see is a small red car. My dad stops the camper and climbs out. He's halfway to the stranded vehicle when the door opens and a kid not much older than me steps out. A few words are exchanged, and then both walk toward us.

"This is Kyle," my dad says. "We're going to give him a lift."

Fine by me. We can pick up a Kyle anytime. Six feet tall and broad shouldered, with honey hair and green eyes so bright the color is clear from ten feet away.

He scans the inside of the trailer. Oz is buckled in beside the door, holding Bingo. My mom, Aunt Karen, and Uncle Bob are on the Bentley seat in the back. Chloe and Vance, buds blasting in their ears, sit at the dinette against the window, while Natalie is on one side of the table and Mo on the other. He smiles when Mo's eyes catch his and takes the seat beside her, proving he's smart as well.

We start to roll again, making our way carefully around Kyle's car.

Kyle is lucky we came along. I can't imagine many cars will take this shortcut tonight, and it would have been a long, cold hike into town.

Behind me, Mo's already reeling him in, and though I can't make out the conversation, I know Kyle is done for. A string of heartbroken guys has been left in Mo's beguiling wake. She's a love-them-and-leave-them-devastated-and-dizzy kind of girl.

I glance back to confirm it, and sure enough, Kyle is turned sideways in his seat, completely captivated as Mo weaves her web, mesmerizing him with her beauty and her sweet questions that seem so genuinely curious, listening to his answers as if he's the most fascinating guy in the world.

Across from them, Natalie stares, tongue-tied, and I actually feel the smallest bond of sympathy with her, glad I'm not the girl stuck across from those two, feeling completely invisible while Mo does her thing.

My dad steps on the brake, and my head whips around to see the blink of a buck's startled eye in front of us. The camper lurches, then skids, the front tires gripping as the back ones slide. It all happens very slowly. We are barely moving. The back end thuds against something solid, and the front tires lose their grip. It feels like only a few inches, but it must be several feet because the front bumper scrapes against the guardrail, the metal creaking as it bends, and we stop.

I breathe, relieved someone was smart enough to think to build a guardrail on this dangerous narrow strip. And the small exhale does it. Like stitches ripping, the pylons that hold the ribbon of steel snap from the mountainside—pop, pop, pop.

And we fall.

There's no time to scream. Like a missile, we plummet, my seat belt suspending me over the windshield as mountain and snow and trees fly past. The tire on my dad's side glances off something hard, and we ricochet forward, then down again, no longer straight, my shoulder lodged in the corner between the dash and the door.

In the next second, the camper is on its side, and I watch as it continues to slide, skidding over rock and snow. I look up, unable to believe how far we've fallen, the road above a distant ridge I can no longer see.

I'm outside but not cold, confused, but only for a second.

6

I am dead.

It's obvious as realizing you are bleeding. You look down and see blood. In my case, I look down and see nothing but the snow and forest around me, too instant and too real to be a dream. I feel my body—my limbs, my heart, my breath—but no longer anything of the world, not the cold, wetness, gravity, or air.

It's shocking yet entirely natural. *Like birth,* I think. I do not remember being born, the pain of entering the world, yet I knew to breathe, to suckle, to cry. Death is a lot like that—I have no recollection of the exact experience, the trauma of dying, but my understanding of this new state is innate. A bit difficult to accept and slightly unbelievable, but intuitively I recognize that I am dead and that my body is no longer a part of me.

The wind howls, and it's strange to hear it but not be affected by it. I follow the camper. It's not difficult. Like telling your hand to grip, my intention is to follow, so I do. My soul exists, but I no longer have any physical form to restrict it. I move freely wherever my thoughts take me. No white light or black hole beckons, and as far as I can tell, I am alone. And though I'm no longer alive, I still feel like I am part of the world, my emotions as desperate as if I were living.

The camper slams against a boulder that spins it into a tree, and finally it stops.

My panic shifts to Mo, and suddenly I am inside looking at her. She is on her side, her eyes wide and her hands clenching the seat. Natalie is across from her in a similar pose, except she is screaming.

Oz hangs by his seat belt from what is now the ceiling and howls at my dad to stop. He holds Bingo, who wriggles to get loose but amazingly still does not bite at Oz to release him.

Chloe and Vance and Kyle, the boy we picked up, are piled against the driver's seat along with all the board games that are kept in the cabinets. Monopoly money and cards and Scrabble score sheets swirl in the air. My mom, Aunt Karen, and Uncle Bob lie jumbled together halfway back.

My dad moans, causing me to move to the cab.

I scream out for my mom. I scream and scream. My dad needs help. My voice is silent.

The front end of the camper is crushed against him, his body sideways and wedged between the driver's side window and the steering wheel. His leg is broken, the bottom half of his femur sticking through his jeans, blood leaking through the denim. His face is slashed from shards of glass and frozen with crystals of ice. Blood is everywhere.

Please, I beg, *please help him.*

His eyes flutter open, and he moans again, wincing in pain and panic as his vision blinks into focus. He mutters my name, turns, and lets out a horrible cry. I turn to look with him and quickly turn back. My death wasn't instant or painless as I thought. My eyes and mouth are frozen open in a silent scream from my half-severed head, which hangs grotesquely toward my dad. Blood, so much of it I can't believe my body was capable of holding it, drips and pools beside him.

He reaches for me and struggles to free himself, causing himself immense pain, and I scream at him to stay put, that I'm fine, that it didn't hurt. I scream these things. I yell them, I think them, but he cannot hear me. Desperately he continues to try to free himself, his muscles straining and his face contorted in agony, and all I can do is watch and pray, until finally my prayer is answered and he passes out from the pain.

In the back, my mom has freed herself from the pile. She winces as she staggers forward, her hand pressed to her ribs and her body not quite upright. Stumbling across the sideways camper, she glances at Mo and Natalie in their seats, then at Oz dangling above her. Ignoring his screams and Bingo's yelps, she crawls to the bodies bunched behind the driver's seat.

Kyle rolls free and sits up, dizzily, holding his left arm. Vance shifts Chloe off him and sits up as well. Blood is everywhere, splattered on the wall of the cabin, soaked into the bench, dripping down Chloe's face.

Vance flinches and scans himself to see if the blood is coming from him as my mom pushes Chloe's bangs away from her closed eyes. A two-inch gash along her hairline gushes red. My mom pulls her scarf from her neck and presses it against the cut, and Chloe moans.

"You're okay," my mom says.

Uncle Bob has crawled up beside her.

"Take her," my mom says, and Uncle Bob wraps his arm around Chloe, lays her on the backrest of the dinette bench that is now on the ground, and gently pulls the scarf away to examine the wound.

Behind them, Aunt Karen has made her way to Natalie. She helps Natalie from her seat and leads her to the back of the camper.

My mom pushes past Vance and Kyle into the cab and freezes, her gasp so sharp that, though no louder than a whisper, it resounds like thunder above the wind and the hail and Oz's screams. Kyle closes his eyes, and his lips move in silent prayer. Vance stares at Chloe, his skin pale. Mo strains to see past my mom, panic and worry etched on her face. Uncle Bob looks up, grabs Vance's hand, forces it to hold the scarf to Chloe's wound, then quickly moves to the front to help my mom.

"Oh shit," he mutters when he gets there.

My mom stumbles back, and Uncle Bob catches her.

My death is horrible to look at, and I think she is going to collapse, her entire body quaking and her breath huffing violently from her open mouth, but then my dad moans, and like a switch, it snaps her back from the brink, and I watch as she squeezes her eyes shut to draw on some internal strength, steeling herself before turning to look at my dad.

His arm is still extended, reaching for me. She crawls over the center console to get to him. "Jack," she says, smoothing back his hair.

"Finn," he moans.

"Shhh," she soothes, and he does, passing out again.

In the back of the camper, Aunt Karen and Natalie cling to each other.

"Mom?" Natalie says, her head craning from her mother's embrace to look toward the cab.

"Shhh, baby. Don't look. It's going to be okay. Just don't look." Aunt Karen pulls Natalie's face against her.

Vance sits beside Chloe, holding my mom's scarf to her head. Mo is still in her seat, struggling to get her seat belt undone, and Oz still dangles from the ceiling, holding Bingo and yelling for my dad.

Kyle reaches toward Oz to help him.

"No," Mo yells, stopping him.

Kyle turns to her.

"Leave him," she says.

Oz kicks and screams, but Mo is right. It's not cruelty but necessity. Oz can't be dealt with right now, and he is better off where he is.

Kyle turns from Oz and instead helps Mo try to release the clip of her seat belt.

At the moment, adrenaline is keeping everyone warm, but in a matter of minutes, they are going to become very cold. The windshield of the camper is gone, and wind and snow whip and swirl through the cabin. My dad is frosted with white, and my dead body is half-buried.

My mom has her cell phone out. "Shit," she says, panic flashing across her face. No reception. Uncle Bob swallows, pulls out his own phone, shakes his head.

"We need to get him to the back," my mom says, processing the situation quickly and realizing, as I did, that at the moment, the cold is the greatest danger.

My dad cries out as my mom and Uncle Bob, with Vance's and Kyle's help, wrench him free and pull him into the back. They lay him on the paneling above the seats. He's in bad shape, his face cut in a dozen places and his jeans drenched with blood. My mom and Uncle Bob kneel beside him, and Vance returns to Chloe, and Kyle returns to trying to free Mo from her seat belt.

"My purse," Aunt Karen says. "There are scissors."

Kyle crawls to Aunt Karen's giant handbag, which flew to the front with everything else, and rummages through it, pulling out her enormous collection of purse paraphernalia—cosmetics, tissues, antibacterial wipes, two packages of saltines, her cell phone, her address book, a bag of M&M'S, thank-you notes—and finally unearthing a small pair of manicure scissors, and he hustles back to cut Mo loose.

As soon as she is free, she crawls past him to the cab. Kyle follows.

When she sees me, she cries out and falls backward. Kyle catches her and turns her away, pulling her face to his chest as he tries to lead her back into the trailer. But she refuses. Pushing from his grip, she crawls forward again and takes my hand. Her lips move quietly, talking to me as tears run down her cheeks, and already I miss her so much it's as if my heart is being torn in two, and I cry with her, wishing desperately for this not to be happening.

Chloe's eyes are open now, and she has taken the scarf from Vance and now holds it to the wound herself as she stares, dazed, at the scene around her. She looks at my dad beside her, then glances toward the cab, and tears fill her eyes. Her jaw trembles, and I watch as she slides it forward to stop its quiver.

Bingo yips, and Chloe looks up at him. "Vance, help Bingo," she manages.

Vance wrestles the dog from Oz's grip, causing Oz to scream even louder, his face ham red from his tantrum and from hanging upside down.

Kyle stares at Oz, and I feel how much he wants to release him, his jaw clenching and his muscles coiled with his desire to help.

"What do you think?" my mom says to Uncle Bob, who squats beside my dad examining his wounds.

Uncle Bob's eyes flick back and forth, and it's obvious he has no idea how to deal with the injuries in front of him. He is a dentist, not a doctor, a specialist in cosmetic repairs, and what he's looking at has nothing to do with teeth whitening or veneers. But after a telling momentary pause, he says, almost convincingly, "We need to set the leg and stop the bleeding."

I can't be certain if it's ego or strength that causes his bluff: whether he's too arrogant to admit he doesn't have a clue or whether he's protecting the women from worry. Either way, I am grateful for the latter, his confidence calming, and even Oz stops screaming and now merely hangs and whimpers.

Behind them, Natalie and Aunt Karen huddle tighter, both having begun to shiver. Mo shivers as well, and I want to tell her to move to the back, where it is warmer, but she continues to sit beside me, holding my hand and crying.

Nothing that I want to be happening is happening, and all I can do is watch. It's the most frustrating, awful thing in the world. *Please*, I beg, *help them*. But if there is a God in this new world, he is as invisible as when I was mortal, and there is no answer whatsoever to my plea. *Mo, move to the back.*

Mo remains oblivious, but Kyle reacts. I'm not certain if it's because he hears me or if it's only that he realizes he can do something useful.

Whatever the reason, mercifully, he crawls forward and gently leads Mo away from my body and the swirling, freezing wind.

My dad screams as Uncle Bob pulls on his mangled leg to straighten it, causing Uncle Bob to release it, his false bluster dissolved instantly into panic. "Maybe it's better if we leave it," he stammers, the truth plain for all of them to see. He makes his living making people's smiles pretty and is no better equipped to deal with this than any of the rest of them.

7

When the initial shock wears off, reality sets in. They are stranded in a blizzard miles from help. I am dead. My dad is in bad shape. Uncle Bob has an injured left ankle, and Chloe needs stitches. These are the wounds that can be seen.

More frightening than the injuries are the cold and wind blasting through the windshield. Kyle and Oz are dressed best for the weather, both in full outdoor gear with snow boots and gloves. Mo is dressed the worst, her thin wool jacket, torn jeans, and designer boots useless against the cold. She shivers in the back beside Aunt Karen and Natalie. Mother and daughter hold each other tight, Natalie whimpering, Aunt Karen shushing her and telling her it's going to be all right.

"What's the plan?" Vance says. "Who's going for help?"

Everyone looks at my mom, but it's my dad who speaks through clenched teeth. "No one. We need to stay put until morning."

Panic shudders through each person in turn. It's not even seven, morning at least twelve hours away.

"No fucking way," Vance says.

Aunt Karen speaks up. "I don't think we can wait that long. It's freezing."

"We have to," my dad says, shivering more from pain than cold. "It's pitch black and blizzarding. Walk out in that, and you won't know which way is up."

"Up is the opposite of down," Vance says. "And there's no fucking way I'm staying out here all night."

"Vance, Jack is right," my mom says. "We need to wait until it's light."

"I'm hungry," Oz says, still hanging from his seat.

"Oz, you need to wait," my mom answers absently.

"You promised pancakes."

This time she simply ignores him.

"Pancakes!"

Ignoring Oz doesn't work.

Vance pulls on his hat. "You want to stay here, that's your business. I'm going for help. Chloe, you coming?"

Chloe's face is striped with blood, and she still holds my mom's scarf to her wound. Her eyes dart from Vance to the others and back again.

"No, Chloe's staying here," my mom says. "And Vance, so are you. Jack's right. We need to wait until morning."

"Chloe?" Vance challenges, his nose flaring and his eyes squinted in defiance.

Chloe stands, wobbling slightly with dizziness.

"Chloe," my mom says, fear lacing her voice. "You need to stay here."

Vance pulls Chloe to him and wraps his arm possessively around her shoulders.

My mom reaches for her. "Chloe, we need to stick together." And though she doesn't know it, her words tip Chloe's decision over the edge. Setting my mom's scarf down, she turns and staggers toward the shattered windshield, careful not to look at my body as she goes, her body wavering and her jaw clenched tight. Vance follows and nearly pushes her into the night.

"Ann, stop her," my dad moans, but there's nothing my mom can do. She is standing at the edge of the cab, staring through the broken windshield into the darkness, but the snow has already swallowed them, and they are gone.

"Pancakes," Oz continues to scream. "I'm hungry."

Everyone pretends he isn't there, except my dad, who mumbles, "Oz, no pancakes, not tonight. You need to take care of Bingo. Bingo's hungry also, but there's no food. He's going to be scared because he doesn't understand, so you need to take care of him."

With this final exertion, my dad's eyes roll back in his head, and he passes out. But what he did was amazing. He's the only one who truly understands Oz. My brother has stopped screaming, his attention diverted to his new task.

"Mo, let me down," he says. "Dad says I need to help Bingo."

I'm a little surprised Mo is the one he asks. But when I scan those who remain, she is the best choice. My heart pinches with the realization that already I've been replaced.

Even now, my mom doesn't look at her son, avoiding him the way some people avoid their reflections, not wanting to see what the world does. The cruel joke is that Oz looks the most like her—light-golden skin and hazel eyes with long lashes. But like a fun house mirror, Oz is distorted, a grossly enlarged version of her, and since he was born, she has refused to face him.

My mom continues to stand and stare into the night, her fists clenched, and I know she is weighing the decision of whether to go after Chloe or stay. I feel her making the choice. Impossible. One daughter gone in the wilderness. Her injured husband and son here. And Mo. Selfishly, I beg her to stay.

Mo stands, her body convulsing from the cold as she walks carefully around my dad to get to Oz. Kyle leaps up to help her, and together they release his seat belt and help him down.

Oz takes a spot in the corner behind the driver's seat and calls Bingo onto his lap. He whispers to the dog, "I know you're hungry, but you need to wait. It's okay. You'll be okay. I'll take care of you." He strokes the dog's fur, and Bingo lets him.

"We need to close off that window," Kyle says with a glance at the shattered windshield, snapping my mom from her trance, the decision made for her, too much time passed for her to do anything but remain.

"He's right," she says, blinking away her tears. "The only chance we have of surviving the night is to somehow block out the storm."

Everyone looks around. The Miller Mobile doesn't offer much in terms of supplies. It's not the kind of camper used for camping. It's more of a surf-mobile, an inexpensive way to travel and cart toys like surfboards, kayaks, and bikes, a metal box with a few seats and a table.

"Snow," Mo says. "We can use the game boards and sticks if we can find them, then pack it with snow like the Eskimos do."

Mo is brilliant. Someday she will do great things. Like MacGyver, give her a paper clip and a roll of duct tape, and she could make a jet airplane.

Kyle doesn't need to be told twice. Jumping into action, he pulls on his gloves and crawls toward the opening. Uncle Bob hobbles forward on his damaged ankle, and my mom and Mo follow behind him.

My mom turns, the twist causing a jolt of pain that freezes her. With a measured exhale, she straightens the wince from her face and says, "Mo, stay here."

"I can help," Mo says, her teeth chattering inside blue lips.

"Stay," my mom says more firmly, and Mo doesn't argue again.

When my mom is gone, Mo turns her attention to my dad. Her hands shake uncontrollably, but she manages to unzip his jacket and wrestle his arms from the sleeves. She crosses them over his body, then rezips the coat and ties the sleeves, his jacket now a cocoon and his bare hands protected.

Her manipulation rouses him. "Finn?" he mumbles, disoriented, his eyes fluttering open.

"It's me, Mr. Miller," Mo says, her voice cracking.

And when my dad realizes it isn't me, his eyes leak, the tears freezing on his cut cheeks. "Thank you," he says, then falls back to unconsciousness.

She looks down at his leg and winces at the injury. It's not the blood that makes her cringe; her wince is in sympathy for his pain, and I see her pray that he stays unconscious. As her eyes travel back to his face, she notices something sticking out from his jacket pocket—the edge of a glove—and I watch as she pushes it out of sight.

8

As cold as it was inside the camper, it's impossibly colder outside. The wind howls ferociously, whipping the snow into hard balls of ice that slash and cut the skin. My mom raises her face to the onslaught, her eyes peering through the razor gauze as she searches for Chloe, but not a trace of her or Vance remains.

Only Kyle wears gloves. My mom wraps her scarf around her hands. Uncle Bob crawls back into the camper, and I follow.

"Oz, I need your gloves," he says when he reaches my brother.

Bad idea.

Oz still holds Bingo and is stroking him with his gloved hands. Oz is dressed for the cold because my dad promised they would build a snowman in front of the restaurant after dinner, a tradition they follow every time we eat at Grizzly Manor.

Mo's eyes slide to my dad's pocket, but she says nothing.

"Oz, I'll give them back," Uncle Bob says. "But I need to use them so I can block out the wind."

"No," Oz says in his blunt Oz way, crossing his arms and tucking his hands into his armpits.

"Oz, give me your gloves," Uncle Bob orders, trying a different approach, his hand held out with authority.

I roll my eyes. Trying to argue, reason, demand, or cajole Oz into doing something he doesn't want is a complete waste of time. It's simply not going to happen. But Uncle Bob, for being as smart as he is, can be pretty dense. And though he's known my brother since he was born, he doesn't really understand his disability.

I describe Oz as simple. Some would say he's dumb, but it's more than that. My brother's mind works in a very rudimentary way, relying more on impulse than thought to get by. If he sees a cookie, he eats it. If he needs to go to the bathroom, he pulls down his pants and goes. His cognition does not extend to calculated thought or complex emotions such as compassion, empathy, or sympathy. He understands his own needs and acts on base instincts to fulfill them. This isn't to say he doesn't love or care. His heart is large as an elephant's, but things need to be presented in a way he can understand. If Uncle Bob asked him to help close up the window, Oz would work until he collapsed and wouldn't complain a lick. Or if he asked Oz to "share" his gloves, "one for you, one for me," Oz might do that as well. He might even "take turns" with the gloves. These are concepts Oz has been taught and that he can understand.

But Uncle Bob doesn't know this. He sees Oz only as a simpleton with gloves he needs so he can close the window. He steps toward my brother impatiently, all his feigned kindness gone and his eyes hard and dark.

Oz is only thirteen, and Uncle Bob mistakenly thinks therefore he can commandeer the gloves. This is foolish. Although Uncle Bob is two inches taller, thirty years older, and a whole lot smarter, it's like believing that because you're taller, older, and smarter than a grizzly, you will win in a fight.

Uncle Bob grabs Oz's sleeve to pull his gloved hand toward him, and quick as a shark, Oz bends down and bites him. Hard.

Uncle Bob yanks his hand away, teeth marks imprinted on the skin. "Animal," he snaps. "Goddamn animal."

Oz tucks his gloved hands back into his armpits, and Uncle Bob hobbles back outside, gloveless and swearing.

He finds my mom and Kyle beside the undercarriage. They have pulled my dead body from the cab and carried it to the downhill side of the camper so it won't get buried when they fill the windshield with snow. I've been laid behind the front wheel, where I will be somewhat protected.

My mom weeps as she unclothes me, stripping off my UGGs and socks and sweatpants. Kyle removes my parka and sweatshirt. I watch, thankful it is dark so Kyle won't see my nakedness, which is ridiculous since I am dead, yet I feel embarrassed just the same.

When they are done, my mom carries the clothes back through the windshield.

"Mo, put these on," she says, setting the pile beside my friend.

Mo swallows hard and shudders from more than the cold. Even in the darkness, the blood on my jacket shows.

"Are those Finn's?" Natalie asks, her voice hiccupping, and I realize she might have just realized I'm not there or just remembered it, her brain not fully processing what is happening.

My mom lifts her head, almost surprised to see Aunt Karen and Natalie, as if she had forgotten they were there.

Aunt Karen's eyes flick side to side, the pupils wide. "Natalie should get the boots," she says, her wild gaze skittering over the clothes as she hugs Natalie against her.

My mom's face tilts to process Aunt Karen's words as if trying to reroute her thoughts to include the additional data. Both Mo and Natalie wear boots that offer little protection from the cold. My mom's own feet are sheathed in ankle-high combat boots that aren't much better.

Perhaps it is the fierceness with which Aunt Karen is looking at my mom, or maybe it's the fact that she's not making any move to help close the window, or maybe it's because I'm dead and Mo is my best friend, or maybe it's because she made a promise to Mrs. Kaminski to look after Mo, or maybe it's because my mom can't reprocess the decision. Whatever the reason, my mom turns from Aunt Karen and repeats, "Mo, put these on." Then, without a word, she pivots and walks back into the fray.

Mo can barely get her body to work. Her muscles convulse violently, and her fingers are frozen into claws. Finally she manages to pull on my sweatshirt and parka. Then she unzips her boots, pulls my sweats over her torn jeans, and jams her feet into my too-small UGGs. My socks she uses as mittens. Lastly, she cinches the hood of my parka at her chin, blocking out the wind and Aunt Karen's glare.

9

My mom and Uncle Bob and Kyle work valiantly to close off the camper from the storm—an arctic tantrum so violent it makes me think of stories I've read of ocean squalls that swallow great ships whole. The force of it makes me cry out for Chloe as I think of her stuck in its fury, and suddenly I am beside her, my breath catching as I realize the trouble she's in.

Vance and Chloe made a mistake, a terrible mistake. Already they are so lost it is impossible for them to know which way to continue. The darkness is absolute, the wind and cold pounding them as they blunder blindly on, stumbling across the uneven tundra, sinking in spots up to their knees, then tripping and sliding on slicks of granite and ice. Vance tries to divine up from down, but it is impossible, as up becomes down quickly or becomes too steep and impassible.

Logic should tell them to stop, to find shelter behind a tree and wait out the night, but desperation and cold have frozen all reason from Vance's thoughts, and so he forges forward, checking on Chloe often, helping her when she stumbles and assuring her they will be okay.

She is not doing well. Her cut no longer bleeds, but there is something wrong. Her balance is off, and she wobbles as she walks like she is drunk. "Go on," she says at one point when her foot sticks in a drift and Vance returns to help her.

There's a beat of hesitation that chills me to my core before he says, "No, I'm not leaving you."

She whimpers and nods, and they continue on, trudging forward, Chloe staggering behind and trying to keep up as Vance stubbornly and bravely blazes a trail, still believing he will be a hero and somehow save them all.

10

My mom, Uncle Bob, and Kyle are shaking badly when they climb back into the camper through the door that is now on the ceiling. Kyle lowers himself through first, moving with the grace of an athlete. My mom climbs in next, wincing when Kyle grabs her waist to help her down. Together they help Uncle Bob, who awkwardly lowers himself, then stumbles when they set him on his feet, his left ankle giving out and sending him to the ground.

Aunt Karen jumps up, helps him stand, then guides him to the back to sit between her and Natalie. She rubs his hands between hers and wraps her scarf over his red ears.

My mom collapses beside my dad, her body quivering so violently she looks like she's having a seizure.

Kyle finds a spot in the corner, pulls his knees to his chest, and trembles alone.

It's eight o'clock.

"People will come looking for us," Aunt Karen says after a few minutes have passed and true misery has set in.

All eyes turn with hope to Kyle and Mo, the disenfranchised orphans of the group with families at home to worry about them.

Kyle shakes his head. "My roommates will assume I went to my girlfriend's. My girlfriend will think I went home."

Mo's bottom lip trembles as she confesses, "I made my mom swear not to call, and I told her I wasn't going to call her. We got into a huge fight about it."

The hope deflates. No one will be looking for them: not tonight, not tomorrow. They won't be discovered missing for at least two days. My mom squeezes her eyes shut, and I know she is thinking of Chloe. I watch her jaw lock as she grits her teeth to hold it together. Mo doesn't bother to hide her emotions, tears leaking as she buries her face against her knees.

The minutes tick by slow as hours, the cold and wind rattling through the camper. In the beginning, each deals with it differently. Natalie complains and cries against Aunt Karen, who shushes her and tells her to hang in there. Uncle Bob fidgets and moves constantly in an attempt to keep warm. My mom and Mo form a sandwich against my dad, one on each side of him, silent tears escaping as they think of me and worry about my dad and Chloe and Vance. My dad mercifully remains unconscious, his wheezing breath and occasional groans confirming he is still with them. Kyle burrows deep into his parka and, though shivering, seems to be doing better than the others, with the exception of Oz, who sleeps with Bingo on his lap, seemingly immune to the cold and the drama around him.

I watch from above, feeling their suffering and desperate to help but unable.

For the first few hours this is how we remain, until, near midnight, the world gets impossibly colder, and the differences of how each suffers diminish until they all endure it in a uniform state of survival. No one fidgets or complains or cries anymore. All have their eyes closed, their chins tucked, their bodies balled tight as they pray for morning and for the endurance to bear the misery until then.

When I can't watch their suffering a moment longer, I return to Chloe, offering a prayer of my own that some sort of divine guidance has intervened and miraculously led her and Vance to salvation and that help for the others will be arriving soon.

11

God is cruel, or God is not listening.

Chloe and Vance continue to trudge through the freezing, vast darkness, which is completely indistinguishable from the freezing, vast darkness they've traveled through for the past six hours. The distance between them has grown wide, Chloe losing ground with each step and Vance looking back less often.

I stay with Chloe as she staggers forward, her strength nearly gone and her body wavering dangerously. We step into a drift, and she stumbles, falls to her knees, doesn't get up.

Get up, Chloe.

Her hands are in her pockets and her face dropped so her chin is bent to her chest. Vance looks back, sees her, takes a step, sinks to his calf. With enormous effort he pulls his foot free and steps back to solid ground. For a long moment he stands there, looking at her through the veil of snow, and I feel the conflict within him, his hesitation and his fear. A hundred feet separate them: a virtual ocean for the amount of effort it would take to cross.

Tears freeze on his blistered cheeks, until finally he wipes them with the back of his frozen hands, turns, and staggers away. And as much as

I hate him, part of me also understands. He is only a boy, and he is lost in a blizzard, and he doesn't want to die. And if he stays, that is what will happen. Both of them will die. And so he takes one step away and then another.

After a dozen, he stops, and I watch as he realizes what he has done and his shame slams into him. He spins, his face a mask of panic as he squints into the swirling darkness, desperate to figure out the way back so he can undo it and reclaim the man he thought he was. But like so many things you wish you could undo, it is simply too late—his footprints are erased, and she is gone.

He thinks he sees the path and follows it, but he is a few degrees off: close but too far for her to hear him and too far for him to see her. I see them both and want to guide him, but though I am with him, he is alone and has no idea he is so near.

Finally, defeated and numb, he gives up, and I watch as he staggers back in the direction he believes is the right one, his only hope now for salvation to somehow find a way out so others can come back and save her.

As I watch, I consider for a moment that perhaps this is hell, an invisible and silent existence where you have no ability to help those you love, forced to watch them struggle and suffer. In life, I did not pray, and my family did not go to church, and I wonder if this is the reason for my damnation, punishment for not worshipping the way I should have or for not offering repentance for my sins.

I offer it now. With all my heart I pray, begging God to spare my family and Mo and Aunt Karen and Uncle Bob and Natalie and Vance and Kyle from any more suffering and to deliver me from this world, if not to heaven then at least to a place where I can find peace, to relieve my anguish and to save me from having to witness any more of the destruction of everything I love.

Chloe remains as she was, kneeling in the snow, her hands still in her pockets and her breath puffing in front of her.

Fight, Chloe, I plead. *Please, Chloe. You have to. You have to try.*

And she does. With heroic effort, she pushes to her feet, staggers to a great pine to her right, and slumps against it, sliding into a hollow at its base and curling into herself so she can rest.

12

Finally the eternal night begins to brighten from black to gray, and when it's light enough for my mom to see her breath steam in front of her, she rolls stiffly from my dad and forces her frozen muscles to unfurl.

My dad is so pale I worry he's dead, and grief begins to overtake me, but then Mo lifts herself as well, and he moans. I sniff back the tears and watch as my mom does the same.

Injuries from the accident have settled during the night, and this morning it is obvious that my mom is in serious pain, her body crimped at the waist from her damaged ribs. My dad's face is swollen and so bruised he is unrecognizable. His jeans are black with blood and his breathing shallow. Uncle Bob pulls Natalie's feet from the sleeves of his coat, a creative idea to stave off the freeze of her toes, and he winces as he lifts his damaged foot, his ankle swollen to twice its normal size.

The left side of Kyle's face is bruised, and he rolls his shoulder to work out the soreness. Other than that, he seems okay. The others—Aunt Karen, Natalie, Mo, and Oz—are fine other than exhaustion, thirst, hunger, and cold.

Uncle Bob hops to the door, climbs onto the edge of the table, and manages to push it open, letting in a gush of cold air. He's tall enough that his head sticks through the opening, but with only one leg, he's not strong enough to hoist himself out. He fidgets uncomfortably, his bladder in obvious need of relief.

Kyle climbs onto the side of the bench beside him, makes his hands into a stirrup, and gives him a boost.

"You need to go to the bathroom?" Kyle asks Oz.

Oz nods, and Kyle says, "Come on then."

"Bingo too," Oz says.

"Bingo too."

Mo watches, her eyes welling with Kyle's kindness.

Oz doesn't need a boost. He climbs onto the table edge, then easily pulls himself out. Kyle lifts Bingo, and Oz reaches down to pull the dog onto the camper. Then Kyle hoists himself out behind them and closes the door.

My mom examines my dad. She looks at his maimed leg and checks his pulse, and then, more tenderly than I've ever seen her with him, she brushes her lips over his. "I'm going to get help," she whispers as she reaches into his pockets, pulls out his gloves, and tucks them beneath her coat.

For a flicker I wonder how she knew about them and why she didn't wear them during the night, but the answer is in the slide of her eyes toward Mo, who still looks at the door where Uncle Bob, Kyle, and Oz disappeared a moment before. *Trust.* Mo told her about them. They trust each other, but neither entirely trusts the others.

The boys are back. Kyle comes in first and holds his arms out for Bingo, who Oz lowers, and then they help Uncle Bob.

"Stay out there, Oz," Kyle says. "It's the girls' turn, and you need to help them up."

Kyle gives each woman a leg up, and Oz pulls them out the door. Each time, Kyle says, "Good job, buddy," and Oz grins with pride.

The blizzard is only half as bad as it was last night, and though still blustery and cold, it is possible to see the trees and to differentiate up from down.

Aunt Karen and Natalie finish their business quickly and hustle back into the camper. My mom holds Mo's sleeve to keep her from following. Oz stands beside them, waiting to give them a boost onto the camper.

"I'm going for help," my mom says.

Mo bites her bottom lip to stop the quiver as she fights to keep the tears in her eyes, and my mom pulls her into her arms, causing the dam to explode. Mo weeps against her shoulder, and it is strange for me to witness, to watch the way my mom holds her and strokes her hair. I cannot recall my mom ever holding me like that or being so tender. As far as I know, she's never held Chloe or Aubrey that way, either, and a pang of jealousy strikes as I wonder, if it were me, if she would be as gentle.

My mom's voice is low as she says, "You need to take care of Oz and Jack. Until I get back with help, you need to look out for them." There's warning in the words.

Mo pulls away and wipes the tears from her cheeks, and then she does something remarkable, something so incredibly Mo-like I miss her even more. "You need to wear the boots," she says as she plops to the snow and wrenches off the UGGs, keeping her feet in the air so they won't get wet.

"Mo . . ."

"There's no argument. You need to get help, and Finn's boots are going to get you there." The words were chosen carefully, and my mom nods, then sits beside her so she can change boots. My UGGs fit my mom perfectly. For two years, we've worn the same size shoes.

Kyle's head pops from the camper. "What's going on out here?"

"As much fun as it's been hanging out here in the cold," my mom says bravely for Mo's sake, "I think it's time to call in the cavalry. I'm going to get help."

Without hesitation, Kyle pulls himself out the door and says, "I'm coming with you."

My mom nods, and that's all the preamble there is before they begin to trek back in the direction the camper fell. Oz helps Mo onto the camper, then clambers up after her, and together they watch until my mom and Kyle fade away in the gauzy film of white. Only I notice that my mom did not say goodbye to Oz.

13

"Where are they going?" Oz asks.

"To get help," Mo answers.

"I'm hungry."

"I'm hungry too," Mo answers, and amazingly this plain shared understanding works, and Oz nods.

Aunt Karen, Uncle Bob, and Natalie stare from their huddle at the back of the camper when Mo and Oz return inside.

"Where's Ann?" Uncle Bob says.

"She went for help."

"Oh, thank God," Aunt Karen says as Uncle Bob's face grows concerned, his eyes drifting to the snow-packed window of the camper. He flexes his ankle with a wince, confirming for himself or the others the reason he's not the one being a hero.

"The kid went with her?" he says, his voice tight with worry for my mom.

"Kyle," Mo says as she lowers herself beside my dad, her lip sucked in as she works to hold it together. Oz returns to his corner and pulls Bingo onto his lap.

Uncle Bob continues to look at the snow while Aunt Karen watches Mo pull off my mom's too-small combat boots to replace them with her own icy boots, her frozen fingers struggling to grip the stiff leather.

Residual bitterness over my UGGs being given to Mo instead of Natalie lines her face.

Natalie's expression is harder to read. There's a slight wrinkle in her brow, and it's hard to be certain, but if I'm not mistaken, beyond the outward expression of scorn that mirrors her mom's is a shadow of respect, perhaps knowing that had my mom given my boots to her instead of Mo, Natalie would not have made the offer to give them back.

After Mo gets her boots zipped, she crawls toward the cab. My mom's purse and Chloe's purse are still where they landed, thrown against the driver's seat with the playing cards and poker chips and Scrabble letters. Aunt Karen has retrieved her own purse, and it is tucked beside her.

Mo goes through my mom's bag first—a few hundred dollars in cash, credit cards, sunglasses, makeup, a hairbrush, two dozen receipts, six pens, tampons, and a menu for our local Thai restaurant. Chloe's bag proves more bountiful—in addition to all the nonuseful makeup and empty candy wrappers is a worn copy of *Pride and Prejudice*, a pair of black tights, and a BIC lighter. Mo slyly pockets the tights and sets aside the book and the lighter along with the receipts and cash. She continues into the cab, swooning slightly when she sees the blood-soaked seats, and rummages through the console to find a few maps, my dad's hat, and a carrot he had probably put there for the snowman he was going to build with Oz. The carrot goes in her pocket with the tights, and she carries the hat along with the kindling back into the trailer.

Uncle Bob's face darkens when he sees the hat; his own head is bare, and my skin prickles with concern. The subtle shift in the dynamic with my mom and Kyle gone is unsettling. Uncle Bob, Aunt Karen, and Natalie now on one side. My dad, Mo, and Oz on the other. I look to where Aunt Karen's purse was to see that she has pushed it farther beneath the seat to conceal it.

Mo unties my dad's hood, and I watch Uncle Bob snap out of it like a switch. He shakes his head as if waking from a daze, then pushes to his feet. "Let me help," he says. Keeping his ankle lifted, he hops to squat beside her and lifts my dad's head so Mo can pull the hat over his hair.

"Thank you," Mo says as she recinches the hood.

Uncle Bob rests his hand on my dad's chest. "Hang in there, Jack." Then he hobbles back to his family while Mo remains huddled beside mine.

14

My mom and Kyle realize quickly that hiking straight up the way we fell is not an option. The icy sheet of granite offers little in terms of footholds and less in terms of shelter from the fierce wind that blasts against its face the moment you rise above the tree line and that could easily blow even the strongest climbers to their deaths.

Instead, my mom and Kyle traverse at an angle, my mom being careful to keep the glow of the sun behind them to ensure they are heading north, the general direction of town. When possible, they travel upward, but often as not, they hit an impasse and are forced to backtrack to lower ground.

At first my mom hikes in front, but soon it becomes clear that Kyle has better traction, and he takes over the lead. On the steeper parts, he digs in and uses my mom's scarf to help her up.

They make slow, inconsistent progress, which I can see is leading them closer to the road, but they have no way to know this. My mom's lips are blistered and her cheeks raw, but the exertion seems to have warmed her, and only her feet appear in pain from the cold.

Kyle seems unaffected, or perhaps he just isn't the type to complain. Stoically he marches forward, forging a path and looking back often to check on my mom. And the more I watch him, the more my admiration grows and the more I find myself wondering about him, about who he is, his family, his girlfriend, how he ended up living in Big Bear, what he's thinking about, whether he's scared. It seems so strange that he is part of this and that we know so little about him.

My mom's eyes slide side to side as she walks, scanning like a hawk, and I feel her hope that somehow they will stumble upon Chloe and Vance. Only I know they are nowhere close, a vast forest of snow, rocks, and trees separating them, Chloe still huddled in the hollow of the tree she stumbled to last night as Vance continues to stagger farther into the wilderness.

15

"Oz, can you lift me out again?" Mo says.

"Where are you going?" Uncle Bob asks, suspicion lacing the words, a new undercurrent of distrust between them that grows with each minute that passes.

"I'm going to get us some water."

Natalie perks up, and Aunt Karen licks her lips. The group hasn't had anything to eat or drink since we left the cabin fifteen hours ago.

Uncle Bob blinks, and his distrustful squint is replaced with a flash of shame. "Do you need help?"

Mo shakes her head a little too quickly. "I just need to get some snow."

My brother weaves his hands into a stirrup like Kyle did and hoists Mo through the door. She closes it behind her and blinks into the blinding glare from the day, which is now dazzlingly bright. She scoots onto the door, which is snowless from being opened and closed, and I shiver as I watch her shed my sweats and her pants to pull on Chloe's tights.

I smile at her brilliance, knowing she purposely waited for enough time to pass that the others would not think about what else she might have retrieved from the purses and console.

Quickly she re-dresses, both of us feeling the guilt of her wearing a layer that Chloe desperately needs. I watch as she closes her eyes in a silent prayer, and I pray with her, hoping Chloe can feel me.

When she is dressed again, she takes two quick bites of the carrot, returns it to her pocket, then scoops snow from the top of the camper into Chloe's purse. She climbs back through the door, and Oz helps her down.

Uncle Bob, Aunt Karen, and Natalie watch curiously as Mo crawls over the seat to the side window of the trailer that is now on the ground. She breaks my mom's sunglasses case apart, pulls off the felt lining, and picks off the glue as best she can. Using the pages of *Pride and Prejudice* and the BIC lighter, she builds a small fire, which she uses to melt snow in the sunglasses case. The case is shallow and barely holds a few ounces, but the method works, and after a dozen pages, she has a small dish of precious liquid.

She pours the water between my dad's parched lips, and I cheer when I see him swallow.

The next vessel she gives to Oz, who guzzles it greedily and again says he's hungry.

"Me too," Mo says.

The next drink she gives to Natalie, who thanks her.

"Bingo," Oz says as Mo returns to the flame with another small mound of snow.

Uncle Bob and Aunt Karen watch silently as they wait for Mo to make her decision of who to give the precious drops to next, them or the dog. Mo has yet to take a sip for herself.

When the snow is nearly transformed, Mo looks up at Oz. "Oz, Bingo is a dog," she says. "He can last much longer than people can without water."

"No," Oz says, pulling Bingo tighter. "He's thirsty."

Mo holds the case out to Aunt Karen, who carefully takes it from Mo's trembling hands.

No, I scream. *It's Mo's turn. She is the next CHILD.* My hate for Aunt Karen is instant and overwhelming. Of all the things she has done or not done since the accident, this is the one that pisses me off the most.

She lifts the case to her lips, but she is too slow. Oz lunges and grabs hold. Aunt Karen pulls against him and bends to try and slurp the water out.

And that's when it happens. Over less than a quarter cup of water, Oz hits her. It's more like a club than a punch, his fist glancing sideways across her cheek, but the force is enough to snap her face sideways.

With a yelp, she lets go, and half the water sloshes out.

Oz doesn't notice. Carefully he carries the remaining water back to Bingo, who eagerly laps it up.

Uncle Bob wraps his arms around Aunt Karen and stares in horror at my brother.

Oz holds the case out to Mo and demands, "More."

Mo's whole body shakes as she complies. Her fingers, white with cold, fill the sunglasses case with snow, and then she rips more pages from the novel and sets them ablaze.

"He's going to be the death of us," Aunt Karen whimpers into Uncle Bob's chest. "He's either going to kill us, or we'll die because of him. Just like he hurt that dog."

My blood goes cold at the mention of the dog. Three months ago, Oz got it in his head that Bingo was lonely and needed a friend, so he decided to find him one, a beagle puppy that belonged to a neighbor. When the neighbor came out and found Oz in his backyard, he confronted him, and Oz freaked out, squeezing the dog too tight and dislocating the poor animal's shoulder and breaking several of his ribs.

A lawsuit was filed, the community association issued our family a warning, and my mom went ballistic. She said Oz was too much for us to handle and that it was time to start looking into alternative solutions, which sent my dad into a fever. He added childproof locks to all the doors, installed monitors in every room, and spent two weeks sleeping outside Oz's door. It was horrible and tragic and extremely distressing.

Mo glances at Uncle Bob, then at Oz, her worry for my brother and about my brother lining her face. My own worry matches hers. Oz would never hurt anyone on purpose, but that doesn't mean he isn't dangerous.

Mo hands the sunglasses case to Oz, who holds it out for Bingo, and the dog drinks. Then she fills it with snow again, and Uncle Bob says, "Oz, do you think you can give me a hand out so I can go to the bathroom? Maybe Bingo needs to go as well."

I smile at his plan. *Good job, Uncle Bob.* Distraction is a great way to deal with Oz.

There is a universal sigh of relief when the three leave the camper, and Mo uses extra pages of the precious book to make the flame bigger so the snow will melt quicker. She hands the next ration to Aunt Karen, who greedily gulps it down, and I pop outside to see if Uncle Bob will come up with a way to delay Oz's return for a few extra minutes so Mo will have time to make a sip for herself.

"Finn," Oz says, noticing my body near the tire. Snow has drifted and fallen over my body, so I am completely buried except for my face.

"She's sleeping," Uncle Bob says, hopping around on his uninjured foot to ward off the cold, his hands jammed in his pockets and his chin buried in his coat.

Oz squints. My brother is not smart, but he is strangely perceptive, and lying to him is usually not a good idea. His face gets heavy, and his bottom lip pushes forward as his head shakes back and forth. "My Finn," he says, causing my heart to swell. Then he does something extraordinary. Without a word, he walks to where I am, kneels beside me, and buries my face with snow. "Good night, Finn," he says when he is done.

When he stands, Uncle Bob says, "Oz, I'm worried," and something in his tone makes my hair stand on end.

Oz tilts his head.

"Your mom's been gone a long time. I'm concerned she might have gotten lost."

Oz's brow furrows, and my pulse pounds.

"I think someone should go and look for her," Uncle Bob says.

Oz nods.

"I would go," Uncle Bob says, "but my ankle's busted pretty bad."

I shake my head, disbelief making my panic slow.

"I could go," Oz volunteers enthusiastically, as if the idea is brilliant.

NO! I put myself between them, directly in front of Uncle Bob so my nose is nearly touching his. *Don't do this.*

"You think you could find her?" Uncle Bob says, his brow lifting as if impressed by Oz's thinking.

"Bingo could go with me," Oz says. "He can find anyone. When Finn and I play hide-and-seek, Bingo always finds her, and Finn is really good at that game."

"That's a good idea."

Please, I beg. *Please, Uncle Bob, think about what you are doing.*

"If Bingo went with you," Uncle Bob goes on, "then he would also be able to help you and your mom find your way back."

I turn to Oz. He is nodding seriously, his face mimicking my father's when my dad is having a serious, manly conversation.

Mo, help, I cry.

But Mo is oblivious. She is inside, melting water as quickly as she can and hoping Oz won't come back too soon.

"Before you go," Uncle Bob says, "I have an offer to make you."

Oz, still wearing my father's expression, nods again, and my panic turns cold. I'm unable to imagine how things can get worse yet certain they are about to.

"You and Bingo are going to need food so you'll be strong as you search for your mom."

"I'm hungry," Oz says.

"Exactly. So here's the deal. I have two packages of crackers." Uncle Bob pulls the cellophane-wrapped saltines that were in Aunt Karen's purse from his pocket. "I'll trade you these for your gloves."

I don't bother pleading again. All I can do is stare in horrified disbelief as Oz takes the deal without a second of hesitation, whipping off his gloves and handing them to Uncle Bob as he swipes the crackers like he just made the world's greatest trade.

"Give me a boost," Uncle Bob says, and Oz makes his gloveless hands into a stirrup so he can lift Uncle Bob onto the trailer.

Uncle Bob doesn't look back or wish Oz good luck. Opening the door, he lowers himself inside, leaving Oz and Bingo outside with the impossible mission of hiking into the wilderness to find my mom.

16

The wind is getting stronger. I can tell by the way it pulls the skin of my mom's face and by the way she leans into it as she forces herself on. Her strength is fading, and so is her confidence for their success. It's early afternoon, and they've been hiking all day with no way of knowing whether they travel closer to or farther from civilization, making it difficult not to give up hope. My mom has been careful to keep the sun behind her, but they've been detoured so many times she's not even certain whether the town is still to the north or whether they've passed it entirely.

When they stumble upon a gully of deep snow that winds like a white snake up the jagged mountain, I scream for them to follow it. The road is above. Every ounce of energy I possess I send to my mom, willing her to turn.

My suggestion isn't needed. "Kyle," she croaks, her voice parched with dehydration and exhaustion. She points to the serpent. The sun is too far to the right. In order to stay on course, they need to turn.

Without protest or question, Kyle changes direction, forging a path into the deep, winding drift.

They make an oddly great team. Kyle has a good sense for climbing and for choosing forgiving paths, and my mom keeps them on course.

They've spoken less than a dozen words since they started, yet a natural synergy has propelled them farther than either would have gotten alone.

With each step up the powder-filled crevice, my mom's feet sink, and the loose UGGs fill with snow. She no longer winces at the ice burning her skin, and I think the flesh must now be frozen and numb.

Kyle moves steadily in front, stopping every few yards to wait for my mom as she claws and crawls her way forward, slipping occasionally, then having to reclaim the ground she lost.

At one point the incline becomes too steep, and my mom loses her footing altogether and slides down nearly twenty feet. For a second she lies in the snow, her body heaving, and then, with superhuman strength and no other choice, she pushes back to her feet and staggers on.

Kyle climbs down to meet her halfway. "Give me your scarf," he says.

My mom unwraps the strip of wool from her throat and hands it to him. Kyle cinches one end to my mom's right wrist, then holds out his right hand so she can do the same with the opposite end. Barely enough space remains between them for my mom to take a step, but a hundred feet later, when she slips again, Kyle digs in and holds tight to the scarf, and my mom only falls to the ground.

They inch their way forward, hope returning with each step that leads them farther in the direction they want to go and that doesn't send them back to the start.

~

It happens suddenly. They are more than halfway to the top, my heart celebrating each inch of progress, when Kyle steps around a boulder and the ground gives way, the patch he thought was solid nothing but a chunk of ice and snow.

I watch as he tumbles, his right foot plunging into air and pulling him sideways off his feet. The scarf catches him, stopping his fall and swinging him like a pendulum back into the face of the mountain and yanking my mom off her feet. Wildly she flails as Kyle's weight pulls her toward the ridge, her right hand clutching the scarf as her left swims, searching for something to grab hold of.

Her shoulder is over the edge when she catches hold of a small sapling that sprouts from beneath the boulder. The tree is less than two feet tall, but already its roots are strong, and I watch as she jerks to a stop and then as her limbs tremble as she struggles to hang on. Her head rolls from the gloved hand that holds the sapling to the one that holds Kyle, and I watch as her mind spins, the calculation made impossibly fast, his weight versus her strength.

Kyle sees it as well, his mouth opening and my own scream unheard as the fingers on my mom's right hand unfurl.

Kyle falls. But only an inch. The knot on her wrist cinches instead of loosening, and before my mom can shake it loose, Kyle is climbing up the wool, and quick as the decision was made, it is reversed, my mom reaching down to close her hand again, gripping the scarf with all her strength as Kyle's weight literally pulls her limb from limb.

A second later, he hoists himself over the edge and collapses beside her, his breath frosting in front of him and his eyes widening from the shock of how close he came to dying.

My mom rolls onto her back, and I watch as she lifts her hand in front of her, the fingers opening and closing as if she hasn't a clue how the mechanism works, her chin trembling.

"Ready?" Kyle says, pushing to his feet, his eyes avoiding hers.

Her mouth opens to say something, but there are no words. How do you apologize for choosing to let someone die so you could save yourself?

The scarf still tethers them as they continue on, but Kyle now picks his way up the trail more carefully, checking each step before he takes it and slowing their progress to a crawl.

17

Oz did not hike in the right direction. He looked at the camper and walked away from the taillights, either forgetting that we did not drive to the spot where we landed or mistakenly believing taillights are like a compass and always point back home.

At first he called out for my mom. When he was deep in the trees and utterly lost, he began to call for my dad.

For two hours Bingo has loyally trudged beside him, but now I watch as the dog groans and stops, sitting and then flopping down on his belly on a piece of snowless granite.

Oz looks down at him. "You tired, Bingo?"

Bingo puts his head between his paws and looks at Oz like he is sorry.

"It's okay," Oz says as he sits down beside him. "We'll rest."

Bingo is nearly eleven. A psychiatrist recommended we get a dog to keep Oz company, and the dog has been a fiercely devoted companion to my brother ever since.

Oz pulls the two packages of crackers from his pocket. One package he feeds to Bingo; the other he eats himself. Then he lifts Bingo's head onto his lap, puts his freezing hands in his pockets, and tells the dog that things are going to be okay.

18

Mo is utterly alone now.

She continues to sit beside my dad, shivering, every few minutes forcing her fingers and toes to move and grimacing with the pain. Her eyes continually slide to the door as the minutes tick by, her panic growing as she realizes that something has gone horribly wrong and that Oz is not coming back.

Uncle Bob, Aunt Karen, and Natalie sit huddled together in the spot they've been since my mom and Kyle left, Natalie now wearing Oz's gloves.

Natalie fidgets from Mo's glance, sliding her hands beneath her thighs, then, a moment later, wedging them into her armpits, while Uncle Bob glares defiantly.

Mo looks away and sucks in her bottom lip, a habit she has when she is in trouble or caught in a lie. Guilt. Grief. Fear. All of the above.

Mo has a giant soft spot for my brother. Oz has always had a crush on her and constantly does sweet, dopey things to prove it. Last summer he spent over three hours and a year's allowance at the fair throwing rings at bottles to win her a giant stuffed cheetah with spots shaped like hearts. The game was rigged and nearly impossible, but Oz was crazy determined because he knew Mo loved cheetahs. Finally the kid working the stand took pity on him and nudged a ring onto a bottle when Oz wasn't looking. Oz's grin when he gave Mo that cheetah was priceless.

Mo sniffs back the tears and wiggles her toes again, the pain temporarily stopping the emotions that threaten to overflow and destroy her.

Meanwhile, Uncle Bob's guilt festers. He sits beside Aunt Karen seething, his agitation growing. I can see it, his shame like acid that consumes him before spoiling into anger. Mo knows he did something, and he knows Mo knows. I see his mind ticking. If they get out of this, when they get out of this, because she knows, others will find out. He didn't consider that when he tricked Oz, but now he does. He sits beside his daughter and wife with nothing but miserable time to contemplate what will happen when they are saved.

Mo has now melted enough water that none of them are thirsty. Half the novel and the maps remain if they need to make more. It's a sad realization to know that, had they all stayed calm, there would have been enough for everyone, including Bingo and Oz.

The afternoon settles into an excruciating monotony of awful existence, and the hope of being rescued before nightfall begins to fade. My mom and Kyle have been gone since morning. If they had been successful, help would have already arrived.

They all hold their dwindling faith differently. Mo worries over my dad, soothing him with quiet promises that help is on the way. He doesn't respond. For hours he hasn't moved, not even to moan. Natalie stares blankly ahead, no thoughts at all, relying wholly on her parents to worry for her. Aunt Karen's mind spins endlessly and goes nowhere. Completely overwhelmed with the idea of being stranded for another night, she mutters in circles, "We need to get out of here. Maybe we should start a fire. No, we need to save our supplies. Maybe someone should look for Oz. We need to stay put. Someone's going to find us. Oh God, we won't make it another night . . ." Every half hour she pulls off Natalie's boots and rubs her daughter's toes, murmuring about circulation and blood flow. I wish she would shut up. I think everyone wishes she would shut up. Uncle Bob has given up on responding and just lets her blather, his mind now occupied with the shifting future and the looming reality of facing another night in the cold and the hard choices that will need to be made. I watch as his eyes slide to my dad, roaming over his North Face jacket, his wool hat, his jeans, and his snow boots.

Mo shifts slightly, obstructing his view.

"We need to get out of here," Aunt Karen wails.

Uncle Bob doesn't answer. He's already explained half a dozen times that leaving is not an option. Five have tried, and none have returned. Uncle Bob is a smart man. Five of the ten who survived the accident remain, his wife and daughter among them.

The minutes tick toward another night of hell, and the factors and probabilities for survival continue to shift, Uncle Bob's eyes sliding again to my dad, his face unreadable as he studies the thin mist puffing from my dad's lips, the only proof he's still alive.

19

There is no celebration when Kyle and my mom finally reach the road, only the briefest shared pause and tremble of relief.

Now that they are on solid ground, the scarf between them is untied, and they quicken their pace. Every few minutes my mom pulls out her phone to check for service, and twenty minutes later, the screen mercifully lights up with a single bar, and her eyes leak with gratefulness.

After that, things move quickly. Within minutes a sheriff's car finds them and details of the accident are being broadcast to various agencies. The deputy wants to take my mom and Kyle to the hospital, but my mom insists he drive them to the rescue site. Kyle agrees, claiming he's fine.

The staging area, a parking lot beside a sled park, is dramatic. Already a dozen ambulances, sheriff's cars, and forest ranger jeeps are gathered, along with at least fifty people in different uniforms. My mom and Kyle are ushered into a waiting ambulance, where they are wrapped with heated blankets and given bottles of water. A paramedic follows them in to assess their condition.

I watch as the man examines my mom first. She has mild frostbite on her fingers, several of her toes, and patches of her calves where snow and ice have lodged in her boots and frozen the skin. Warm compresses are wrapped around the damaged areas, and her feet are submerged in a tub of warm water. The paramedic also suspects my mom has several broken ribs, and he advises she go to the hospital for X-rays. She shakes her head and asks again if he will call the captain on his radio for an update on the search.

He makes the call, hangs up, shakes his head, then turns to Kyle, who patiently drinks his water and eats a McDonald's cheeseburger that was bought for him. My mom has a bag of food as well, but she hasn't touched a bite.

Kyle sets his food aside and removes his jacket and shirt.

I gasp, and so does my mom, her eyes bulging. The entire left side of Kyle's body, from his shoulder to his hip, is one giant swollen bruise, the skin a mottled, sickly purple blue.

"Ouch," he says with an ironic smile when the paramedic lifts Kyle's arm.

I'm overwhelmed with his heroics. His body was battered to a pulp, and he never said a word.

My mom swallows. She had no idea. She never asked. A boy the same age as her daughter in a horrible accident, and she never even asked him if he was okay. I didn't think of it either. Only in retrospect does it seem so incomprehensible. I want to tell her it's okay, remind her of how much she was already dealing with. But I know that even if she could hear me, it wouldn't matter. Regret is a tough emotion to live with, impossible to move on from, because what's done is done. Only delusion can protect you from it, somehow altering history into something easier to accept, and my mom is not capable of delusion.

"You okay?" the paramedic asks, noticing her pallor.

She nods and turns away, locking out the future that will be haunted by this moment to focus on the horrible present as she prays for no more regret.

"You need to go to the hospital," the paramedic says to Kyle. "Those bruises need to be looked at, and I think you dislocated your shoulder. It popped back in, but you probably need a sling."

Kyle nods and shrugs like what the guy is telling him is a bummer but no big deal; then in a tone that's weirdly everyday, he says, "Do you think someone can give me a lift?"

"There's a second ambulance outside," the paramedic says.

Kyle cringes. "Kind of a pricey ride."

The paramedic opens the door and hollers out the back, "Hey, Mary Beth, you think you can give the kid a ride to the hospital on the house?"

A woman's voice says, "Sure, there's a special hero rate running today—no charge for trips to the ER."

Kyle blushes as he pulls on his jacket and stands. "Thanks," he says to the paramedic. Halfway through the door, he hesitates and turns back to my mom. His words thick, he says, "I hope they're okay."

His kindness nearly destroys her, and I watch as her expression tightens, the muscles straining against her emotions. She manages a nod as her right hand opens and closes on her leg, and then she opens her mouth to say something, but it's too late. Kyle is already gone, and I think it almost would have been more merciful had he not turned back. A sob escapes, and my mom bites her knuckle to stop it, pushing it deep inside to keep the dam from exploding.

I watch as Kyle disappears into the other ambulance and wonder if I will ever see him again. I doubt it. Like soldiers who fought beside each other, once the war is over, they return to their separate lives, their only bond a tragic shared memory all would rather forget.

20

Mo hears it first. Her head lifts, and she looks at the ceiling and tilts her head. Thump, thump, thump, too consistent to be the wind. Her posture straightens as the thrumming grows closer, and I watch as she listens harder. She leaps to her feet but then falls back to the ground, her feet too frozen to hold her. On hands and knees, she crawls onto the side of the seat below the door.

"Help," she cries meekly, her voice cracking.

Her croak causes Uncle Bob and Aunt Karen and Natalie to become aware. Their tucked heads lift, and then their ears, too, catch the sound of the helicopter. Uncle Bob scrambles from his seat, hobbles up beside Mo, and manages to push open the door.

Through the opening, a man who is being lowered from a helicopter signals for them to stay put. Mo crawls back to my dad.

"Help is here," she cries. "You're going to be okay. Help is here."

My dad doesn't answer, and I pray she's right, that they arrived in time and that he's going to make it.

The man is in the doorway. Perhaps thirty, he looks like a marine, his body squat, tight, and muscular, his hair buzzed short and stick straight. He scans the interior, then lowers himself inside, and Uncle Bob shakes the man's hand as the man surveys the scene.

"Five," he says into his headset. "Four responsive, one unconscious."

"Confirm five. Supposed to be six and a dog," someone squawks back.

Uncle Bob's eyes slide to the ground, then return quickly. "The sixth and the dog left this morning," he says. "He went looking for his mom."

Mo's eyes dart to Natalie's gloved hands, but she says nothing.

Aunt Karen and Natalie are so delirious with being saved that they are oblivious to everything else. They hug each other and cry, blubbering and swearing how they're never going anywhere with snow again. I wish they would shut up. *SHUT UP!*

Within minutes, the snow wall my mom, Kyle, and Uncle Bob constructed to close up the windshield is cleared away, and two more rescue workers carry a gurney into the camper. A few minutes later, my dad is carried out and hoisted into the sky. The helicopter does not wait to lift the others before leaving. As soon as my dad is on board, the chopper races away, heading toward a level-three trauma center in Riverside, where a team of doctors is waiting.

A second helicopter arrives a few moments later. Natalie is lifted first, and then Aunt Karen steps forward, but Uncle Bob stops her, saying, "Honey, Mo needs to go next." Aunt Karen's face turns crimson, and she steps back.

Once everyone is on board, the helicopter leaves for the hospital. There was a brief discussion about bringing my body along, but it was decided that they would come back for it.

I'm glad. Mo's been through enough. The last thing she needs is a ride along with my frozen, mutilated corpse.

As they fly, Mo stares out the window, her eyes squinting through the snow at the endless forest, tears streaming down her face as she takes in the vastness and the hopelessness of spotting Chloe, Vance, or Oz.

21

My mom sits alone in the ambulance, waiting for news.

The San Bernardino County Sheriff's Department is in charge of the rescue operation, and the man running things is a guy named Burns. He's the kind of man you want to be running things. Medium built with the quickness of an athlete, he has a sharp assertiveness that's comforting, especially when it comes to dealing with my mom. Half an hour ago, he ordered her to stay in the ambulance and not interfere, and when she opened her mouth to protest, his stern look stopped her.

Burns runs the operation from the back of a sheriff's van, barking commands to his team with an urgency that conveys the essence of time but without panic. Every few minutes, he steps outside to peer at the horizon, gauging the darkness and the impending storm, both approaching far too quickly.

When he gets the news of the rescue, he hurries across the parking lot to the ambulance and steps inside.

"What's wrong?" my mom says to the grim expression on his face.

"We found the camper. Your husband is on his way to Inland Valley Medical Center in Riverside. He's alive, but his condition is serious."

She squeezes her eyes shut and sighs in relief that he's still alive. She thinks this is the bad news Burns came to deliver, and it takes a minute for her to realize he's not done.

"Maureen and the Golds—Bob, Karen, and Natalie," he continues, "are being taken in a second helicopter to Big Bear Medical Center."

My mom nods. Burns pauses. Her head tilts.

"Your son isn't with them. He wasn't in the camper when we arrived. According to the others, he and the dog left this morning."

My mom's eyes widen in confusion. "You must be mistaken. Oz wouldn't leave. He just wouldn't. It's just not something he would do. My son, he's . . ." She always has a hard time with this, unsure how to describe Oz. "He's simpleminded," she says finally. "He doesn't think for himself that way."

Burns's jaw twitches, a small but telling sign of his emotions. "I'm sorry," he says. "But he's not with them. The search party has been instructed to look for him as well."

My mom stares at her red, chapped hands, her head shaking back and forth in either denial or bewilderment or overload.

"The K-9 units will be here soon," Burns says. "And we still have an hour or so left before we need to stop for the night, hopefully—"

"An hour," my mom yelps, stopping him. "What do you mean, an hour? My daughter and son are out there. You can't stop for the night."

She says nothing about Vance.

"Mrs. Miller, we are doing everything we can to find Chloe, Oz, and Vance."

My mom flinches as she is reminded that hers are not the only children lost. I do not hold it against her for not thinking of him. I have not thought of Vance since last night, my thoughts occupied entirely with Chloe, Mo, Oz, my dad, and my mom—consumed with mine, mine, mine, with no room left for concern for the others.

"I need to help," my mom says, starting to stand.

"Mrs. Miller, the best way for you to help is for you to let us do our job and to be here in case we need you. And what I need from you right now is a better understanding of your son—anything that might help us in locating him, in figuring out how he might have gone about trying to find you."

"He was trying to find me?"

"According to Bob, that's why he left. So right now, I need you to tell me a little more about Oz."

My mom's face is in her hands, her elbows on her knees.

I can't tell if it's a distraction or if Burns actually needs the information, but giving my mom a task is a good idea. It gives her something to focus on and keeps her from going mad. She thinks for a second, then begins, and I am stunned.

My mom never looks at Oz, or never seems to, yet her description is chillingly detailed. Somehow, without anyone knowing, she has studied him. Her eyes are closed as she describes the mole below his left ear, the birthmark that looks like California on his wrist, the scar on his temple from when he fell off his bike two years ago, the cowlick at his hairline that swirls his hair to the left. She knows that he is wearing wool socks—one gray and one brown because his left foot is larger than his right and the brown sock is thinner and he likes his shoes to feel even. She is certain he will walk down instead of up because this is what will make sense to him, just as she is certain he will hide if the rescue workers come near.

She tears up when she talks about how strong he is and when she warns Burns not to go near Bingo unless Oz gives permission. Oz is fiercely protective of those he loves. Her description is so vivid I see him in her words. Her voice quivers with pride when she describes his kind heart, then grows soft when she speaks of his devotion, and as I listen, I wish my dad could hear it or that Oz could know it.

22

I watch as the brave rescue crew, dressed in bright-orange parkas, waits at the edge of the accident site for the order to rappel down and begin the search. A dozen of them stand with their backs to the wind, gusts of hail peppering them and the wind drowning their voices. None complains or shows any sign of surrender, and when they get the word that the operation has been suspended because of the storm, I feel their despair. These people all carry photos of Vance and Chloe and Oz on their phones, and none of them wants to leave them out there another night. Reluctantly each returns to the jeeps that brought them here.

It takes three officers to restrain my mom from storming the woods herself when Burns tells her the news.

"Haldol," Burns barks to the paramedic who has run over to assist.

My mom is flailing wildly, her eyes bulging.

The paramedic pulls out a syringe and jabs it into my mom's thigh before she can kick him away. Nearly immediately she slumps in his arms, and the men carry her to the ambulance, where she is strapped down and transported to the hospital.

I am relieved. It's been over thirty-six hours since my mom has slept.

23

I go to the hospital in Big Bear to check on Mo.

Numb. That is the word the doctor keeps using. "There will be tingling, and for several days you might not have feeling . . ."

I wish the word were restricted to Mo's fingers and toes. But numb is what Mo is all over, inside and out. She nods to the doctor's questions and follows his simple commands, but she doesn't speak, her pupils are the size of pinheads, and her body slumps like a rag doll as he prods and pokes her for damage. Valium is mentioned by a nurse, but the doctor shakes his head. Maybe later, if necessary. He prefers her to remain unmedicated while her body reacclimatizes.

Mo's injuries are limited to damage from the cold. Her lips are swollen and raw, her ears are blistered, her hands and feet are splinted and wrapped in gauze to treat the frostbite, and her body temperature was, at first, a few degrees below normal. Despite all that, she is beautiful, and the sight of her sitting safe in the hospital, wrapped in a heated blanket, brings incredible relief.

Mrs. Kaminski bursts through the door, and Mo looks up slowly.

"Mommy," she mumbles, her whole body quivering, the trembling starting at her lips and spreading outward until her whole body shakes violently. Then she is in her mother's arms, and Mrs. Kaminski is holding her up, absorbing the shock waves as she kisses Mo's head and assures her that she is here and that Mo is okay.

"Shhh, baby," Mrs. Kaminski says, gently guiding Mo to lie back on the bed. As she tucks the heated blanket around her daughter's curled body, she sings a Polish lullaby that I remember her singing when Mo and I were little. Within minutes, Mo's eyes close and her breath settles. Mrs. Kaminski doesn't stop singing. Pulling a chair from the wall to the rail of the bed, she settles into it and sings and sings and sings.

An hour later, Mo stirs but doesn't wake, and when she cries out, sobbing my name, it's too much to take, and I leave.

24

My dad is in surgery.

At least a dozen people surround him, all of them in gowns and masks. His head is wrapped in gauze, and there is a breathing tube in his mouth. A surgeon on his left seems to be working on his chest, while the one on his right is focused on an open incision above his hip. My dad's right leg is in a brace, and the gaping wound from where the femur broke the skin is clean but exposed. Like Mo, his feet and hands are in splints and wrapped in gauze.

You don't have to have a medical degree to know he's in bad shape. It's been four hours since he was airlifted from the crash site, and it looks like they've barely begun. They are in for a long night.

25

I decide to visit Burns for an update on the search plans for tomorrow and am surprised when I wind up in a room with Uncle Bob, Aunt Karen, and Natalie.

From his bed, Uncle Bob shakes the captain's hand as Burns introduces himself.

"How are the others?" Uncle Bob asks.

Aunt Karen is in the bed beside the window, her hands wrapped with warm compresses but not splinted, and I'm guessing her frostbite is less severe than my dad's and Mo's. Natalie curls in a recliner chair in the corner, the skin on her fingers chapped but otherwise unharmed. Both are asleep.

Uncle Bob's ankle is in a neoprene boot and elevated on a foam block.

If I were a good person, I would be happy that they are not seriously injured, that their fingers and toes and ribs and lungs and legs are fine. But at the moment, I am not a good person. I am an angry spirit who is dead and whose family and best friend are suffering, and I hate that the three of them are so damn fine.

Burns gives Uncle Bob a rundown on my family and Mo. The color drains from Uncle Bob's face when Burns tells him the search was suspended and that Oz and Chloe and Vance are still out there.

From the way Burns says Chloe's name, I can tell she is the one he's most worried about. Perhaps he has a daughter, or perhaps it is because of the description my mother gave, with Chloe the least athletic and she and Vance in the elements the longest. He has every reason to be concerned. Chloe is not doing well; slowly she freezes in the crook of the tree as the seconds tick by, so slow I cannot bear witnessing it, each tick a dagger to my heart.

"Mrs. Miller was brought in a few minutes ago," Burns says.

"Ann is here?" Bob says, straightening. "In the hospital? Is she okay?"

"She needed to be sedated," Burns says. "It's not serious, but for the moment, the doctors are recommending keeping her on Versed until the morning so she can get some rest. That's why I'm here. Because Ann is sedated, there's no one from the family available to speak with the press, and I was hoping perhaps you could talk on their behalf. The more public interest we can generate, the more support we'll get for the search."

Uncle Bob nearly leaps from the bed, then stumbles with dizziness from rising too fast.

"Take your time," Burns says. "Get dressed, gather your strength, and meet me in the lounge when you're ready."

Uncle Bob nods, and Burns walks toward the door. Halfway there, he turns. "One more thing. There's something I'm not quite clear on. The boy, Oz—his mom was certain he wouldn't have left on his own. You told the ranger that he left to look for her. Why would he do that?"

Uncle Bob's eyes flicker side to side as the options of how to answer tick through his head. "Oz is . . . well, I'm sure Ann told you . . . he's off."

Off, I scream. *What the hell does* off *mean?*

"And when he gets upset, he gets emotional and can't be reasoned with."

Burns's face shows nothing, his sharp eyes steady on Uncle Bob's.

"I think the situation was just too much for him, and when he got violent—"

"He got violent?" Burns interrupts.

Uncle Bob nods. "He hit Karen." He nods toward his sleeping wife. "It was her turn for a sip of water, but Oz wanted the water for the dog, so he grabbed it from Karen, and when Karen didn't let go, he hit her."

Burns glances at Aunt Karen, the left side of her face exposed—pale, white, unmarked.

"That's when I took him outside. I asked if he needed to go to the bathroom to get him away from the others, hoping it would calm him down. But when we got out there, he got it in his head that he needed to find his mom. I tried to stop him, but there was nothing I could do."

Burns nods, starts to turn, then hesitates and turns back. "How did you get back in the camper?"

Uncle Bob tilts his head. "How did I what?"

"How did you get back in the camper? Ann said Oz and Kyle were the only ones strong enough to pull themselves onto the camper in order to climb back inside. She was concerned that Oz was the only one left to boost the rest of you, worried he'd climb in without remembering to lift the others first."

The beat before Uncle Bob answers is all the confirmation Burns needs to realize something is off with the story. "I never got down from the camper," he says. "Like I said, Oz was upset, and when Oz is upset, it's best to steer clear. So when he and the dog got down, I stayed on top."

"Hmm," Burns says, nodding. "So he left while you were still on top of the camper?"

Uncle Bob nods.

"That could be helpful. Which way did he walk?"

I swallow hard. Surely Uncle Bob isn't going to answer and send the rescue crew in the wrong direction. He has no idea which way Oz walked. Oz hoisted Uncle Bob onto the camper, and Uncle Bob was already inside before Oz chose his path.

"He went the same way as Ann and Kyle," Uncle Bob answers, and panic and rage turn my vision red. Oz walked the complete other way, downhill like my mom said, in the direction of the taillights.

"Good to know," Burns says. "I'll see you in a few minutes."

The sound of the door closing wakes Natalie, and she sits up sleepily.

"Angel, can you give your old man a hand?" Uncle Bob says.

Together they manage to get him dressed, and then she helps him stand and hands him his crutches. He chuckles when he cannot figure out how to use them. To Natalie's credit, she doesn't laugh along with him. She actually looks like she might be sick. Either that, or there's a tinge of disgust on her face as she watches her dad amuse himself as he practices his crutch walk for his fifteen minutes of fame.

26

Mrs. Kaminski still sits beside Mo singing her lullaby, so soft now it is merely a hum. I'm about to leave to go to the news conference when a phone rings, a single cow moo, the signal from my iPhone that lets me know I've been messaged. Mo must have taken my phone from the accident. It's on the side table beside her own.

I drift over to look at the screen. Though *drift* is really the wrong word, because it implies movement and air and feeling, and there is none of that. I do not actually move; I simply exist where I choose, invisible and silent—a witness, an awareness, nothing more.

The screen glows. My mom wants to know what color ur dress is so she can buy a matching tie. Hope ur having a great weekend. C u Tuesday. Charlie.

I swallow hard, and my eyes fill with tears. And I know I shouldn't be feeling sorry for myself when there are so many others to feel sorry for, but I can't help it. I want to go to formal. With Charlie. I want to sit beside Mo and distract her by talking about my dress and what color I should wear, because Mo cares about those sorts of things. I want to help Burns search for my brother and sister and Vance. I want to tell my mom I'm sorry about wrecking her car and to tell her what Uncle Bob did to Oz. I want everyone to be found and for all of us to go home.

I want to go back to school, go to college, then go on to be the first woman Major League Baseball manager. I want all these things.

I stare at the screen of my phone, which is now blank, thinking of the dress I would have chosen, maybe green because it would match Charlie's eyes. I think of him taking my hand and leading me to the dance floor, about me giggling as he wrapped his hand around my back and him smirking back. I know we would laugh because he's funny. His friends are always laughing at the things he says.

Mo stirs and moans and calls my name.

I'm here, I sob, though I'm not.

She shifts again, her face grimacing as if in pain. Worried it is my distress that is disturbing her, I leave.

27

The room is the size of a classroom and is jammed with reporters and cameramen. Near the door is a podium with a microphone. Burns stands behind it, giving a statement. It's the first time I've seen him uncomfortable, and I realize, confident as he is leading his team, being in the spotlight is not his thing.

Stiffly he explains the situation, along with the search plan for tomorrow, while Uncle Bob and Natalie stand behind him. Uncle Bob has shaved, and Natalie has brushed her hair and wears lip gloss and blush.

Burns wraps up his statement, then introduces Uncle Bob, who crutch hops forward.

"Mr. Gold," a reporter with bright-blonde hair says, "what can you tell us about the ordeal you and your family have been through?"

Uncle Bob blinks several times, blinded by the lights and the pretty woman speaking to him. "Uh, um, well, our priority, uh . . . was to just get through the night."

"So your decision was to stay put?"

Uncle Bob nods. "We had fallen a long way, and it was pitch black and snowing. Finding our way out at night would have been impossible."

"But . . ." The reporter looks at her notes. "Chloe Miller and Vance Hannigan chose to try? Was it a group decision to send them for help?"

Uncle Bob swallows at her slightly accusatory tone, and his eyes narrow as a shield of self-preservation goes up. "No, that was their decision," he says, "a decision we tried to stop them from making, but Vance was determined to go, and Chloe was determined to go with him." He stops and shakes his head. "There was nothing any of us could do." He looks back up and, with genuine heartbreak in his voice, says, "They're just kids. I'd give anything to have them here and safe with the rest of us."

The reporter nods with sympathy, and the gaggle around her nods as well. "And the third child who is missing," she says, "the boy, Oz— did you try to stop him as well?"

"I did," Uncle Bob says with shocking sincerity. "I begged him to listen, but he wanted his mom." He stops as his emotions get the better of him and then, with a deep breath, continues, "Oz has an intellectual disability. He has a strong will but not a strong mind. I pray the rescuers find him. His parents are my best friends, and they left their son in my care. If something happens to him, I'll never forgive myself." He looks away as tears fill his eyes, and he is so convincing even I almost believe him. And as I watch the reporters, expressions of great sympathy and understanding on their faces, I know they believe him as well, and I wish I could smash him over his head with an Oscar for his Academy Award–worthy performance.

"Mr. Gold," the reporter goes on, her voice now gentle, "on a more positive note, your family, Jack Miller, and Maureen Kaminski were rescued."

Uncle Bob nods and, following her lead, changes the subject. "Yes. Hearing those choppers overhead was God answering our prayers."

"The rescue crew mentioned that aside from the injuries sustained during the crash, the five of you were in remarkably good shape thanks

Suzanne Redfearn

to some smart survival choices. Is it true you packed the windshield with snow to block out the storm?"

"We did. The snow acted as an insulator. It's the same technique the Eskimos use."

I bristle that he does not mention Mo or give her credit for the idea.

"And you melted snow into water?"

"We had a lighter, a sunglasses case, and the novel *Pride and Prejudice*," he says, still with no mention of Mo. "Thank goodness Jane Austen was so long winded."

Small chuckles from the audience.

"Very ingenious," the woman says. "You're a real Indiana Jones."

"Not really," Uncle Bob says with a blush. "When you're in a desperate situation, you figure things out. You have to."

Behind Uncle Bob, Burns frowns, but remarkably it is Natalie who steps forward and says, "Dad, we should go. I'm tired."

Uncle Bob snaps back to reality, and a shadow of shame crosses his face. "Of course, baby," he says, his eyes not quite meeting hers as he wraps his arm around her shoulder and gives her a supportive kiss on the side of her head. Then he readjusts his crutch and finally does something right. Turning to the cameras, he says, "Three kids are still out there. The search resumes tomorrow. Please send your prayers and any support you can to find them."

With Natalie beside him, he hobbles away. Looks of admiration follow from everyone there, except for Burns, whose eyes reveal nothing but whose mouth is drawn tight, the corners pulled down in a look of suspicion and distrust.

28

I spend the night with Chloe. I checked on Oz, but I could not stay, his cries for my dad too much to bear. He is still on the rock where he stopped to rest with Bingo, though Bingo is gone, fading paw prints traveling back toward the camper.

Chloe huddles in the crook of the hollow tree, her hooded head buried against her knees. She makes no noise at all. I feel her cold, her pain, and her misery, and I know she has given up. If it were up to her, she would stop her heart from beating and her lungs from breathing. But despite her wish, her blood continues to pump, and air continues to flow.

I sit beside her and pray that my soul still has energy and will give her some warmth, and as I wait with her, I talk. I tell her what it's like to be dead and what happened to the others. I tell her about Uncle Bob's stupid news interview and what a schmuck he is even in the face of disaster. Chloe has always disliked Uncle Bob, so she will appreciate this.

When I run out of serious things to talk about, I tell her about Charlie's text. I confess I was thinking of green for my dress because it would match Charlie's eyes, blushing at admitting to my girliness. *Don't tell,* I warn her. *Don't want to ruin my badass reputation now that I've made it to the finish line.*

I tell her how I hoped Charlie would wear his cowboy boots: the black ones with the red stitching, not the brown ones. Then I apologize for all the things I did that weren't nice. I tell her I'm sorry for ratting her out to the principal when I saw her smoking pot behind the gym. Then I bark at her to stop smoking pot, telling her how stupid it is and that she's way too cool for that. I tell her that the sunglasses she thought she lost are in my bottom drawer beneath my practice shirts. One lens is broken from when I borrowed them without telling her and then sat on them by accident.

I talk and talk and talk, then abruptly stop. Voices, not mine, followed by the bark of a dog. Chloe doesn't hear. She doesn't move. She doesn't realize she is being saved.

Over here, I scream. *Here, here, here.*

A husky or a shepherd or some sort of amazing beast with long gray hair sticks his muzzle into her hood, causing Chloe to whimper. The dog pulls his nose out and howls. Two minutes later, two men in orange parkas are squatting beside us. One talks into a walkie-talkie.

"We found her. We've got the girl." His voice is brittle with emotion.

The other presses his fingers against Chloe's neck and gives a thumbs-up.

"She's alive," the one with the walkie-talkie says.

"Copy that. Chopper's on its way," it squawks back.

I cheer and clap and spin and whoop and holler, and I don't care that no one can hear me. They found Chloe. My sister is going to be okay.

29

I go to where my mom is. I want to be there when she gets the news.

I'm not surprised I end up at the staging area instead of the hospital. My mom sits in the same spot she sat yesterday, in the back of an ambulance, stone still and staring at nothing. Beside her, holding her red, chapped hand, is Uncle Bob.

Uncle Bob's plea for help worked. Over a hundred volunteers and personnel from various agencies have joined the search. There are ambulances, fire trucks, sheriff's cars, and dozens of jeeps and vans from the Forest Service.

In the distance, dark clouds heavy with unfallen snow threaten but for the moment hold their load.

Over the valley, two helicopters circle. I hold little hope for them to spot Oz. He is hidden beneath a thick canopy of trees, and because of Uncle Bob's misinformation, the search is focused in the opposite direction from where he walked.

Burns opens the door to the ambulance, and a gust of wind blows in with him. My mom leaps up, her eyes trying to read Burns's expression.

"We found Chloe. She's alive," he says, a smile cracking his weathered face.

My mom throws her arms around him. "Thank you. Oh God, thank you. Where is she?"

"They're flying her to the same hospital as your husband."

"Is she okay?"

His pause is a pulse too long, and the hesitation sucks the air from the ambulance. "She has a pretty severe concussion, and they're not sure about her hands and feet," he says.

My mom's fingers go to her mouth, and she stumbles back into Uncle Bob, who catches her. Her head shakes back and forth as if trying to erase the news like a bad drawing on an Etch A Sketch, and Uncle Bob helps her back to her seat.

"Should I go there, or should I stay here?" she asks numbly of no one in particular.

I don't know if I've ever heard my mom ask for advice. It's a sign of how distraught she is.

Burns speaks up. "They've given your daughter a sedative, and she won't wake up for hours. So for now, you should stay here."

The news delivered, he pivots to return outside.

My mom's voice stops him. "And Vance?" she says.

Burns turns back and shakes his head, and my mom buries her face in her hands. Uncle Bob rubs her back and tells her it's going to be okay.

But it's not going to be okay, because as Burns steps from the ambulance, his eyes scan the dark horizon, and his mouth sets in a deep frown as he studies the leaden clouds rolling toward them and the snow that has begun to fall.

30

I wait with my mom and Uncle Bob. The storm has arrived, and the hail on the roof peppers the metal like a drum brush, a constant reminder that they are dry and warm while Oz and Vance remain at its mercy.

It's hard to believe today is Presidents' Day, the third day of the three-day weekend I was so looking forward to. It occurs to me how happy I was supposed to be right now—my final morning on the slopes—possibly snowboarding, most likely skiing. I was supposed to be having the time of my life, flying down the mountain, whipping past Mo on the bunny slope, racing Vance, riding the lifts with my dad, all while taking the day, the fun, and the moment for granted, the way every mortal does.

Uncle Bob is incredibly kind as he sits with my mom. He rubs her back, doesn't yap like he normally does, and keeps watch out the window for any sign of change.

"How's Karen?" my mom asks at one point when the hail is particularly bad.

"Okay," Uncle Bob answers. "The doctors want to keep her in the hospital one more day just to be sure, but she's fine."

My mom's mouth tightens into a thin line, her lips disappearing, hurt mixing with all the other emotions she is dealing with. Aunt Karen hasn't called, and she isn't here. My mom's injuries are worse than Aunt

Karen's, and her ordeal is a thousand times worse, but Aunt Karen has yet to even offer a condolence.

"She's not like you," Uncle Bob says. "Karen's not strong. She'll come around. She just needs to process things."

"Come around? Process things?" my mom hisses, the hurt transforming quickly into bitterness. "What the hell is that supposed to mean? Last I checked, she has all her children."

"She's upset," Uncle Bob says. "And she's worried about Natalie. You know how she gets. She obsesses."

My mom wraps her arms around herself.

"Give it time," Uncle Bob says.

My mom doesn't answer. There are some things time can't heal. She and Aunt Karen have been friends twenty years, but in a lifetime, this moment won't be forgotten.

Mary Beth, the ambulance driver, turns from the cab to face them. "They found Vance," she says. "Helicopters spotted him near Pineknot Campground. He was still walking, which is a good sign."

Uncle Bob kisses my mom's hair and hugs her tighter, both of them grabbing hold of this news as a promising sign for finding Oz.

A few minutes later, their newfound hope is dashed when Mary Beth turns again and says, "Helicopters are grounded for the day. Too much weather."

My mom barely reacts, one more lash after a thousand, and she has nothing left to give.

"Hang in there," Uncle Bob says. "Oz is strong, and the search parties on the ground are still out there looking."

~

It's noon when Burns walks toward the ambulance, the wind biting his face and causing him to tuck his chin into the collar of his coat.

Uncle Bob nudges my mom when he sees Burns through the window, causing her to lift her head. This time she doesn't wait for Burns to get to them. Stepping out from the warmth, she rushes forward, her face so hopeful my heart aches with the cruelty.

Burns's eyes slide left, then down to a spot on the ground beside her, and she stops abruptly, her breath catching as her hand goes to her mouth and her head shakes, the other possibility of why he's coming to talk to her suddenly filling her mind.

"We found the dog," he blurts before she can finish drawing the wrong conclusion. Not allowing her hope to be obliterated completely— not yet, anyways.

She blinks several times rapidly as she absorbs the news, and then, without a word, she pivots and returns to her vigil. Bingo was found. Oz is still out there.

31

"What do you think?" a deputy says, walking up to Burns. The man's hands are shoved in his pockets, his shoulders hitched to his ears to protect his face from the snow that now falls sideways.

"Twenty more minutes," Burns says. "We'll give it a little longer."

An hour later, when the world is in total whiteout, he makes the decision he was praying he wouldn't have to make and suspends the search for the day.

It is a death sentence for my brother, and everyone knows it—the rescue crew, Burns, my mom. Another storm front is moving in, and it will be at least a day, probably two, before the search will resume. No one could survive that long.

It's the worst possible outcome, worse than had they discovered him dead. I watch as the search team shuffles to their cars, their heads bent in defeat and their prayers shifting from hope that Oz is still alive to pleas that he is dead and will therefore be spared any more suffering.

He is not dead. He is curled on the rock where Bingo left him, no longer calling for my mom or my dad. Alone and terrified, he trembles, and watching him destroys me.

Though I know he cannot hear me, I tell him I love him and that Bingo is safe, and then I leave, deeply ashamed for being too much of a coward to stay.

When Burns delivers the news to my mom, she barely reacts. She thanks him for keeping the crew out as long as he did, then gathers her things from the ambulance and walks with Uncle Bob toward the waiting deputy's car. It will drive her to the trauma hospital in Riverside where my dad and Chloe are being treated.

She is shell shocked, I tell myself, shaking away the other impression that struck me when she received the news: *relieved.*

No, I scream. *Resigned.* She knew it was coming and was therefore expecting it; the news wasn't a revelation and therefore wasn't devastating like it would have been had her hopes been high or if she'd been surprised. Her only crime is not having the energy to fake it, to pretend she is destroyed as everyone expects her to be, including me.

"Do you want me to go with you?" Uncle Bob asks as he opens the door to the deputy's car for her.

My mom shakes her head. "Karen and Natalie need you."

He pulls her into his arms, and she melts against him, her head against his chest and his chin resting on her hair.

"I'm here if you need me," he whispers, and the tenderness between them makes me wonder if more than friendship might exist between them. Uncle Bob's affection for my mom is clear. It always has been. Her sentiment toward him is not as defined.

32

My mom startles at the sight of Chloe in her bed. Her hair is buzzed around her forehead, a swatch of gauze covering the gash. Her eyes are closed. A white sheet is draped over her, her bandaged hands on top of it. Moonlight streams in from the window, glancing off her pale skin and making it glow. She looks like a wounded angel, and I feel my mom's chest loosen with the relief of seeing her, so much she scarcely notices Chloe's blistered ears or the blue hollows around her eyes or the black tips of her fingers and toes that extend beyond the splints.

I sit with my mom as we wait for her to wake, nurses coming in often to check on her and change her dressings as the machines hum and whir around her, the steady bleeping and scrolling squiggly lines reassuring. Though she burns with fever and her breathing is sometimes erratic, her pulse keeps a steady, comforting rhythm.

Aubrey arrives a little before eight. She is strangely unchanged, and it is disconcerting to see her. Like staring directly into the sun, it hurts to look at her yet feels amazing at the same time.

My mom stands, and they fall into each other's arms.

Aubrey is my mom's. She loves my dad, and my dad loves her, but Aubrey is my mom's. They have one of those cute, comical, easy mother-daughter relationships. Both like to shop and go to sappy movies, and both could spend every day at a spa being pampered and every evening checking out the latest restaurants in Orange County. We always kid them that they should become mother-daughter food critics. They would be great. Aubrey would be generous, and my mom would be nitpicking and harsh.

They sit beside each other, mirrors of each other, feet on the floor, hands clasped on their thighs. Aubrey has been crying. I know because her eyes are red and she is not wearing mascara, a trademark sign that her sensitive tear ducts are inflamed.

But now, sitting beside my mom, she is stoic. She says little, worry lining her face as she watches Chloe and thinks about me, absently turning the engagement ring on her finger as she silently counts the stones. When she first got the ring, she proudly announced it had twenty-two small diamonds around the center stone to symbolize each month she and Ben had been together before he'd proposed. I examined it and, just to mess with her, said there were only twenty-one. She must have counted those diamonds a hundred times after I said it, and it became a running joke, everyone teasing her and asking if she was *sure* there were twenty-two diamonds.

"They put Dad in a medically induced coma," she says after some time, "to help with the swelling in his brain."

My mom nods. The doctors updated her before Aubrey got there. The surgery went well. His leg was put back together and his spleen removed, but they won't know the extent of the head trauma until he wakes up, which they are hoping will be in a week or so.

"He's going to be okay," Aubrey says. "So is Chloe."

She doesn't mention Oz or that he is still out there and that there is still hope, and neither does my mom. And the longer I wait for them to do so, the more upset I become, until, unable to take it a second longer, I leave.

33

I arrive in Mo's room as the door opens and Aunt Karen walks in, causing Mrs. Kaminski to turn from her vigil beside the bed. She stands quickly and guides Aunt Karen back into the corridor.

"How is she?" Aunt Karen says when the door closes, her face lined with concern.

Aunt Karen suffered first-degree frostbite on her fingers and mild shock. But after a day in the hospital, she is nearly fully recovered. Her hair is styled and her makeup neatly applied, and other than the glossy salve on her hands, she looks exactly as she did before the accident.

Mrs. Kaminski studies her for a long moment before answering the question with one of her own. "Natalie is not hurt?"

"No," Aunt Karen answers. "She was lucky."

Mrs. Kaminski's eyes remain steady on Aunt Karen's as she says, "Maureen was lucky as well, though perhaps not as lucky as Natalie, whose fingers and toes are fine. Yes?"

Aunt Karen nods, her concern for Mo stiffening as Mrs. Kaminski continues to look at her for a long moment before saying, "I shudder when I think how cold it must have been out there, and how scared my daughter must have been."

Aunt Karen shifts her weight.

"Have you seen Maureen's toes?" Mrs. Kaminski says.

Aunt Karen swallows as she shakes her head.

"They are worse than her fingers." She looks at Aunt Karen's feet. "Her toes cannot bear weight like yours."

I feel Aunt Karen curling her toes inside her shoes.

Natalie's seven-hundred-dollar coat turned out to be worth every penny. The long, thick down not only protected Natalie from the cold but spared her parents' feet as well, Aunt Karen and Uncle Bob able to wedge their shoes beneath it.

"Her fingers are still mostly white," Mrs. Kaminski goes on. "Which I'm told is good. The paleness means only the skin was frozen. Black is bad: it means the circulation was cut off in order to conserve heat for the vital organs."

Aunt Karen swallows, and the color drains from her face.

"Maureen's toes are mostly black. Like stone. As if made of hardened lava instead of flesh and bone."

She stops, her eyes remaining on Aunt Karen's for a full second before she goes on. "It is hard to imagine the cold that caused that. But yes, as you say, our daughters were lucky. I need to remind myself of that, of how *lucky* they were."

Aunt Karen opens her mouth as if to say something, but Mrs. Kaminski isn't done. Her words honed like daggers, she says, "Every second I sit in that room, I remind myself that my daughter is here while Finn is dead and that we are lucky. But when I look at Maureen's toes and I think of the cold, I can't help but also think of Natalie and wonder why my daughter's toes are so black while your daughter's are not. And I think, if it is luck, then luck is cruel and unfair. Both of them were in that camper, both of them cold and scared, both wore boots that did not protect them, and yet only my daughter is in danger of losing her toes, and it is hard for me to understand why your daughter was so *lucky* and mine was not."

Not waiting for a response, she pivots and returns into the room, leaving Aunt Karen alone and trembling in the hall. I watch as she reaches for the wall to steady herself, her breath shallow as she sucks air through her open mouth and shakes her head as if trying to wake herself from a dream.

I always wondered how it was possible that Mo was Mrs. Kaminski's daughter, how such a mild-mannered woman could be the parent of such a spitfire. Now I know. Appearances are deceiving, and people are not who they seem. Aunt Karen will never again look at Natalie's toes without thinking of Mo or look in a mirror without hearing Mrs. Kaminski's words: *It is hard for me to understand why your daughter was so* lucky *and mine was not.* Mrs. Kaminski is not meek, and Aunt Karen is not caring and generous, though if you ask a thousand people who know them, almost all would disagree.

34

If Mo was not as lucky as Natalie, Chloe was outright damned.

The doctors are careful not to tell the truth to the loved ones, their honesty reserved for when they talk among themselves. Chloe is going to lose some toes and possibly some fingers. How many is not clear, but they will not be able to save them all. They are also concerned about her ears, and a plastic surgeon has been called in to consult.

I leave the doctors in the hallway and return to her room to see for myself how she is doing. I am there only a minute when she jerks suddenly and her eyes fly open. Her pupils dart from side to side, her face twisted in panic, and then she collapses back to the pillow and slips away again.

"What was that?" Aubrey asks.

"Fear," my mom mumbles, sliding her chair closer and taking hold of Chloe's wrist above her bandaged hand to let her know she is there. She touches her carefully, as though she might shatter, which she looks like she might. Chloe's skin is so white it looks like crystal and her body so small beneath the sheet it appears brittle as twigs. Chloe mumbles, and my mom's brow furrows. Only I understand what she said, and it makes my eyes bulge and my heart pound. Clearly she said, *Black boots, red stitching.*

Chloe groans, waking again, this time more slowly and writhing in pain.

"Get the nurse," my mom barks, and Aubrey leaps up and darts from the room. Then softly to Chloe, she says, "I'm here, baby. Mom is here."

Chloe pulls her wrist from my mom's hand and squeezes her eyes shut, begging to return to unconsciousness, and mercifully a nurse charges forward and injects something into her IV that answers her prayer.

35

I go to Oz. Chloe heard me—*black boots, red stitching*. In her sleep, she heard me.

I curl beside him and tell him I am here. I tell him about Chloe being found and that she is going to be okay. I tell him Dad is in the hospital and has been asking about him and that Bingo is safe. I tell him how good he did and that he was a big help. I tell him that thanks to him, Mom was found and that his trail led the rescuers to her. I tell him how special he is and how strong and brave. I tell him how much he is loved and how much he will be missed. I tell him about heaven and that it is a beautiful place with no rules and that no one gets mad at you if you make a mistake. I tell him he can put marshmallows on all his food, even steak if he wants, and that all the angels are as pretty as Mo and that they have beautiful gold wings and that they love to have water fights and build snowmen. I talk until the blackness lightens to gray and the horizon glows.

I am still talking when his shivering stops, his death so quiet I almost don't notice. His chest rises and falls one last time, and then his mouth drops open and he is still.

I pray for his soul, asking God to carry him away quickly to a heaven like the one I promised him, a place that is kind and understanding, a place more tolerant and less confusing for a special boy like Oz.

When my grief turns to hate, I go to the source of it, wishing equally for a hell that will punish Uncle Bob for what he did.

36

It is deceiving. The ones who have survived, you think are okay.

It's been a week since the accident, six days since my mom climbed out for help, five since Chloe and Vance were found.

Oz was never found. The search resumed the moment the storm lifted, then was called off two days later.

Two died. The others are healing and can resume their lives, pick up where they left off.

This is what you think. Right?

Wrong.

Like a quilt of thorns, an injurious aftermath has settled over the survivors, the urgency of staying alive morphing into something else entirely. Adrenal glands no longer fire in overdrive; exhaustion and shock no longer numb the brain; and the reality of life-after has seeped into consciousness like a slow bleed, a silent haunting of the cold and suffering that tears at each of them with every breath.

Dread coils my stomach in a constant ache as I realize the worst is yet to come. Denial and regret, shameful gratefulness and guilt, grief and hopelessness spin through the thoughts and dreams of my mom, Chloe, and Mo—each so terrorized by what happened they avoid sleep for fear of remembering.

I think of the deer in the road, his startled marble eye blinking through the windshield, and I wonder if he is aware of the damage he caused, or if he is oblivious, ignorantly going about his life completely unaware of the price that saving his life has cost.

Uncle Bob, Aunt Karen, and Natalie have returned home to Orange County. I'm glad they are gone. Though Uncle Bob's presence was comforting to my mom, it was infuriating to me. It seems grossly unfair that the same lack of conscience that allowed him to do what he did also guards him against the posttraumatic effects from which the others are suffering. Already his ankle is almost healed, his family is healthy and whole, he's being heralded as a hero, and he sleeps easy at night.

If I could play for him my brother's suffering, I would. Every time he closed his eyes, I would torture him with an endless reel of Oz's cries, his confusion, and his pleas for my dad, for me, for Mo—the entire soundtrack of his lonely, awful, slow death. Sometimes I would wait silently, allow him to believe he was being spared, and then I would blast the recording full volume, mercilessly haunting him until he was terrified of sleep.

But I can't replay Oz's suffering, and so, like the deer, Uncle Bob continues on, oblivious and without repentance. His thoughts never venture back to that awful night or to the moment he sent Oz away, never reflect on his role in the chain of unfortunate events, and therefore he suffers no ramifications for what he did and feels no sense of responsibility or remorse.

The others are not blessed with his lack of retrospection. Constantly their consciences roar, should-haves and could-haves blaring in their brains. They cannot bear how they see themselves now—the reflections too clear, too unflattering, too brutal and honest—and I realize we are not meant to see ourselves so plainly, without the guise of ego and ignorance, not meant to have our true characters revealed.

My mom and Mo and Chloe suffer from different regrets, though the root cause is the same—fervent desire to turn back time, reverse fate, and be better than they were.

My mom mostly thinks of Oz. *Did I say goodbye?* she mumbles to the mirror out loud.

She didn't, but she's not sure, and desperately I hope she convinces herself she did.

She also tortures herself with what happened to Chloe. She sobbed uncontrollably when she told Aubrey about it, and no matter how many times Aubrey said it wasn't her fault, she could not be convinced. Uncle Bob also reminded her that she did try to stop her. He said it forcefully, almost angrily, telling her in no uncertain terms that there was absolutely nothing she could have done.

I hate him, but I was glad he said that.

Unfortunately Chloe doesn't feel the same way. Openly she hates my mom, blame radiating whenever she is near. My sister spent nearly thirty hours huddled in the hollow of that tree, and that is a long time to be alone with your thoughts and for your perspective to become distorted. I cannot be sure how Chloe remembers things, only that her altered view leaves no room for forgiveness.

It is hard to know what Chloe thinks because Chloe doesn't talk. Since she was rescued, the only time she's spoken was to ask about Vance, her eyes filling when she heard he was alive, then her heart breaking when she asked the nurse to call him, and Vance's mom told her he wouldn't take her call.

Since then, she hasn't said a word, hasn't done much of anything. All day she lies on her side, her face toward the window. Sometimes her eyes are open, though most of the time they're closed. She refuses to eat or go to the bathroom. An IV feeds her, and she wears diapers, and even when she soils herself, she does not move.

It is horrible to watch, and I think the smell must be vile—gangrenous flesh, urine, and feces. My mom must be used to it because she doesn't react, but all the others wince when they walk in and hurry to finish their business quickly so they can escape.

Already one toe on Chloe's left foot and two on her right have been amputated, along with the top third of her left pinky finger. A plastic surgeon removed several infected blisters on her ears, and her lobes are now lopsided and misshapen. The toes that remain are black and look like they could snap right off, though the doctors are hopeful they can be saved.

Through it all, my mom remains, sitting vigilant at Chloe's side, her stare nearly as unblinking. Only I see the effort it takes each morning for her to walk into the room, the deep breath she takes before opening the door.

But once she is there, in the chair beside her bed, she is stoic: silent and unmoving as she watches Chloe breathe, a look of such devotion on her face that it twists my heart and makes me wonder how someone can love another so much yet desperately not want to be near her. It was that way before the accident as well, the two of them in the habit of hiding from each other, listening for which direction the other went and avoiding the path.

"Oil and water," my dad once said, but Aubrey shook her head. "Oil and oil," she corrected. "Can't you see how much they're alike?" I think they might both have been right: the two are completely opposite on the outside but have the same stubborn mettle on the inside, making it impossible for them to get along.

Sometimes my mom thinks of Kyle. I know because I see her right hand open and close as her face contorts. And a lot of times she thinks of me, tears brimming in her eyes as her lip trembles.

And on and on it goes, an endless cycle of sorrow and torture as she waits for my dad and Chloe to recover—regret over Oz, Chloe, and Kyle, worry for my dad, and grief over me.

Mo's suffering is different: so much lost so quickly she cannot wrap her head around it, her glass bubble shattered and the world now incomprehensible. Her perfect life, her perfect best friend, her perfect fingers and toes. Her fearlessness, her blessed ignorance, her indomitable spirit. Her belief in goodness and optimism and right and wrong. Her belief in herself and how she saw herself. All of it obliterated into a million razor-edged shards that make no sense and paralyze her to move beyond this.

"I was glad it was Finn," she wailed to her mom the morning she woke in the hospital. "How . . . how could I think that? Finn was dead, and my first thought when I saw her was relief that it wasn't me."

"Shhh, baby," Mrs. Kaminski soothed. "We do not control our reactions, only our actions."

"Fine," Mo answered. "Oz didn't come back with Bob, and I didn't do anything. Nothing. Inaction. I. DID. NOTHING."

To this Mrs. Kaminski could only nod, wetness filling her eyes.

Mo cries a lot. She rarely sleeps, and when she is awake, she cries.

Her doctor has given permission for her to be transferred to Mission Hospital in Laguna Beach, where she will need to stay until her toes are no longer in danger of infection: at least another two weeks.

The doctors say her feet are getting better, though they look worse. Like a rotten onion, the top layer of skin is mottled brown and gold with splotches of black, and it is cracked and blistered, patches of the dead flesh peeling to reveal tender pink skin below.

Mo refuses to look at her feet or her new life, unable to accept that the grotesque parts belong to her.

37

The doctors have decided it's time to wake my dad. The swelling in his brain has finally gone down, and his vitals are stable. It's late evening: a time chosen for its proximity to night, since regaining consciousness can take time, sometimes hours, and the quiet and darkness will minimize the stress.

His right leg is in a complicated contraption with straps and bolts and springs, and dozens of tubes and wires grow from his arms like jungle vines. I marvel at it, amazed at modern medicine and the brilliant doctors who were able to save him.

His face is concealed by a week of thick beard, and he has lost a lot of weight, his cheeks sunken and his normally robust body almost frail beneath the sheets. But he is still him, a noble strength in the set of his jaw and a remnant of laughter in the lines around his eyes, and looking at him, I miss him so much I want to scream at the doctors to hurry up.

My mom stands beside the bed, holding his hand, her face a mixture of terror and concern, and I wonder what she is thinking.

The anesthesiologist injects his IV with a syringe.

Minutes pass, and finally the pulse on the machines grows quicker, and my dad begins to stir. His uninjured leg shifts beneath the sheet, and then the hand not held by my mom clenches. The vein on his neck begins to pulse, and his mouth screws up as it says my name. Then he calls out for Chloe, and the anesthesiologist looks at my dad's doctor, concerned.

"Jack, it's okay," my mom soothes, stepping closer and wrapping her other hand around the first, and as if her words were laced with chloroform, he slumps back to the sheets. I sniff back my tears, fully realizing the pain he will face when he wakes again and discovers all that has happened.

Everyone exhales, realizing it as well, and minutes later, when he stirs again, the anesthesiologist stands ready, a syringe in his hands. But this time is only half as bad as the first, and I watch as his eyes dart around frantically as my mom says his name, then cling to her once they find her.

"It's okay," she says. "We're okay." It's a lie, but it's the perfect lie.

"Chloe?" he rasps.

"She's here. She's okay."

My dad closes his eyes in deep relief. He doesn't know to ask about Oz. He assumes Oz is fine, that my brother was rescued when he was.

"Mr. Miller," the doctor says, stepping forward and causing my mom to step back. The doctor asks a battery of questions to assess whether there's brain damage, which thankfully there doesn't appear to be.

"You're a lucky man," he says when he finishes.

I'm not certain my dad agrees. My dad holds his emotions tight but trembles with the effort. He is not listening as the doctor tells him that he no longer has a spleen, that his leg will take four to six months to heal, that he will have a permanent limp, that he will be in the hospital for another two weeks and confined to a wheelchair for five, that he will need physical therapy several times a week for at least a year.

My dad hears none of it, his eyes still fixed on my mom, holding her gaze and offering her all the strength and courage he could not offer on the mountain. His guilt is enormous; I feel it. Not so much that the accident happened—my dad is a firm believer that we do not control luck—but that he couldn't stop it once it started, change things or fix them and somehow protect his family.

Finally, the doctor leaves, and when the latch clicks closed behind him, my mom begins to cry, great sobs that flow unchecked, her shoulders shuddering as her grief overwhelms her.

With a wince, my dad shifts a few inches to the right and holds out his hand, and like a small child, my mom clambers onto the narrow bed beside him. Her body shapes itself to his, her left leg draping over his uninjured one and her arm wrapping across his chest. He takes her hand in his and rests his chin against her hair.

All night that is how they remain, entwined together, my dad slipping in and out of consciousness as my mom sleeps deeply for the first time in a week.

38

Aubrey sits in Chloe's room paging through *Modern Bride*. When the door opens, she shoves the magazine beneath her chair.

I do not blame Aubrey for her distraction. It's been ten days since the accident, and life goes on. Her wedding is three months away, and it is far better to think about that than the death and suffering around her. So I understand. And I also feel bad. All the joy that was swirling around her and her big day has been sucked away and reduced to a guilty indulgence she needs to hide from everyone.

The woman who walks in is the psychiatrist assigned to Chloe by the hospital's social worker. I do not like her. Short and wide with puffy brown hair and small bird eyes, she talks to Chloe like she is five and has tried everything from bribery to threats to get my sister to respond, a Hail Mary approach to headshrinking that has zero chance of success. To put it mildly, she sucks, and I know Chloe thinks so as well.

"May I speak to you outside," she says to Aubrey.

"Uh, sure," Aubrey says and follows her out the door.

For the most part, Aubrey has been uninvolved in the aftermath. She's here because my dad was wakened last night, and my mom didn't want Chloe to be alone, but since her first visit directly after the accident, she's been home, she and Ben taking care of Bingo and the house while my mom was here looking after Chloe and my dad.

"I'd like you to tell me a little about your sister," the woman says.

Aubrey scrunches her brow. "What do you mean?"

"I mean, what she likes to do. What are her hobbies, her interests? I'd like to get a better understanding of her so I can figure out a way to connect."

Aubrey's eyes move left and right as she thinks, and as I watch her, I realize how little she might actually know about Chloe. While Aubrey and I got along great, and Chloe and I got along great, the two of them never really vibed. Five years divide them, and when Aubrey went off to college, she pretty much disconnected from everyone except my mom.

Come on, Aubrey, I encourage. *Chloe. She likes to listen to music and walk on the beach. She collects shells and rock and roll albums from the seventies. She likes anything with cinnamon and loves to bake. Snickerdoodles are her favorite because they're made of cinnamon and the word is fun to say. She likes words like that and sprinkles them into her sentences:* shenanigan, debauchery, phlebotomist, Zimbabwe. *She's a sucker for anything pathetic and helpless—stray cats, bunnies, lizards—and she loves those ridiculous reality shows like* The Biggest Loser *or* Love in the Jungle. *She's a hopeless romantic and was crazy in love with Vance until he abandoned her in the snow. Come on, Aubrey, think!*

Aubrey shakes her head. "I'm sorry," she says, looking at the woman with genuine apology in her eyes. "I don't know."

The psychiatrist frowns, causing Aubrey to squirm, and desperate to add something of value, she blurts, "She listens to awful music, the kind with screaming guitars and lots of drums, and a month ago she cut off her hair and dyed it black."

"So she's angry?" the shrink says, lighting up as if this is some kind of breakthrough. "Do you think she was depressed?"

"Uh . . . uh, I . . ."

No, Chloe wasn't depressed. She was the happiest she's ever been. She was graduating in four months, head over heels in love, and openly revolting against convention, society, and my mom. She was rebel-without-a-cause, goth, snarky-and-loving-it happy.

"Maybe," Aubrey says.

I groan in frustration. *Jesus, Aubrey, really? Are you kidding me?*

"Yeah," Aubrey says. "Now that I think about it, maybe she was."

39

When my parents wake, still wrapped together, the day is so beautiful it makes me want to cry. Through the window, blue sky stretches to the horizon, vagrant clouds lazily drift along, and the sun shines with arrogance.

My mom unfurls from my dad without a word, and the desperateness that drew them together evaporates in the bright glare of the morning and the awful reality they face in front of them. Like a magnetic force, even while they still touch, dark energy repels them, and within minutes, they have returned to the isolated realms they've grown accustomed to over the last few years.

With the heels of her hands, my mom blots the sleep from her eyes, then stretches her arms over her head to wake her body as she stands, wincing slightly from the pain in her damaged ribs.

"Where's Oz?" my dad asks, squinting at her through the brightness.

For the past two years, nobody except my dad has taken care of my brother. I would relieve him for brief periods, like when he needed to shower or when they went to the barber and it was my dad's turn to get his hair cut, but other than that, my dad was the one who watched him. Oz had grown too strong for anyone else to manage.

The lack of freedom this caused created a rift the size of the Grand Canyon between my parents, and they fought about it constantly. My mom wanted to look into a long-term solution: a home or at least part-time care. My dad refused.

"You want him drugged up and chained?" my dad would argue. "Because that's what they'll do to him, Ann. That's what you're suggesting."

"I'm suggesting that at least on the weekends, we place him somewhere where he's safe so we can have a life."

"We have a life, and Oz is part of it."

"I get that, Jack, but he's becoming all of it. We can't go out. We can't do anything together. And he's getting dangerous."

"He's not dangerous."

"He hurt that dog."

"He didn't mean to."

"But he did. Whether he meant to or not, he hurt that animal. He doesn't know his own strength, and he's going through puberty. Think about what a dangerous combination that is."

It was true. I'd seen it. Oz would get this lovesick look in his eyes whenever a girl walked by, especially blonde girls with large breasts, his features melting into desire and an unsettling yearning to touch.

"I'll watch him," my dad said.

"You can't watch him every second."

Their voices were hushed but heated, the way their arguments always were: angry rasps that lashed and slashed and filled the house with tension that lasted for days, until eventually the tension faded into deafening silence that made you almost miss the fighting.

My mom doesn't know it, but my dad and I once took Oz to check out one of the homes she had talked about, a facility in Costa Mesa. We never made it through the front door. Oz took one look at the tenants walking the grounds, rocking on the grass, and mumbling to themselves, and he freaked out. My dad needed to tackle him in the parking lot to keep him from running into the street.

We never told my mom, and my dad never considered it again. Neither did I. Oz was ours; he didn't belong in a place like that.

"Is he with Aubrey?" my dad asks, not particularly concerned. If absolutely necessary, Chloe or Aubrey could watch Oz, so long as he was sedated on something like Benadryl.

My mom sways slightly and grabs on to the rail of the bed to steady herself.

My dad's head tilts.

My mom opens her mouth to speak, but the words don't come out. Finally she shakes her head and lowers her eyes.

I watch as my dad's face transforms from question to confusion to alarm and back again.

"I hiked out to get help," my mom stutters. "And he went looking for me."

"You left him?" my dad says, his distress transforming into something else entirely—color rising in his cheeks and his features narrowing, such fury on his face I can't bear to watch it—and as I leave them, I wonder what we did to deserve such suffering.

40

We are home. My dad and Chloe were transferred by ambulance this morning and are now at Mission Hospital, two miles from our house.

I watch my mom as she walks into our empty home, Bingo at her side. Seeing Bingo makes me extraordinarily happy. He survived unharmed, and I almost can't believe it. Aubrey and Ben have been looking after him, and by the looks of his round tummy, I'd say Ben has been spoiling him rotten.

The quiet is shocking, so unlike our house it feels foreign. The living room is still a mess from preparations for our trip thirteen days ago. The storage bins that hold our ski clothes lie open in the living room. My school backpack is thrown beside the staircase. Oz's plastic soldiers are lined up on the floor preparing for war. Chloe's combat boots are kicked off beside the couch.

I stare at the boots, remembering her last-minute choice to switch them out for her ancient felt-lined Sorels. A choice that in retrospect probably saved her life.

My mom walks past it all and stumbles up to her room. She peels off the clothes she's lived in for the past ten days, throws them in the trash, then takes a shower that lasts until the water turns cold. Wrapping herself in a thick robe, she rubs lotion into her chafed hands, then returns downstairs and pours herself a glass of wine. Then another. After the third, she climbs back up the stairs, curls into her bed, and almost sleeps.

Tomorrow is my funeral.

41

I didn't realize I was so popular. I scan the room, taking in the large collection of mourners. The pews are full, and so are the aisles. The church is packed to capacity, overflowing with nearly everyone from my school—parents, teachers, students—hundreds of neighbors, teammates from a dozen years of sports, and miscellaneous family members from around the globe. Only half the faces are familiar, and less than a quarter do I know well.

Thankfully it's a closed casket. I am done looking at my cold dead body and have no desire for anyone else to view it. It's not my most attractive look. I'm also thankful my dad and Chloe aren't here. They would hate this, being the center of attention at such a large spectacle and having their mourning on display. My mom hates it as well. She sits rigid in the front pew between Aubrey and Ben, her eyes fixed on my coffin as the audience scrutinizes her to gauge how well she's holding up.

Her eyes are dry and her expression unreadable. She will not cry, not here in front of all these people. Only I know that this morning she sobbed uncontrollably, ghastly grief so violent I was afraid she would pass out and the sheets clenched so tight I was certain they would tear. No one here knows that. To them, she looks like an ice queen, expressionless as she waits for the service to begin for the unfathomable task of burying her child.

Her eyes stare at the sunflowers draped over the polished mahogany, my favorite flower and her choice for the bouquets. I'm proud of her for remembering and wish I could tell her, let her know I see them and that I'm glad she chose them.

Uncle Bob and Natalie are here. Aunt Karen is not—too hard for her or too hard for my mom, it's impossible to know which. Either way it pisses me off, and I decide at this point she is no longer my aunt. I also decide Uncle Bob is no longer my uncle. I am dead. I have that right.

Mo is one of the last to arrive. Necks crane to look at her as her dad wheels her down the center aisle to a reserved space in front, the mourners leering with morbid curiosity at her bandaged hands and feet. After the service, she will return to the hospital. She has a week left before she can go home. Like my mom's, her face is a mask, but Mo's is formed into a perfect guise of humble sorrow, a wounded princess who steals the heart of each person who looks at her.

Only Bob is not infatuated. Mo's eyes slide sideways as she passes him, the slightest shadow crossing over her features when their eyes connect, causing him to look away.

Charlie is in the balcony. He wears a maroon argyle sweater and a dark tie beneath a black jacket. He looks very handsome and very sad. I sit beside him for a while, liking the idea that I can be so close.

The minister is a small man with thin brown hair and a baritone voice, and he does a wonderful job talking about me, considering he never met me. When he is done, he introduces others for the eulogy.

Lots of people speak, and they all say lovely things. I especially like the speech my softball coach gives because he makes it about the pranks I was famous for, and everyone laughs.

Aubrey speaks on behalf of our family, and she represents us well. She looks at Ben a lot, and I know that is how she gets through it. When she talks about me as a sister and my relationship with Oz, a lot of the audience cries.

Then Mo talks. Unable to put weight on her fragile toes, she is wheeled onto the platform and given a handheld microphone. She is dressed in black but looks like an angel. Her hair gleams golden under the church lights, and her skin is luminous from her weeks in the hospital without sun.

She holds the microphone between her bandaged hands and steals the show, the audience swooning with emotion as she regales them with story after story about our lives—a dozen Lucy-and-Ethel, Laverne-and-Shirley, Tom-and-Huck moments—each adventure so hilarious and splendid that anyone would be envious of the grand friendship we shared.

As I listen, my gratitude and admiration for my brave friend grows, every ounce of fortitude drawn upon to make this moment one of celebration rather than sadness, knowing it is what I would want. This morning she could not eat even a bite of toast, her emotions overwrought from knowing the day she faced. Her hands trembled so badly as she applied her makeup that finally her mom needed to do it for her, a thick layer of foundation to cover her bruised, hollow eyes and blush lipstick just light enough to be bright without being happy. She changed it three times, not smiling once. But now, she puts on a show for the audience and for me and perhaps a little for my mom, who she looks at often, reminding everyone who I was and the remarkable life I lived and letting them know how much I was loved. It makes me miss my life terribly and miss her even more.

I don't want to be dead, desperately I don't, and no matter how long it has been, I can't get used to it. Gone. Forever. Permanently. The world going on without me. Mo and I never able to have another fantastic, wonderful adventure again.

When Mo finishes, there's not a dry eye in the house, the audience united in their love and their sorrow, and I have to remind myself it is for me, that I'm the one who died and that this is their goodbye.

42

The doctors think Chloe is doing better. She eats now and goes to the bathroom on her own. She even talks to her new shrink, an ancient woman who forgets a lot but who at least talks to Chloe like an adult. Only I know the truth. Chloe has a plan, and being catatonic doesn't work because then her meds are given intravenously. Now that she is eating, her painkillers and antidepressants are given orally. The ones given in the morning, she swallows; the ones given at night, she palms until the nurse turns away, and then she stashes them in the lining of her suitcase.

When no one is in the room, Chloe flexes her muscles and stretches. She hums the lyrics to songs and has conversations with herself. When she has company, she feigns moroseness that verges on comatose.

Nearly every night she revises her farewell note. The journal beside her bed is filled with them. The latest version reads:

Dad, this is not your fault. The accident was just that, an accident.

Mom, you are who you are, so you also are not to blame. You tried your best, but your best could never make me who you wanted me to be.

Vance, I loved you.

She vacillates on the tense of the second-to-last word: *loved* or *love?* *Vance, I loved you* or *Vance, I love you.* But mostly her edits involve the section about my mom. This is the kindest version, but I still hope my mom never lays eyes on it.

Last night, when my mom was asleep, I tried to tell her what Chloe was doing and about her plan, but at my first word, my mom startled awake violently, hyperventilating and screaming, and I decided not to visit her again.

43

At the door to my bedroom, my mom pauses, draws in a deep breath, then bravely steps inside. Bingo steps in with her. My mess, which before was a constant irritant to her, is exactly the same as it was eighteen days ago, when everything was different. My soccer uniform is balled beside my bed, my shin guards and cleats thrown in the direction of my disheveled closet. Schoolbooks and notebooks and cards and trophies litter my small desk, and several half-finished art projects are piled in the corner.

Chloe and my dad will be discharged from the hospital in a week, and Chloe's room (our room) needs to be ready for when they get home.

I'm slightly appalled by the callous efficiency with which my mom goes about the task. Like a hazmat service disposing of contaminated waste, everything I owned is deposited into trash bags and thrown out the bedroom window to the lawn below to save my mom the task of lugging it down the stairs.

Bingo watches. He lies in his favorite spot, in the square frame of the afternoon sun through the window, the light soaking his gold fur and painting it white, his brown eyes tracking her. When she pulls the chewed-up Frisbee from beneath my bed, his head lifts and his ears perk, and then he flops back to the ground when it is deposited unceremoniously into the trash bag with everything else.

Amazingly, my entire life fits into eight Hefty lawn bags: my clothes, my collection of pigs, my trophies, my scrapbooks, my schoolwork, my Mike Trout–signed baseball.

She leaves nothing.

When the last bag has been tossed out the window, she attacks my bed, ripping the sheets and covers and dust ruffle away with such violence she is huffing and puffing and her shirt is wet with sweat. She throws them, along with my pillow, onto the stack of bags below.

She is pulling down the sash when there is a knock at the door.

With a shuddering breath, she straightens her shoulders, smooths her hair, and marches down the stairs to answer it. She swings it open to find Bob standing there, his face lined with concern, and she falls into his arms.

"I saw you throwing bags out the window," he says, rubbing her shoulders. "Ann, you should have called. You shouldn't be doing this alone."

She doesn't answer, just allows him to lead her to the couch, where she curls against him, her tears seeping into his shirt. And I hate that I'm glad he's there.

44

Mo returns to school today. She was released from the hospital three days ago. The doctors and nurses threw a surprise apple-cider party in her room when they announced the good news that her toes were out of danger. She didn't even wait for the party to be over before she began packing her bag to go home.

I hang out in her bedroom as she gets ready for her first day back. Physically she is better. She has regained the weight she lost, and her skin is mostly healed on her fingers. Her greatest remaining struggle is sleep, her nights continually interrupted with shivering and flinches of terror that make her exhausted when she is awake. She spends twenty minutes blotting out the fatigue that shows in dark circles beneath her eyes, and when she's done, she almost looks like her old self, with the exception of her footwear, an old pair of sheepskin moccasins she bought when we visited Alaska three years ago—the only shoes she owns that fit over her still-swollen toes.

She frowns at her feet in the full-length mirror and then, with a deep breath, flings her hair back over her shoulder and heads out the door.

~

From the moment she steps onto the quad, she's a celebrity, every eye watching as she pretends not to notice and walks boldly toward her first-period class. Some stare directly, their eyes pinched in pity. Others hide their glances, furtive peeks that dart away as soon as she looks their way.

All morning she deflects the unwanted attention with the grace of Kate Middleton, nonchalant and elegant as if immune to it. And only when she goes to the restroom after third period and is alone in a stall does she pull her feet up on the toilet and put her head against her knees, resting from the toll it takes to pretend she's exactly who she was and to survive without me, the one person she was always able to be exactly who she was with.

I sit with her at lunch. She buys a baked potato from the cafeteria and carries it to an empty classroom to eat it in private. Peeling back the aluminum, she slices the potato open with a plastic knife and stares at its open belly as the curls of steam swirl upward, and I know she is thinking of warmth and her mouth is watering.

Like so many things, a baked potato will never be the same. Baked potatoes are the opposite of hunger and cold, an innate comfort factor built in, and when Mo gets older, I bet she will always keep a bag of potatoes in her house just to know they are there. She takes a bite, and I feel the heat and taste fill her mouth, and I smile with her as her eyes close at the pure wonderfulness of it.

Through the window I catch sight of Charlie and decide to hang out with him for a few minutes as well, curious to watch him from this unobstructed vantage point. I'm surprised when he does not head to the bleachers to hang out with his soccer friends and instead walks off campus to a small park behind the baseball field to sit behind a tree where he can't be seen.

He pulls a sandwich, chips, and a bottle of water from his back-pack, plugs earbuds into his ears, and props a notebook on his lap and begins to draw. He smiles as he sketches, and when I see what he is drawing, I smile as well, my grin widening until it fills my face.

The cartoon is of him and me. He wears a tuxedo, the pants rolled up, his feet bare. I wear a poufy dress and hold up the skirt, my feet also bare. Between us is a soccer ball. When he finishes the ridiculous drawing, he titles it *First Dance*, and then he holds it out to admire it and chortles softly.

As he eats his sandwich, he leafs through the other sheets in the notebook, snickering as he turns the pages, and I laugh with him. The drawings are hilarious, and he must have been doodling them for months. Not all are of me. Some are of teachers or of strange cartoon animals that remind me of Dr. Seuss. He's not much of an artist—the proportions are strange and his technique rough—but he's very funny.

In one I am kicking a goal, my leg wrapped around my body in a contortionist pose, the ball headed toward the wrong goal. *Gumby* is the title, and the bubble over my horrified mouth reads, *Oh shit!* Another is of me asleep on my desk, drool dripping from my mouth onto my notebook—*Sleeping Beauty*.

And that's what perhaps stuns me the most. Even with all the exaggeration and less-than-Michelangelo talent, in every drawing, he has drawn me as beautiful. It's something I've never thought of myself as before. Cute maybe, pretty if you're being kind, but I've always been the tall, skinny girl with skinned knees and too many freckles to be attractive in anything but a Pippi Longstocking sort of way. Beautiful is a word used for girls like Mo and Aubrey, girls with curves and lashes and flawless, freckleless skin.

But Charlie didn't draw me in a cute sort of way. Funny, yes, but also beautiful. He exaggerated all my best features—my large eyes, my long legs, the smile dimple that I only have on my left cheek and not the right. Over and over he drew me like I was a genuine muse, a girl worthy of being drawn, as if my too-long chin and bony shoulders were the most gorgeous chin and shoulders in the world.

When his sandwich is finished, he closes the notebook and heads back to the school, and as I watch him go, I sigh with the realization of how perfect we would have been together and what a shame it is that I didn't realize it when I was alive.

Charlie and I only had one conversation, and it was far from meaningful. "Finn, right?" he said as I made my way to the locker room after practice. Blood flooded my face; I was certain that all the fantasies I'd had about him were telegraphing from my brain like a five-alarm siren. I managed a nod.

"Great goal," he said.

"Thanks," I answered and raced away, recounting the syllables as I went. *Four.* Charlie McCoy spoke four words to me. The next day, I practiced my future signature, *Finn McCoy*, scrawling it over and over in my notebook until my hand hurt.

Regret. I wish I'd said more to him that day, that I'd been braver and realized how little time I had. I would have kissed him. I hate that I never kissed him.

45

Mo stands with her friends, a group of three girls from our neighborhood, who, along with Mo, have been known as the Milkshake Gang since fifth grade, luscious and sweet. Though Mo is my best friend, at school we've always hung in different crowds, she among the popular and beautiful and me among the jocks.

"Sure glad you're back," Charlotte says. "Natalie told everyone how awful it was."

Mo tenses.

"Yeah," Claire adds. "She said it was totally gnarly, like you had to boil snow for water and stuff."

"What I don't get," Francie says, "is if you could make a fire, why didn't you just make it bigger so you could stay warm? Natalie said the wood was wet, but if you were there for like a whole day, couldn't you just dry it?"

A shadow falls over Mo's face, the dangerous look she gets when she really doesn't like something. Then it passes, and she smiles sweetly at her friends. "A fire to warm our feet and hands, how silly that I didn't think of that." Then she spins and walks away, leaving them to stare after her.

Francie speaks first. "Bitch. It's like because she was in an accident, she thinks she's too good for us."

"Maybe it was even worse than Natalie said," Charlotte says. "I mean, Mo's pretty smart. If she could have made a fire, don't you think she would have?"

"I don't know. When people get freaked out, you never know how they're going to act. Natalie said a really cute boy was there. Maybe Mo didn't want to go all Rambo on him," Claire says.

"I kind of like her moccasins," Charlotte says.

"Are you kidding?" Francie says. "I wouldn't be caught dead in those. It looks like she's wearing roadkill on her feet."

46

Chloe and my dad are both being released from the hospital tomorrow. I shiver at the thought. Chloe now has a dozen pills stashed in her suitcase. I have no idea if that is a fatal dose, but a single one knocks her out cold, so I think it might be.

I hate this part of being dead but still here. I know things, but there's nothing I can do about them. My only ability is a fuzzy conduit to the sleeping subconscious: an ability that freaks people out so badly and registers in such fragmented garble that I don't want to use it.

Since my night terror–provoking episode with my mom, I've stayed out of the thoughts of the living. But tonight, I have no choice.

I watch my father sleeping, his handsome face so serene, the way it used to be when he was awake, that I am reluctant to break his peace. So I wait a long time—so long I'm worried he will wake and I will lose my chance.

Dad, I whisper. His eyes move behind his lids, and I talk fast to minimize the torture. *It's not Chloe's fingers and toes that are upsetting her. It's Vance. He hurt her and . . .*

My dad's features twist, and he cries out, his eyes snapping open before I can tell him the rest, before I can tell him about the pills and the note.

He sucks in air, and his eyes dart around wildly, and I know I won't visit him again. It's too cruel to allow him to hope I still exist.

47

Bob and Ben lift my dad up the front steps in his wheelchair. Behind them, Aubrey and my mom help Chloe, who winces with each step. Bingo circles and jumps and yips like a puppy, and I wonder how much of what happened he understands. Unlike the humans, he is euphoric rather than sad, celebrating those who have returned and seeming to have forgotten those who are not here.

I grow to like Ben more and more with each day that passes. He's cute in a charming, bookish sort of way. He has a nice smile; a wide, open face; and kind eyes hidden beneath thick wire-rim glasses. I was underwhelmed when I first met him. Milquetoast—I'd always wanted to use that word, and when Ben joined our life, I finally had a reason to use it all the time. The guy was dead-to-rights boring, and I couldn't understand what Aubrey saw in him.

When Aubrey announced she was going to marry him, I actually cried. Mo told me to trust Aubrey, that she must see something in him that we didn't. And now I see it, the side of him I never would have seen in life.

This morning, when he showed up at Aubrey's apartment to drive her to the hospital, he handed her a bouquet of tissue roses. My sister loves flowers, but pollen makes her sneeze.

"And they're practical too," he announced as he plucked one from the bunch and honked his nose on it.

I couldn't decide if it was cheesy or lovely. I settled on cheesily lovely, like the ooey-gooey cheese they squirt on nachos at the movies—strangely wonderful despite how awful it is.

He keeps this side of himself hidden, plodding forward as milquetoast, and I wonder if it's for self-preservation. Now that I'm dead, I realize how awful people are to each other, how a pervasive cynicism exists in most of us that stops us from seeing the best parts of one another. Perhaps this is one of the things I like most about this perspective: my ability to view things more plainly than I did before, to see a tissue rose as brighter and more beautiful than I would have when I was alive.

As Aubrey climbs the stairs with Chloe, she looks over her shoulder at Ben and offers an expression of apology for making him do this. Ben ricochets a crooked smile back, letting her know that no apology is necessary, and I feel it, his tissue-rose heart willing to do whatever it takes to make his girl happy, and again I find myself really liking him.

There's no fanfare or homecoming party for my dad's and Chloe's return, only our family and Bob. The couch is made up with sheets and a pillow, and my dad glares at it as they help him toward it, hating the reminder that he's an invalid. Then his eyes shift to Chloe, who is hobbling up the stairs, and they catch on her hair. It has begun to grow out, a half inch of copper blazing at the roots before abruptly changing to black, marking time and reminding him of me.

"Chloe," he says.

She turns.

"We're home. Hang in there, baby."

She gives the smallest nod, and I give the smallest prayer of thanks. I do not know if it's because of what I said last night or if he would have said it anyways, but Chloe loves my dad, and she'll do as he asks, at least for today.

Aubrey returns a minute later, and when she's near the bottom of the stairs, she and Ben make faces at each other that the others don't see, a silent exchange asking how long they have to stay to not be considered horrible human beings. Ben gives a supportive smile, letting her know he's fine with staying. Aubrey is the one who nearly groans with the thought.

I can't blame them. The house feels like a morgue.

When my dad turns on the television to watch the Angels, they say goodbye.

A few minutes later, Bob returns with Subway sandwiches. He gives one to my dad, then goes to the kitchen to give one to my mom. She invites him to join her outside, claiming it's so they can enjoy the spring weather, but the truth is, like for Ben and Aubrey, mostly it's to escape the misery.

The centerpiece of our backyard is a lemon tree. My parents planted it when they moved in nearly twenty years ago. It was my dad's idea. He wanted a reminder of how far they'd come. There used to be a garden around it, herbs and tomatoes and carrots and pumpkins, practical plants my mom would use when she cooked. Sometimes I forget that she used to garden and cook. It's been a long time since she's done much of anything but work.

Weeds and neglect overtook the garden years ago, but my mom still tends to the lemon tree. Every spring she prunes it, and every month she sprinkles fertilizer around its trunk. Even now, as she and Bob talk quietly and eat their sandwiches, she walks absently around the tree, pulling off dead fruit and breaking off small twigs.

I hate that they are out here talking and my dad is inside alone. I hate that Bob is here at all. He spends too much time here, too much time alone with my mom. I should be grateful he has been so supportive, and if I didn't hate him so much, maybe I would be. But I do hate him, and so I want him to go home.

He lies to Natalie and Karen about where he goes, tells them he's off to the golf course or the gym, and then he parks behind the Laundromat on the Coast Highway and sneaks back to our house to console my mom. I'm not sure if he lies because his intentions are impure or if it's because of the silent feud between my mom and Karen. So far he's done nothing but be a good friend, and only the naked devotion in his eyes betrays that he feels more.

As my mom tends the tree, she tells him about her cases at work, and he tells her about his patients. He has a funny sense of humor that makes her laugh, which I hate but also love. My mom doesn't laugh anymore except when she's with him. He never talks about the accident or me or Oz, and my mom is careful not to talk about Karen.

When their sandwiches are done, Bob gives my mom a lingering hug and tells her to call if she needs anything.

For a few moments after he's gone, my mom remains alone on the patio, sitting and staring at nothing. Then, with a deep breath, she picks up the trash from their lunch, carries it inside, and goes into the living room to check on my dad. His eyes are glued to the television, focused intently on a flickering commercial for auto insurance as he pretends she's not there.

"Can I get you anything?" she asks.

He doesn't answer but instead clicks the volume louder.

Every ounce of strength my dad has recovered since he woke from his coma two weeks ago has immediately transformed into anger, most of it targeted toward my mom. It's hard for me to watch. My dad, the eternal optimist, who has climbed mountains and conquered oceans, diminished to a bitter, defeated man.

"I'm going to the office for a few hours to catch up on some work," my mom says.

My dad says nothing.

48

I visit Bob, curious to hear the lie he will tell Karen about his absence. He's not dressed for golf or the gym.

"How are they?" Karen asks when he walks through the door, shocking me that Bob told her the truth.

Karen is one of those immaculate people—her house, her clothes, her car, her daughter. She likes white and can't stand dirt, dust, or scuffs. She is the queen of Tupperware and closet organizers. It's why I absolutely hate her house. It's like one of those model homes where nothing is real, the plants made of plastic, the wood floors laminate, every object freshly removed from its shrink-wrap. Only now that I am dead do I see the manic obsessiveness it takes to maintain it, her days filled with compulsiveness that borders on insanity.

Bob ignores the question as he slips his shoes off just inside the door, then places them on the shoe rack inside the coat closet.

She follows him into the kitchen, twisting an antibacterial sanitizer wipe in her hands. "How's Chloe? Is she feeling better?"

Bob grabs a beer from the fridge, pops it open, and swallows half its contents in a single chug.

"And Jack?" Karen continues, still wringing the towelette. "How's his leg?"

Bob wheels on her so quickly she falls back a step. "Why don't you go over there and see for yourself?" he seethes. "They're two fucking doors away. Knock and ask all the goddamn questions you want. Ann is your best friend. Go over there and offer to help."

The wipe in Karen's hands rips, and she looks down at it, almost surprised to see it. She stares for a moment, then folds it neatly into fours. She picks up Bob's beer bottle and wipes away the sweat ring. "I'm making ribs for dinner," she says. "Would you prefer potatoes or rice?"

49

My mom did not go to work like she said she was going to do.

It's amazing how much people lie and how good they are at it. Everyone. Always. They say one thing and then do something else entirely. My mom lies to my dad. My dad lies to Chloe. Chloe lies to my mom. A complete and total circle of deceit.

My mom is at the mall, wandering aimlessly through the stores. She has taken to going to crowded places where she can pretend she is normal and where no one knows the travesty of her life. She window-shops for an hour, then sits on a bench, sipping coffee and watching the happy people around her—families with children, women like her, teenage girls like me and Chloe—all of them going about their lives completely oblivious to how quickly it can all be snatched away.

When her coffee is done, she wanders some more. Outside the Rocky Mountain Chocolate Factory, she stares at the chocolate-covered marshmallows, and I know she is thinking of Oz. A few minutes later, she stops outside Wetzel's Pretzels, and I know she is thinking about me.

She checks her watch often, knowing she should return home but each time granting herself a few more minutes, until finally, reluctantly, she returns to her life.

50

My dad is not on the couch where he should be.

He is not using the wheelchair as he was told to.

He is not resting as his doctor ordered.

Instead, he is in the back seat of a cab, his injured leg propped on the seat, and I have no idea where he is going, but wherever it is, I don't have a good feeling about it.

Twenty minutes later, we are in Aliso Viejo and turning into an area known as the Audubon, where the streets are all named for birds. The cab turns onto Blue Heron and stops in front of a gray duplex with a brown lawn.

The cab driver helps my dad from the seat. "You sure you're okay, man?" he asks.

My dad does not look okay. His breath wheezes, and his body shakes. For two weeks, the most he managed was to hobble from his hospital bed to the bathroom.

"Wait for me," my dad says, ignoring the man's concern. "I'll be back in a few minutes."

My dad bangs on the door to the duplex with his fist. Nothing. He bangs again.

He checks the door handle, and when it turns, he lets himself in.

My heart pounds. Whatever this is, it's not good, and I want it to stop.

"Vance," my dad bellows, and my insides go cold.

Crap. Shit. This is why I need to stay out of people's dreams, I yell at myself, regretting very much last night's intrusion into my dad's thoughts. I knew talking to my dad was a bad idea, but I went ahead and did it anyways. You'd think death would make me smarter, wiser, and more provident, but nope—I'm still the same old stupid me, sticking my nose where it doesn't belong and doing things without thinking. And now, because I'm an idiot, Chloe is home alone with her stash of pills, and my dad, who should be home resting, has broken into Vance's house, looking like a rabid animal ready to kill the boy who hurt his daughter.

"Vance, I know you're home. Get your ass out here."

Nothing.

I go to where Vance is, hoping my dad is wrong and that Vance is nowhere near his home, but I find him less than twenty feet away, in his room down the hall, huddled on his bed listening to my dad holler.

I swallow at the sight of him, unable to reconcile the scarecrow in front of me with the boy Chloe loved, and if it were not for the distinct gray of his eyes, I wouldn't know him at all. He's gone from long and lean to skeletal, his cheeks sunken and his eyes bulging from hollowed caverns of blue. He wears plaid boxers and a torn T-shirt, both stained and loose on his emaciated body. His black hair is gone, shaved to prison camp bald, the thinnest fuzz of ash coating his head. His ears were damaged from the cold and are now misshapen and scarred.

There are no textbooks or notebooks, and I wonder if he's dropped out of school. He was never a great student, but with Chloe's help, he got by, and thanks to his mad tennis skills, he was accepted to UC Santa Barbara on a sports scholarship. I wonder if all that is gone now.

On his bureau, in front of his dozens of tennis trophies, is an ashtray filled with crushed cigarettes, and beside that is a wooden box, its lid open and a small baggy of lavender pills with smiley faces inside. Ecstasy. I know this from the "say no to drugs" lecture they made us attend our freshman year—smiley faces, handprints, and peace symbols engraved on pretty pastel tablets, a gateway drug to oblivion and addiction.

"Fine. I'll come to you," my dad yells.

Vance's eyes twitch around in his head, and it isn't solely from fear. He's drugged out of his mind. I know he and Chloe smoked pot sometimes, but Chloe would never be into this.

Vance pulls his knees to his chest, and that's when I see it: the tops of all his fingers except his index fingers and his thumbs are gone. I swallow at the sight, my throat swelling as I glance at his tennis bag in the corner.

The door bursts open, and my dad charges in, adrenaline propelling him forward and giving him strength he didn't have a moment before. And of everything I've witnessed since Oz's death, I've not watched anything as sad as this moment—one man and one boy, both in love with my sister and both utterly wrecked by that day and their failure to protect her.

My dad doesn't slow. Storming the bed, he lunges onto his left crutch as the right one swipes Vance across the temple, knocking him sideways and spinning him off the bed. Vance lands on his knees, and the crutch whips back to strike him again in the ribs. The wind goes out of him as he collapses to the floor and curls into a fetal position, his deformed hands wrapping over his head.

My dad winces when he sees Vance's fingers, so much worse than Chloe's—his pinkies half-gone, his ring fingers remaining to just below the first knuckles, his middle fingers trimmed to the length of his index fingers—a progression of loss that has left his hands resembling a bar graph.

My dad's pity lasts less than a second. The crutch rises again before slamming down on Vance's back.

Stop, I scream, but my dad has only just begun, his rage blinding him as he carries out his wrath on the one person besides himself he can blame. Vance grunts with each blow, but other than to cover his head, he doesn't even try to defend himself. Blood trickles from his lip, and welts rise on his arms and legs. I am thankful my dad is so weak, the blows a quarter the strength they would be if he were in full form.

The power diminishes with each strike as my dad's strength drains, until finally, too wasted to lift his crutch again, he stops. "You arrogant little prick. You led her out there, and you left her." His breath wheezes, making the words barely audible.

Vance actually nods in agreement, which enrages my dad, and he finds the strength to hit Vance across his forearm with the crutch, metal cracking against bone. My dad stumbles with the blow and nearly collapses, catching himself awkwardly on his crutch as his chest heaves. "You goddamn son of a bitch. She almost died because of you. My girl almost died." Mucus and tears stream down his face. Unsaid but blaring is the statement, *Finn died BECAUSE OF ME. Chloe almost died BECAUSE OF ME. Oz died BECAUSE OF ME.*

Vance curls tighter, says nothing, and wisely doesn't nod again.

If my dad had the strength, he would continue, but he's barely able to hold himself. "Rot in hell, Vance. Rot in fucking hell."

Like a drunk man, dizzily he staggers away.

A foot from the door, his eyes catch on the pills on the dresser, and he glances back at the destroyed boy sobbing behind him. His face curls in disgust, and he swipes the pills to the floor, then continues out the door. And as I watch him go, I wonder if this brutal act of vengeance helped, if it diluted his rage or if this is only the first step toward greater destruction. I feel a chill shudder my spine, the answer etched in the ugly expression on my dad's face.

51

My mom walks into an empty house, and it takes her a second to remember it's not supposed to be empty.

"Jack?" she calls.

His wheelchair is beside the couch, his crutches gone.

Bingo follows her into the kitchen and then out the sliding doors to the backyard. Her pace quickens as she climbs the stairs and looks into her bedroom and into Oz's room. At Chloe's door she stops, takes a breath, then steps inside.

Chloe turns her face from the window and says nothing.

"Where's your dad?" my mom says.

Chloe turns away.

"Damn it, Chloe. Where the hell's your dad?"

Chloe's head snaps back, her eyes hard and dark.

"Answer me."

Chloe squints in hatred, and my mom squints back, the fierceness of their gazes clashing with such force it's nearly audible. Then, for the first time since the accident, Chloe speaks to my mom. "How the hell am I supposed to know?"

The answer stuns my mom, and I can tell she can't decide whether she should hug Chloe or yell at her. She chooses the latter, since it's what got the response in the first place. "Well, get out of bed and help me look for him," she barks.

Chloe blinks several times rapidly, like my mom just asked for her right kidney instead of her help in finding my dad.

"Get up," my mom says again. "This is serious. Your dad is gone."

Surprisingly, Chloe does. She wavers a little as she pushes herself up, slightly dizzy from the sudden redistribution of blood.

My mom pretends not to notice. "Go down to the beach to look for him. I'm going to drive around the neighborhood."

Chloe continues to blink like a warning light but also continues to respond. She grabs a hoodie from the hook beside her bed and pulls it on as my mom heads out of the room.

As Chloe shuffles past the dresser, she startles at the sight of herself in the mirror. Her hair is very strange, an inch of bronze and an inch of black, like the ends were dipped in ink. Her skin is ghostly pale, hollowed blue circles ring her eyes, and the scar on her forehead is broiled and pink. And she's lost so much weight her cheekbones stick out sharply from her face. She tilts her head, sticks her tongue out at herself, tries out a couple of cockeyed expressions, then continues on her way.

By the time she reaches the stairs, my mom is already storming out the door. At first I think this is mean. After all, Chloe is still weak, her toes are damaged, and it hurts when she walks on them, but then I realize that this is the only way it can work. Without an audience, Chloe ignores all those things. As a matter of fact, she pays so little attention to them I wonder as I watch her if her toes even hurt at all or if it's just an act so she can continue stockpiling her pills.

52

From her house, Mo must have seen Chloe hobbling down the ramp toward the beach, because she is running to meet her.

The Kaminskis live in a home overlooking the ocean, and Princess Maureen has a gorgeous view from her room.

Mo hasn't seen my sister since the night of the accident, and she stops short when she sees her up close for the first time—the strange hair, emaciated body, her slippered feet wrapped in gauze. Mo erases the shock from her face and hustles to catch up, which isn't difficult since Chloe shuffles forward tentatively, unsure of her three-toes-short-of-whole grip on the sandy concrete.

"Clover," Mo says, using the nickname she's called Chloe since we were toddlers.

Chloe turns, her face set in a mask of determination. Something like relief washes over her when she sees it's Mo. Mo is like the easiest person in the world to be around.

Chloe surveys Mo for damage, scanning her head to toe. Mo helps her out. She holds out her hands front and back, then kicks out her bare feet. The skin on her hands is peeling, a mottled relief of waxy-yellow dead skin chafing off over new pink skin. Her feet are uglier; the digits are still attached, but patches of brown and vermillion still bruise the tips. Chloe holds up her own wounds, and Mo frowns and nods when she sees how much Chloe's decision to follow Vance cost her.

"That sucks," Mo says, stating the fact so plainly it erases every trace of bitterness from Chloe's face, and for the first time since that awful day, Chloe's lips curl at the corners with the smallest hint of a smile.

"What are you doing down here?" Mo asks, changing the subject.

"My dad's gone AWOL," Chloe says. "And my mom thinks he might have come down here."

Mo's brow creases. "Isn't he in a wheelchair?"

"Supposed to be."

Mo doesn't ask anything more because she doesn't want to break Chloe's concentration now that they've reached the sand, each step my sister takes suddenly precarious, and I gain a new appreciation for toes. I never knew how important they were for balance.

When they've shuffled far enough to see beyond the ridge of rocks to the open ocean, they stop. Chloe takes a deep inhale of the salty air, and I'm so jealous I groan.

I love the ocean, every part of it—the water, the waves, the sand, the wind, the constant ebb and flow—but mostly I love the smell, the briny tang I inhaled almost every day I was alive, a scent that conjures up a million memories of hot dogs and s'mores and volleyball and surfing and dolphins and collecting seashells and building sandcastles and burying my brother in the sand.

Chloe's lower lip trembles, and Mo folds her arms around herself. It would be impossible for them to stand there and not think of me. This was my playground.

"I miss her," Mo says.

Chloe closes her eyes and nods.

"It's like there's this great big hole with her gone. This enormous emptiness."

Chloe pinches her nose, and I know she is on the brink of losing it. Since my sister was rescued, she has not cried, and I don't know if it is a good thing or not that she is on the verge now.

Mo doesn't notice. Her eyes still on the ocean, she goes on, "And it's like it is all around me all the time, and it sucks away all the light and absorbs all the sound so everything is less bright . . . less fun . . ." She sighs, lowers her face, then lifts it again to return her gaze to the water. "Less, I don't know, less everything."

Chloe's eyes leak, tears rolling down her cheeks as she pinches her nose tight, trying to hold them in.

"When I think about her," Mo says, "like now, I try to be happy because I know that's what she would want and that she is someplace really good, but it's all the other times, when I'm not thinking about her, that it's hard, because those are the moments I miss her the most, when I feel so alone it's like I'm floating in this great big sea or drifting in outer space, like gravity has deserted me or like I'm going to run out of air."

Chloe sniffles, and Mo's eyes snap to her. "Sorry, Clover," she says quickly, suddenly realizing Chloe is crying.

Chloe shakes her head. "No, it's okay." She blots her eyes and takes a deep breath. "I miss her too. All the time."

"I mean, I get it," Mo says as her own eyes fill. "People die. And I get that I'm still here and that life goes on, and that eventually the hole will get smaller. At least that's what everyone keeps saying."

"Don't you wish everyone would just shut up?" Chloe says.

Mo nods, looks up, almost smiles, looks back at the ocean. "Exactly. Because it's not that I don't get what they're saying. I do. But right now, the hole, it's really, really big, and it's really, really lonely, and I really, really miss her."

For a moment they stand quiet, both of them looking out at the ocean and holding back their emotions, and as I watch them, both so sad, I feel awful. I don't want to be a black hole that sucks away their happiness and makes them cry, and I wish they could see the fullness rather than the void. I am so tired of being missed and of people being miserable every time they think of me. *Don't just try to be happy when you think of me—be happy. Look at the ocean and smile. Inhale the scent and celebrate. Remember me. Remember that I was never sad for more than a day, rarely for more than an hour. Remember the amazing times we had and what a goofball I was. Remember that I was scared of anything with more than four legs but fearless of adventure. Remember. Carry me inside you as a light that brightens your world and makes everything better. I don't want to be a void, a hole, a shadow. REMEMBER ME!*

"Do you know what I think about?" Chloe says. "When I dyed and cut my hair. Not one person commented on it—not my family, my teachers, my friends. Everyone just pretended I had always had butch black hair. But not Finn. Finn comes right out and says, 'Wow, very Buttercup.' You know, from *The Powerpuff Girls*. She didn't lie and pretend she liked it, but she also didn't pretend it didn't happen. Thing is, she didn't care that it happened. It didn't matter if my hair was black, green, or purple—I was still exactly who I'd always been to her. There's no one else I know like that."

"She hated your hair," Mo says with a sniffly laugh.

Chloe manages another small smile, and I cheer for Mo. In ten minutes, she's accomplished more than a slew of psychologists and doctors have been able to in weeks. Then I laugh that Chloe's single precious memory of me is one I don't actually remember myself. It's strange and wonderful, the things we do that we don't realize we've done.

"That second night I was out there," Chloe says, her voice tight and her eyes fixed on the silver line of the horizon, "I wanted to die." She shudders with the memory of the cold, and Mo wraps her arms around herself. "If I could have stopped my heart, I would have. People think burning to death is the worst way to die, but they're wrong. Cold burns worse than flame, and it takes longer, each part of you freezing one cell at a time, so painful your mind can't deal with it."

Mo's face goes pale with her own memory, but Chloe doesn't notice, completely lost in the confession she's refused everyone who's asked.

"You'll do anything to stop it," she says. "And you realize what a coward you are, how little your life means to you. You just want it to end. So much so I envy Finn—that the decision was made for her, and that it's just over."

Mo stands frozen, and I know she heard it, Chloe's use of the present tense. And unfair as it is for this burden to be put on her when she has already endured so much, I am glad, and I pray she will not dismiss or ignore it.

Chloe straightens, and her focus returns. "Finn was there," she says. "The second night, she was with me. I know it sounds crazy, but she was. She came and sat with me."

Chloe glances at Mo, looking for judgment, but all she finds is compassion.

"She talked to me," Chloe says. "It's vague, and I don't remember the things she said, but it was her, and she was totally Finn, chattering a million miles a minute, moving from one subject to the next without finishing what she was saying about the thing before."

I laugh because I totally do that.

"You saw her?" Mo asks, a hint of envy in her voice.

"No, but she still visits sometimes."

"She talks to you?"

"No."

"Then how do you know?"

"I just do. Sometimes she hangs out in our room with me."

I pirouette and cheer. Chloe knows I'm here.

Mo's about to respond when a voice behind them interrupts.

"Chloe."

Both Mo and Chloe turn to see Aubrey walking down the ramp.

"They found him. Dad's home," Aubrey yells. "Mom told me to come and get you. Hey, Mo."

"Hey, Aub," Mo says, her face transforming into a mask of the perfect, well-adjusted teenager, exactly who Aubrey expects her to be, and Chloe transforms back into the damaged, dysfunctional teenager who is suddenly barely able to take a step without nearly collapsing, exactly who Aubrey expects her to be.

Mo doesn't say a word about Chloe's act. Coolly going along with the charade, she takes Chloe by the arm and supports her as they walk back across the beach, Chloe wincing with each step.

"I'll bring the car around," Aubrey says.

When she's out of sight, Chloe turns back to the ocean and says to Mo, "The ocean is going to miss her."

And I smile and cry a little because she's so right.

53

I return to our house and to the middle of a heated argument.

"Damn it, Jack, are you trying to kill yourself?"

"Yeah, that's what I'm trying to do," my dad barks from the couch, where he lies gray and drenched with sweat, his leg propped on a pillow.

"Where the hell were you?"

"None of your business."

"It is my business. Aubrey's looking for you. Chloe's looking for you. I called Bob."

"Yeah? You called Bob?" he spits. "What a surprise. Good old Bob's been quite a pal to you lately."

"What the hell's that supposed to mean?"

"You know exactly what the hell that means. The question is, does your best friend, Karen, know what a pal he's been, or do you just not tell her when you call him and he comes running?"

My mom's nose flares, and I swear if it were possible, steam would be blowing from her ears. "Nothing is going on between me and Bob, and for your information, Bob's been amazing. He practically ran the search for Oz—"

"GET OUT," my dad roars. The explosion causes a violent coughing fit that leaves him breathless. He spits his words through it. "Get the hell out. Don't you dare stand there and tell me what a big help Bob was in looking for my son. Oz is dead. You left him, and Bob didn't watch out for him."

My mom falls back a step.

"NOW." My dad tries to push himself up, but his strength is gone, and all he manages to do is incite more coughing.

My mom flees to the kitchen, where she leans against the counter, her shoulders, her neck, and her body stooped in a way I've never seen before, both my parents older and smaller than I remember them.

54

Aubrey stayed the night, and it was a godsend. When she is around, my family is on their best behavior, my parents doing a remarkable job of acting like they did before the accident, like the poster couple for a difficult but remarkable marriage. My dad calls my mom *hon*, and my mom brings him beers and teases him about being his servant. It's all pretend for Aubrey's sake, but I'll take faking it if it means a day better than yesterday.

For breakfast, my mom serves up lemon-ricotta pancakes in the living room on the coffee table, and my dad pretends to be in good spirits. He jokes with Aubrey about the old priest Ben's mom is insisting marry them.

"Don't worry," he says. "I know CPR, and if he collapses during the ceremony and I can't resuscitate him, I'll marry you myself. I have a license to wed."

It's true. Before my dad married my mom, he was the captain of a private yacht, and his boss asked him to get licensed so my dad could officiate his fourth wedding.

"Not gonna happen," Aubrey says.

"It could. I'd be great. *Dearly beloved, we are gathered here today to join this incredible, lovely, amazing woman with this not nearly good enough man . . .*"

Aubrey socks him in the arm.

"You punch like a girl," my dad says. "Chloe, will you teach your sister how to punch?"

Chloe gives half a smirk.

She actually came down for breakfast. Mostly because my mom refuses to bring her meals up to her anymore, and she won't allow anyone else to, either, which has forced Chloe from her bed.

"I love these pancakes," Aubrey says. "I swear that's what I miss most about not living here. No offense, everyone, you're great and all, but seriously, living without Mom's cooking is a major hardship."

My mom's cheeks flush. "Maybe you want to take some lemons home with you," she says. "The lemon tree is bursting with fruit." She looks at my dad as she says this, the overture to their life together, their history, and their marriage transparent. Her glance ricochets off his fixedly congenial expression of stone.

Aubrey misses it all. "That would be great. And can you give me the recipe for these pancakes? Ben would love them."

Despite everything that has happened, Aubrey remains remarkably unchanged. Like a time traveler thrown into a post-Armageddon world, she is aware of the tragedy but also oblivious to it, unaltered and therefore impervious to the fact that everyone around her has mutated into strange new creatures, alien beings teetering on the brink of destruction.

And remarkably, her blindness is like a magnetic pole of ordinariness that pulls everything back toward normalcy. She chatters about her wedding and the flowers and the invitations, and my mom, my dad, and Chloe cling to it, participating more than they ever did before, thankful or desperate to be focused on something other than the travesty they've been focused on for the past twenty-six days.

To some extent I think Aubrey realizes it more than she lets on, her blitheness exaggerated. No one knows it, but right after the accident, she and Ben talked about postponing the wedding. A celebration in the wake of so much tragedy felt wrong, and Aubrey was distraught about it. She talked to her future mother-in-law, who talked to the priest, but ultimately it was Karen who cemented her decision to go forward with it.

The day my dad and Chloe were transferred back to Orange County, a package arrived at Aubrey's apartment. The card read, *You are going to make the most beautiful bride, a ray of light in a time of darkness. I'm sorry we will be unable to attend your wedding. All our love, Aunt Karen, Uncle Bob, and Natalie.*

The Tiffany Blue box contained a stunning pair of pearl-and-diamond drop earrings: exactly the sort of earrings my mom and Aunt Karen had been clucking over in the bridal salon the day before we'd left for the mountains. Aubrey closed the box and held it in her hands for a long time, and then she set the earrings and the note in the top drawer of her dresser and called my mom to tell her she had found the perfect earrings to go with her dress. And my mom forced lightness into her voice as she asked about them. And Aubrey forced herself to be upbeat as she described them.

And after that, there was no longer any discussion about canceling the wedding, and Aubrey became determinedly perky each time she was around my family, resolved to be the "ray of light" my family needed, despite how often she didn't actually feel that way.

"Ben and I are completely lost on the song list for the reception," she says now. "Neither of us knows music. I swear our guests are going to be groaning."

"I can help," Chloe says, causing my parents to turn in surprise and Aubrey's eyes to bulge.

Chloe rolls her eyes. "Don't worry, sis; I know you don't dig grunge. I got it, pure Adele and Maroon 5—cheesy Taylor Swift romance fluff."

My mom's expression pleads across the table, begging Aubrey to say yes.

With a brave smile and as much false enthusiasm as she can muster, Aubrey says, "Great."

I slap her on the back, then do a jig. *Way to go, Aubrey.*

From the moment Aubrey announced her engagement, I was sick of it, but now I'm loving it. Let's talk ribbon and lace and garters and bridesmaids. My mom is smiling as my dad jokes that he wants to help Chloe with the music, add a little Michael Jackson and Madonna to the mix, and Chloe rolls her eyes, and Aubrey holds her fingers up like a crucifix warding off the devil. And watching them, they almost look like a normal, happy family.

55

The moment Aubrey leaves, the air deflates, a united exhale of exhaustion from feigning happiness for nearly a day. Chloe disappears into her room. My mom washes dishes. My dad watches TV.

When my mom's phone buzzes, she goes into the backyard and sits beneath the lemon tree to answer it. "Hey," she says softly. "Okay . . . yeah, he's okay . . . I don't know where he went. He wouldn't tell me . . ." She laughs. "I don't think so. He can barely get it up to pee."

I cringe.

She listens and laughs again, a shy giggle. "Thanks for checking in. Karen and Natalie doing okay? . . . Good . . . Okay . . . Yeah, I'll call you tomorrow . . . After work? . . . Yeah, that would be good . . . I could use a drink." She laughs again. "You're right—I could use several."

She clicks the phone closed and, with a deep breath, returns to the house.

"Was that *Bob*?" my dad asks, surprising my mom as she walks through the patio doors to find him leaning awkwardly against a counter stool, his leg sticking out like a post.

"He was just checking in," she says defensively.

"I bet he was. Good old Bob," he spits. "You two sleeping together again?"

I rear back at the same time as my mom, and then her face goes red with outrage. But the reaction took a beat too long, the accusation not denied for a single revealing pulse. "How dare you?"

"How dare I what? Accuse you of what I know, that you slept with him, or question what I'm not certain of, whether you're sleeping with him again?" my dad lashes back.

My mom stiffens.

My dad stares.

"You knew?" she says finally, her eyes dropping and her voice small.

"Of course I knew," my dad spits, but I feel the steam draining from him, horrible hurt replacing it, and all of me is on fire, for him, at her, and for her.

My mom stares at the tile between them. "You stayed," she mumbles.

"Where was I going to go?" he says. A dagger to the heart would be less painful than his declaration that the only reason he didn't leave was because he had no choice, and I feel the last of my mom's air go out of her. She staggers to a chair beside the table and collapses into it, her elbows on her knees, her face buried in her hands, and my dad turns from her. His eyes stick for a second on the lemon tree through the window, and then he continues on his way, hobbling back to the living room and away from her.

I knew they were unhappy, but I had no idea the depth of their misery.

56

I torture myself by starting the morning with Mo at school. The hardest thing about being dead is watching the world move on without me. It's been four weeks since the accident.

My soccer team is in the playoffs. I'm thrilled for them and sad for me. Most of the kids in my grade have their licenses and have new cars. And last week was formal, and everyone is talking about it.

Mo now hangs with the drama kids, a development I view with great horror. We hate . . . hated the drama group. They're always so dramatic. I think this is why she chose them. They're the only group so wrapped up in their own crises they don't dwell on hers. At least most of the time. Today is the exception.

"Hey, Mo, why didn't you tell us about the cute boy who was with you in the accident?" Anita, the head diva of the group, asks when Mo joins them. "Natalie says he was hot and that he was, like, totally heroic and pulled her back from Finn's body when she was, like, freaking out."

Natalie says seems to be the start of a lot of conversations these days. The novelty of the accident has worn off, and with it so has Natalie's newfound popularity, her irritating personality spiraling her quickly down the social strata. So in order to hang on as long as possible, Natalie's been blabbing more and more about that day and straying further and further from the truth.

"Excuse me," Mo says, standing, and I watch as she walks across the quad to the table of jocks, where Natalie sits at the end beside her new boyfriend, Ryan, a grade A jerk whose greatest claim to fame is getting thrown out of more football games for unsportsmanlike conduct than he finishes.

"Looking fine, Mo," Ryan says as his squinty eyes rake over her.

Mo ignores him. "Natalie, can I talk to you?"

"I'm eating," Natalie says as she pushes her salad around on her plate.

Ryan uses his hip to nudge her off the bench so she falls to her butt on the concrete. "Mo wants to talk to you, babe," he says through his laughter. "Don't forget to discuss that threesome you've been promising me."

Natalie picks herself up, pretending not to be humiliated.

"What do you want?" she seethes when she and Mo are around the corner and out of sight of the tables.

"Why do you go out with that guy?" Mo says.

Natalie's nose flares. "What do you want?" she repeats.

Mo takes a deep breath, then says in a surprisingly calm voice, "I want you to stop talking about the accident."

"I can talk about whatever I want."

Mo studies her and says nothing, her brow furrowed as if trying to figure something out.

"Is that all you wanted to say?" Natalie says impatiently.

On the surface, Natalie seems the most unaffected by what happened, her detachment during the accident seeming to have protected her from any lasting repercussions. Only I see the differences, her constant nervousness that borders on neurotic—how she checks the lock on the door when she gets home at least six times before she will go upstairs to her room, how she walks three blocks out of her way to reach a crosswalk with a light, how she hoards food in her backpack, her locker, and the side table beside her bed. She never did get the MINI Cooper her parents promised her, a dozen excuses getting in the way of her taking the driver's test.

Most surprising is her obsession with my death. An entire shoebox in her closet is filled with clippings about the accident, along with all sorts of information about dying in a car accident and how to avoid being injured. Along with all the morbid reading is the deck of cards we used to play bullshit on the way up to the mountains and several photos of her and me that were taken over the years. She looks at the photos often, and watching her looking at them is heartbreaking. In each she is smiling almost eagerly, while I stand beside her barely suppressing a grimace, and it makes me feel terrible for how unkind I was, realizing now how much she genuinely wanted to be my friend.

Finally Mo says, "I don't get it. Why bring it up all the time? It's so awful. Don't you want to put it behind you?"

Natalie cocks her head, like she's unsure what Mo is asking.

"And the way you're telling it," Mo goes on, "changing it the way you have. It's like your version and what actually happened are two completely different things."

Natalie continues to look confused, and I realize it's possible that in her mind, the truth has actually been altered. I think about how she has pored over the news clippings about the accident, reading them again and again as if trying to make sense of them or glean some wisdom. Then I think about how she was during the accident, the dazed look on her face as her parents took care of her, and I realize it might actually be possible she doesn't really remember it, and now she is struggling to figure it out.

"Is that really how you remember it?" Mo says. There's no anger in her tone, the question sincere, as if she really wants to know.

Natalie looks down at the sidewalk between them, and her head shakes slowly as she shrugs. "Actually I don't really remember much about it at all," she says. "I mean, I do. I know it happened, and I know I was there, but it's blurry, like it happened to someone else a very long time ago. Is that how it is for you?"

Mo stiffens, and I watch as she exhales slowly through her nose, taking a long time before she answers. When she does, the words are slow and deliberate, betraying the effort it takes for her to speak about it. "No," she says. "For me it's the opposite, the memory so real it's like I more than lived it, and so close it's like it happened yesterday or like it's going to happen again at any moment."

Natalie's eyes widen.

"Every detail so vivid that, most of the time, I can't see past it."

"Oh," Natalie says.

Another long beat passes, Natalie fidgeting and Mo still.

"Can you tell me something?" Mo says.

Natalie nods, no longer in a hurry to return to her table.

"How did your dad end up with Oz's gloves?"

Natalie shrugs.

"You don't know?"

"Do you know what happened to that boy who was with us?" Natalie says instead of answering.

"I don't know. I suppose he just went back to his life."

"He was really cute," Natalie says. "Didn't you think he was cute?"

Mo gives a small smile. This is who Natalie is, a girl with the depth of a dime who would rather talk about a cute boy than almost dying in the cold, and who will deal with it in the dark, in the closet of her bedroom where no one can see, turning the story over again and again until finally she gets it right, altered into a version she can understand.

"He was really nice too. Didn't you think he was nice? Do you know what he said to me when he gave me a boost onto the camper after we went outside? He told me it was going to be okay. He was wrong, and I knew he was wrong, but it was nice of him to say it."

"He was wrong?" Mo says.

"Well, yeah? Nothing's okay. I mean, maybe it is for him, but nothing's okay for the rest of us. Finn and Oz died. Chloe's all weird now and doesn't have a bunch of toes. Vance dropped out of school. My parents are a mess. You're, like, not even you anymore."

Mo laughs, a high, lilting sound that makes me smile. "I'm not?"

"No. Just look at you."

Mo looks down at herself. She's wearing Converse sneakers, jeans, and a surf sweatshirt, very unfashionista. She laughs again, and Natalie giggles with her.

"I guess you have a point," Mo says.

"Nat, let's go," Ryan hollers from the corner of the building. "Unless you're arranging that threesome, then take your time."

Mo rolls her eyes and holds up her middle finger. He gives a few hip thrusts in response, then trots off.

"He's a jerk," Mo says.

Natalie toes the ground.

"Well, I guess we should get to class," Mo says.

Natalie doesn't move. "You won't tell?" she says.

"Tell what?"

"Why Oz gave his gloves to my dad?"

It surprises me, but it doesn't, that Natalie has decided to confess. It's amazing how people trust Mo. It has a lot to do with her eyes, wide pools of blue so innocent looking they seem incapable of deceit—at least this is what people believe.

"Crackers," Natalie says. "My dad traded Oz two packages of crackers for his gloves."

Mo's right dimple twitches, but otherwise she doesn't react. Her eyes remain steady on Natalie's, and her rosebud lips still hold an understanding smile.

"He told me one night when he was drunk," Natalie goes on. "He probably doesn't even know he told me. He was completely plastered. He can be such a loser." Then, perhaps realizing she has stepped over a line of loyalty, she says, "You won't tell?"

Mo's blue eyes flutter innocently, and she offers her most engaging smile. "Your secret's safe with me."

57

My mom is at work, which means Chloe and my dad are home alone. If I still had nails, they'd be chewed to their nubs. I have no idea what lies in store, only that both are on the verge of self-destruction and that this is the first opportunity they've had to act on it.

The home health nurse arrives at nine. Her name is Lisa. She's blonde and bubbly, with exaggerated blue eyes and breasts, and I'm glad she's the nurse we got instead of some old biddy. She is like a burst of fresh air each time she steps through the door.

She checks on Chloe first. Chloe sits on her bed, a notebook on her lap and her earbuds in her ears. She is making notes for Aubrey's reception music, a task she's thrown herself into fully.

"How's the pain?" Lisa asks as she examines Chloe's toes.

"I'm almost out of the hydrocodone," Chloe answers.

I swallow hard at the lie. The hospital sent her home with eight tablets, and she has yet to take a single one.

"I'll pick up a refill and bring it on Wednesday," Lisa says without a blink of suspicion. "Toes look good. Need anything else?"

Chloe shakes her head, and Lisa gives a thumbs-up, then canters out of the room and down the stairs to my dad.

"Morning," my dad says brightly.

While Lisa was upstairs, my dad changed his shirt, shaved, and combed his hair.

"Morning, Jack. You're looking better. Bath first or last?"

"First. Go ahead and take your clothes off, and I'll start the water." He starts to get up.

Playfully she pushes him back down. "Very funny. Like I haven't heard that one before." She pulls a blood pressure cuff from her bag.

"But have you heard it from someone as charming as me?" My dad grins with all his teeth.

He's flirting, and I have to laugh. It's absolutely awful but also incredibly funny. Perhaps he's compensating for the emasculation of having a young, pretty woman take care of him, or perhaps it's a little out of spite toward my mom, or perhaps it's just to lighten the boredom of his recuperation, but it's hilarious, him sprawled on the couch with his mangled leg and laying on the charm like Sir Lancelot.

Lisa's teased brows seam together in concentration as she studies the blood pressure meter in her hand.

"You know that's not fair," my dad says.

"What's not fair?" she says absently.

"Taking a man's blood pressure after you make it rise."

She grimaces at the cheesy line but also blushes, and I actually think she might be falling for it.

You've got to be kidding. My dad is twice your age.

"Strong as an ox, Jack," she says, her fingers lingering a second longer than necessary as she removes the cuff.

"So am I cleared for *all* activities?" he says, his eyebrows rising and falling twice and causing me to cringe. Funny is turning gross quickly.

She giggles. "That brace might be a bit of a hindrance."

I leave before he can answer. It's bizarre seeing my dad not as a father but as a man, and I don't think I like it.

58

Hunger drives Chloe from her bed a little before noon.

My dad clicks off the television when she returns from the kitchen carrying a peanut butter and jelly sandwich and a can of Coke.

"Chloe," my dad says, "can you sit with me for a minute?"

She changes course and settles on the love seat across from him, her lunch perched on her lap. My dad pulls himself up so he's sitting more than lying on the couch. He glances at Chloe, then looks away, his eyes stopping on the table between them as he decides on something or figures something out.

"I know you don't want to talk about it," he says finally.

Chloe stops midchew. She's made it very clear she doesn't want to talk about it.

"It's just . . . I don't need to know what happened out there, but . . ." He stops, unsure how to continue.

"You want to know why I went," she says, helping him.

He still doesn't look at her. He can't, the hurt of her decision blaring like a thousand-watt bulb between them.

Chloe looks at the plate on her lap, sighs, and with her head still bowed, says, "I couldn't let him go alone. I knew you were right, but I also knew that Vance *thought* he was right, which meant he was going to go no matter what, and I couldn't let him go alone. It's like if you weren't hurt, even if I was wrong, you would have gone with me. You wouldn't have let me go out there alone." Chloe's eyes slide to the mantel and the photo of my mom and dad on their wedding day, her eyes sticking on my mom's young face, hurt radiating and the reason she's so angry suddenly clear. She believes my mom didn't love her enough to go with her.

"I loved . . . I love him," Chloe says.

My dad's face jerks up at the distressing thought that Chloe still loves Vance, especially after what he saw on Saturday.

Chloe doesn't see it. Her chin has dropped to her chest, and tears run down her cheeks. "And now, he's left me." Her body convulses with her sobs.

"Exactly," my dad says, acid in his voice. "He left you."

Chloe lifts her face and blinks through the wetness. "Not out there. Out there he left me because he had to."

"But you just said he left you."

"After," she cries. "He left me after. He won't answer my calls. He hasn't come to see me . . ."

"Baby," my dad says. "He's going through his own—"

"His own what?" she screams. "I went with him. I followed him. I left you and Mom and Oz, and now he just tosses me aside like I don't exist, like I'm nothing, like I mean nothing."

"Chloe—"

"No," she says, standing and whirling toward the stairs. Before she starts up them, she turns back. "This," she says, holding up her half-pinky hand, "is nothing. I'd give up all ten fingers and all ten toes for someone I love. The problem is loving someone that much and discovering they don't love you back."

She stumbles forward, leaving my dad staring after her, lost, not for the first time, when it comes to dealing with his daughters.

59

Men can't handle stewing in their emotions. At least men like my dad can't. Boredom and emotion lead to irritation and frustration, which, when combined with testosterone, is highly combustible and leads to irrational action, world wars, and mass destruction.

"Get up," my dad says, throwing a sweatshirt that was on the floor at Vance, who lies on the bed in almost the exact position he was in the last time my dad burst into his room two days ago. The only difference is that Vance's cheek is now bruised where my dad slugged him with his crutch, and dried blood stains the side of his lip.

"Now," my dad says.

Vance flops to his side and pulls his pillow over his head.

"The hard way or the easy way, you're coming with me," my dad says. Fueled by my mom's cooking and some newfound purpose, my dad's strength has been miraculously restored.

"Kill me or leave me alone," Vance mumbles.

"Killing you would be my choice, but I can't do that, so get the hell up."

When Vance still doesn't move, my dad hobbles to the bathroom down the hall, empties the waste bucket onto the floor, fills it with cold water, awkwardly hops back, rips the pillow from Vance's head, and dumps the water over him.

"Shit, man," Vance says, rolling off the opposite side of the bed to his butt. "What the fuck's your problem? I told you, leave me the fuck alone."

"Can't do that. Now let's go. You're driving."

"Fuck you."

"Fuck you too."

Vance lunges at my dad, a clumsy charge of a kid who is stoned and was never taught to fight. My dad used to be a boxer, so even with him on crutches, Vance doesn't stand a chance. Vance runs straight into my dad's outstretched crutch, impaling himself on the rubber base, and he collapses to the ground, gasping for air.

"Shit, man. Get the fuck away from me."

"You need to talk to Chloe," my dad says.

What? I'm as shocked as Vance, whose eyes literally bulge from his emaciated face.

"I can't," he stutters, all his badass bluster gone, and suddenly he looks like a scared little boy, his chin trembling as he wipes snot from his nose with his deformed hand.

"Well, you have to," my dad says, pretending he isn't affected. "So let's go."

"She doesn't want to see me," Vance moans. "And I can't see her. I can't."

My dad's fury returns full force, and he slams Vance across the shoulder with his crutch. "Don't you dare tell me what you can or can't do. Chloe needs to see you, so get the fuck up. NOW." He hits him again across the calves.

With a whimper, Vance rolls out of range and stumbles to his feet.

Standing, he's even more pathetic than he was on his bed—bruised and battered, stoned and broken, dripping wet and stained from head to toe.

"Shit, you smell," my dad says. "Shower first. I don't want you to kill Chloe with your stench."

As Vance shuffles toward the door, his eyes slide to the wooden box that holds his drugs. My dad sees it, too, and he shifts to put himself between Vance and his stash.

With a sigh of resignation and maybe a glimmer of hope, Vance continues past him and into the bathroom to shower. My dad collapses to sit on the bed, wincing in pain as he lifts his leg, a moment to let down his guard and catch his breath.

I stare in disbelief. *Is he nuts?* Chloe can't see Vance like this. Forget waiting until Wednesday for Lisa to bring the final fatal dose. This will destroy her. She won't make it through the night. The only hope there is for her not following through with her plan is the deluded hope she still holds for reconciliation with Vance, a naive optimism that things can return to what they were. It's what she clings to, but if she sees Vance like this, all hope will be lost.

Bad idea, Dad. Bad, bad idea.

60

I return to Chloe to wait with her until Vance and my dad arrive, praying she'll take a nap so I can tell her to leave or at least attempt to prepare her in some way for what is about to happen.

She's in the bathroom, and I'm shocked to find her freshly showered and her hair newly buzzed—the black erased, her head now crowned with pretty copper fur. Her foot is propped on the toilet, and she is shaving her leg. Her iPod on the sink blasts "Lovesong" by the Cure, and she hums along.

I am stunned. It's like someone zapped her with happy juice and transformed her back into my slightly narcissistic, carefree sister.

When she is finished shaving, she opens the vanity cabinet and looks through our amazing collection of nail polish until she finds the one labeled Ruby Rebellion, and my stomach grows cold as things become clear. It's a color she bought when we were with my mom shopping for back-to-school clothes.

My mom held it up and said, "Now there's a color for hookers and harlequins."

It's the reason Chloe chose it, and it's the reason she's chosen it now.

I watch as she carefully paints her deformed toes, the seven that remain swollen and peeling, the nails cracked and yellow. The red is gruesome, eruptions of blood from tattered wounds.

I no longer worry that Vance's visit will put her over the edge. Chloe is already there. She walked to the other side the night I sat with her in the cold, and she never came back. Something irrevocably changed in her, a resoluteness not of despair but of something much less malleable, a maladaptive reaction to her lack of control that night. She willed her heart to stop, begged for death, but her pulse continued to beat. Now she has the power to determine her fate, and that's exactly what she intends to do.

She's really messed up, and nobody knows it. They think it's her fingers and toes. I thought it was Vance. It's neither.

I scan her room for clues to why now. No answer exists except *Why not now?* It's probably as simple as the fact that my dad and mom are gone and she is alone. Perhaps this is all she's been waiting for.

She finishes the top coat, admires her morbid creation, then switches her iPod to play Metallica's "Fade to Black," bopping to the music as she applies her makeup. She takes her time, and I wonder what is taking my dad and Vance so long, now wishing for them to get here.

Her makeup complete—her eyes traced in coal liner and shaded smoky gray, her foundation thick and ghostly, her lips painted the color of wine—she dances to our closet and chooses a knee-length satin white dress that was originally Aubrey's. It was bought for Aubrey's debutante ball when she was sixteen. She outgrew it a month later, and it became Chloe's.

It's a little loose on Chloe, but it looks better that way, making her appear waifish, the ivory satin swimming around her arms and draping off her thin hips.

She is pulling up the zipper when the doorbell rings. At first she ignores it, but when it rings again, she pirouettes out of the closet and scrambles down the stairs, surprisingly nimble and unaffected by her missing toes.

"Mo," she says when she pulls open the door.

Mo's eyes pulse once as she takes in my sister's bizarre getup: the white dress, her burgundy lips, the mortician foundation, and her ruby-painted toes.

"Hey, Clover," Mo says, her face revealing nothing.

"What's up?" Chloe asks.

"I need your help."

Chloe's mouth skews to the side. "I'm kind of busy," she says without irony.

"It can't wait," Mo says, the slight quiver in her voice betraying her alarm over realizing she might have arrived in the nick of time. "Please, Clover, you're the only one who can help. You need to come with me."

A beat of less than a second that feels like an hour passes before Chloe shrugs, and Mo pulls her out the door.

Chloe doesn't have shoes on, but they're not going far, only to Mo's backyard half a block away.

They walk across the Kaminskis' thick, manicured lawn to the deck that overhangs the beach below. In the corner is the Jacuzzi. Halfway there, Chloe stops and her head tilts. I hear it as well. High-pitched peeps and squeaks that make my heart jump.

Mo walks ahead of her and lifts the corner of the tarp that covers the Jacuzzi to reveal a shoebox holding four kittens no larger than gerbils. The littermates cluster around each other, crying and stumbling over one another, desperate and sightless.

Chloe doesn't step closer. Instead her toes curl into the grass, clenching the earth.

She's still too far to see them, but their tiny screams are deafening, the sound a torturous, nails-on-chalkboard kind of horrible—God's way of protecting the young, a unique decibel of desperation reserved for babies that is impossible to ignore.

Mo carries the box to the grass and sets it at Chloe's feet, causing Chloe to look down.

"Oh," she says, dropping to her knees. "Look at them. Poor little things."

Mo lifts her face to the starlit heavens and mouths, *Thank you.*

"Where's their mother?" Chloe says, using her forefinger to stroke the back of a gray kitten who is meowing up a storm as he blindly scrabbles over his siblings.

"I don't know," Mo says. "I found them near the steps."

She's lying, but only I know this because I know Mo so well. When Mo lies, the emphasis on certain words is too sharp. *I don't* know. *I found them* near *the steps.*

Chloe picks up the gray one. It's no bigger than her palm. It cries and cries. "Shhh," she says, then to Mo, "It's hungry?"

"You think?" Mo says innocently, still lying.

"Do you have milk?"

Mo nods.

"And an eyedropper?"

Mo jogs toward her house.

"You need to warm the milk," Chloe instructs as Mo opens the door. "Not hot, just warm, like body temperature."

Mrs. Kaminski is in the kitchen, waiting. She sits at the table with a cup of tea in front of her and a book. "Did it work?" she says.

"I think so," Mo says. "She's out there with them now."

As the microwave warms the milk, Mo walks to the table and drops a kiss on top of her mom's head. "Thanks."

Mrs. Kaminski pats Mo's hand. "Anything to help. I'm sorry to hear she's struggling. Sorry it took so long. Finding newborn kittens isn't easy. Most kennels put them down if they're that young. I needed to drive to Oceanside."

The microwave beeps. "Well, let's hope it was worth it," Mo says, grabbing the bowl of milk and the eyedropper and heading back to the yard.

Mo is brilliant, brilliant and beautiful, and I was very lucky to have had her as my best friend. Her greatest talent is knowing people, an amazing ability to suss out a person's core like a hunting dog. While the rest of the world saw what they wanted to see when they looked at Chloe, Mo saw the truth, and then, more importantly, she concocted the perfect plan to save her.

Mo watches as Chloe drips milk into the gray kitten's mouth. "Shhh, you're okay. Shhh, that's it. Good boy." Chloe is in love.

When she finishes with the gray one, she takes out a tabby-colored runt, half the size of her brother but with the roar of a lion.

"Finn," she says. "I'm going to call you Finn."

61

When Chloe picks up the third kitten to feed her, I go to find my dad to see what's keeping him and Vance. It's been hours, and the drive from the Audubon only takes twenty minutes.

Are you kidding me?

I do not end up at Vance's house, and I am not on my way to our house. We're not even in Orange County. We are in Vance's 4Runner a mile from my grandfather's cabin. Vance is driving as my dad snores in the seat behind him.

I shudder as the truck cruises around the curve where the accident happened. Vance doesn't notice, doesn't even glance at the new guardrail or at the hillside that nudged us over the edge. Maybe it's because he was in the back and did not see the deer or experience looking through the windshield as we tumbled over the edge. Strange how each perspective is so different, eleven entirely separate points of view.

The new guardrail is sturdier than before, constructed entirely of steel with no wood to rot over time. If the Miller Mobile were to encounter a deer today, we would be saved. But of course, there is no Miller Mobile anymore or any me or any Oz or any friendship between the Millers and the Golds. Mo would never be entrusted on a ski trip with us again, and Kyle probably never takes this shortcut anymore. Today there is no snow on the road or in the air, the sky blue and the sun shining.

"Mr. Miller," Vance says when they turn the last bend and the cabin comes into view.

My dad grunts.

"Do you really think this is a good idea?"

Vance only looks half as bad as he did. A shower, a shave, and fresh clothes helped. The only change for the worse is the slight jaundice of his skin and the shaking of his deformed hands on the steering wheel.

My dad rubs his eyes as he sits up and ignores Vance's question.

"Where's her car?" Vance asks as he pulls his truck into the driveway.

"Ann drove her, then went home," my dad lies.

Vance nods and, with a hard swallow, bravely steps from his truck.

"She knows I'm coming?" he says as he helps my dad from the back seat.

My dad nods, and Vance starts toward the door.

"Hold up," my dad says, stopping him. "Give me the keys; I left my pills in the truck."

Vance hands my dad his keys and continues on, and my dad clicks the truck open, pretends to grab something from the back seat, then clicks the locks closed again and tucks the keys in his pocket.

"Where is she?" Vance says when they step inside the empty cabin.

"Welcome to your new home," my dad answers.

The cabin is eerily unchanged from the evening we left for pancakes at the Grizzly Manor. Our skis and the coolers are still in the entry, the grocery bags with our food for the weekend still on the counter.

Vance looks at him, his brow wrinkled in confusion. "Chloe's not here?"

"I'm going to sleep," my dad says. "There should be some cereal in the kitchen. There's no milk, but you'll live."

"What the fuck? You told me . . ."

My dad turns, only exhaustion on his face. "I told you, Chloe needs to see you. And she does, but she can't see you the way you are right now. Chloe has a soft spot for pathetic, so before I can let her see you, I need to turn you back into the arrogant punk you used to be so Chloe can realize what an asshole you are and be done with you."

Vance sneers at my dad, the briefest glimpse of his former self.

"Exactly," my dad says. "So welcome to your new home."

I think Vance is going to protest some more, but instead he lunges for the kitchen, barely getting there in time to puke his guts into the sink.

The "say no to drugs" video was surprisingly accurate in its depiction of withdrawal. Vance's skin fluctuates between green and white, his body trembling as he heaves up his lunch—a poster child for staying off drugs.

"Clean that up and make sure you drink some water," my dad says. "Vomiting causes dehydration, and at this altitude, that can cause a nasty headache."

"Fuck you. Give me my keys. I'm leaving."

My dad laughs.

"This is kidnapping," Vance says, clearly not willing to tussle with my dad again.

"You drove."

"Because you told me Chloe was going to be here. You lied."

"Drink some water."

"Fuck you."

"Suit yourself." My dad turns and hobbles toward the bedroom.

"You can't keep me here."

"There's the door." There's cruelty in my dad's tone, a dare for Vance to defy him as he did the night of the accident. Tonight is not as cold as it was a month ago, but it is still brittle, and Vance wears only a T-shirt and jeans.

The door to the bedroom closes behind my dad.

"Fuck you," Vance roars, and then he bends over the sink to throw up again, his body quaking.

His eyes slide to the door, another crossroads in front of him, but this time he is not as naive, entirely aware how much a single step can cost.

62

I decide to check on my mom to see what she thinks about my dad not being home and discover she's not thinking about it at all. My mom sits with Bob at the end of a bar known as the Dirty Bird. Its real name is the Sandpiper, but it's so seedy and infamous for its grunge factor that for twenty years it's been referred to almost exclusively by its nickname.

". . . and I swear, honest to God," Bob says, "the woman's out cold, but the moment I start to drill, her hand shoots out and latches on. And what can I do? I've got a drill in her mouth, and she's got me by the crown jewels."

My mom laughs and takes another sip of her drink.

She's drunk and he's drunk. I can tell by the way they slosh around on their stools as they talk and laugh.

Bob drinks. A lot. I see it now that I'm dead. When he works, he's sober; the rest of the time, he's drunk. On his way home from the office, he stops off for a scotch. The moment he walks into his house, he downs two beers. And with dinner, he drinks wine with Karen. Then before he goes to sleep, he has half a tumbler of something gold.

It must be worse these days because Karen mentions it often. "Sweetheart, don't you think you've had enough?" she said last night when he poured a third glass of wine. In response, he downed it in two gulps, then poured another.

It seems every word from Karen's mouth is an irritant, like the very pitch itches his brain. Meanwhile my mom seems to have the opposite effect, her company a soothing elixir that makes him witty and charming, affectionate and happy.

"Do you need to go?" he asks.

My mom shakes her head. "Jack left. He's gone to stay at the cabin."

Bob doesn't say he's sorry; that would be too disingenuous. Instead he swallows the remainder of his drink and, wobbling slightly as he stands, says, "Let's get out of here."

I beg my mom to say no, but that would be asking too much. Without a flicker of hesitation, she stands, and Bob takes her hand to pull her from the bar toward the hotel across the street.

63

I decide to hang out with Karen, curious to see how she is dealing with Bob not being home this late after work.

Karen does not sit idle. Karen is never idle. Since her return from the mountains, she never stops. She avoids thought through maniacal busyness and avoidance, relying on regimens of activity and obligations that allow no time for reflection. If there is a report of snow on the news, she changes the channel. If there is a car accident on the freeway, she exits and takes side streets home. Her coping mechanism seems to be based on the theory that the past can only hurt you if you let it, only if you stop long enough to consider it. Best not to dwell on things, even better if you don't think about them at all, pretend nothing happened, and live in denial that anything has changed.

This is fine when it's daytime and Karen can run from her PTA meeting to the women's shelter to the grocery store and to the gym. But at one in the morning, when she's awake and the rest of the world is asleep and her husband is not home, none of these distractions are available, and so instead, obsessively, she cleans, pretending not to recognize that Bob isn't there, acting as if he's only a little late and as if it's not in fact very early on another day altogether.

Perhaps she convinces herself that he is having a drink with the other dentist in his practice or that he fell asleep at the office. I don't know. I only know her mind refuses to recognize the truth. She polishes and dusts and straightens. She freshens her makeup and vacuums. She sorts through the bills on her desk. She purges her emails. She polishes and dusts and straightens again.

Only I know how miserable her life is, how alone and lonely she has become, how her marriage has disintegrated to the point where if she walks into a room, Bob walks out. In public, they appear united. Bob, a talented actor, will wrap his arm around Karen's shoulders and regale whoever is listening with tales of his brave family as Karen politely smiles along, no one but me noticing the distress in her eyes from the toll it takes for her to keep up the charade.

Her stomach constantly bothers her now, and when Bob talks about that day, it acts up. Sometimes it's too much, and she needs to excuse herself and go to the restroom, where she locks herself in a stall and pops Tums, hoping it will pass. Normally this is something she would talk to my mom about, but my mom is no longer her friend.

At around three, I begin to feel sorry for her.

Until the accident, I loved Karen. She was like a real aunt, my closest aunt, the first call I made if I was in trouble because I knew she'd do anything for me, the last call I made if I had good news to share because I knew she'd want all the details and that I'd never get to the other calls.

Now, after the accident, I hate her.

Mostly because I feel so betrayed. My whole life Karen has billed herself as a do-gooder, a champion of causes, the first to volunteer for bake sales and to lead the charge for putting shoes on children in Africa or food on the tables of the poor. Self-righteous and pious to the point of sainthood—that is who I believed her to be.

She was supposed to be good, do good, be selfless, and care about others, and she failed. When things got tough, her concern was solely for Natalie and herself. It's like pulling back the curtain on the great and powerful Oz to discover an old man with a bunch of levers and strings and no magic at all. She has no right to claim she's a good person because she's not.

But my conviction wavers because, try as I might to only hate her, the sixteen years we shared before that day still exist, along with all the things I loved about her, and I find myself still caring for her and feeling sorry for her. She's so utterly alone and miserable, and Karen is not a woman designed for loneliness or sadness. She is a woman made for laughter and hugs—buxom and soft, ditzy and fun, loving and good . . . yes, good. Until that day, she was good, and discovering she isn't is very sad.

I grapple with this. Is goodness only true if it is at a personal cost? Anyone can be generous when they are rich; anyone can be selfless when they have plenty. My mom is not known as overly compassionate—some might even say she's a bitch—yet using her bare hands, she closed the window of the camper. She undressed her dead daughter and didn't keep a shred of warmth for herself. Bravely she left her son and husband and hiked out for help. All while Karen sat in the back of the camper with Natalie.

Can I blame Karen for her cowardice? For being selfish because she was scared? Are we born with our strength? If so, then should we condemn those who don't have it?

I watch her shuffle into the kitchen, where she pulls the knobs from the stove so she can scrub them in the sink, and I decide I do not feel sorry for her. Fear is not an excuse. My mom was scared. Kyle was scared. Mo was terrified. Because of Karen, Oz is dead.

She is putting the knobs back on the stove when the door opens and Bob walks in.

She hurries out to greet him. "Late night at the office?" she says.

He looks like death, his hair disheveled, his clothes rumpled, his face red from perhaps still being drunk. He lifts his head to look at her holding a stove knob in her rubber glove and, with a sigh, nods to the charade and then stumbles up the stairs to their room.

Karen stands where she is, her compulsiveness momentarily paused as she watches him go, the reality blindsiding her and causing her to drop the knob as she catches herself on a chair. Because no matter how busy you keep yourself, no matter how much you refuse to talk about the past or face it, no matter how many times you change the channel if the weatherman is predicting snow, there are moments, inevitable lapses and gaps in time, when the past floods into the present with such fury it sucks the wind from your lungs and knocks you off your feet.

Crumbling to the floor, she curls into a ball and sobs.

64

My mom creeps into the house like a burglar. Any other night this might work, but tonight she is caught red handed as soon as she steps through the door.

"Mom," Chloe says from the couch.

"Chloe?" Guilt laces my mom's tone, though it doesn't need to. Chloe is the last one to cast stones. She is also ironclad with secrets.

Chloe still wears the ridiculous getup she had on earlier. Dirt stains the skirt from where she knelt on the grass, and her eye makeup is smudged.

My mom pretends not to notice the oddness. "What do you have there?" she says, stepping closer. "Oh my. They're so tiny."

The four kittens sleep on Chloe's lap. Finn meows and yawns with the disruption, then curls tighter against her brother and two sisters to return to sleep.

Bingo, who lies at Chloe's feet, lifts his head at the yowl and then flops back to the floor.

Chloe nods. "The mom left them."

My mom sits beside Chloe and strokes the back of the gray one. "She probably couldn't take care of them. Are you going to bring them to the shelter?"

"I can't. Mo found them and called the shelter, and they told her that they can't take them until they can drink on their own."

"And Mo can't keep them?"

"Her dad's, like, super allergic."

I see the hint of a smile in my mom's eyes, a grin of acknowledgment and gratitude for Mo's genius. My mom might not realize the exact peril Chloe is in, but she knows Chloe is struggling.

"So you're going to keep them?"

"I have to."

My mom nods in agreement. "How about I watch them for a spell so you can get some rest?"

Chloe yawns and nods, then carefully transfers the small pack to my mom's lap. Each wakes and cries out, a symphony of tiny squeaks.

"They're hungry," Chloe says.

My mom rolls her eyes. "No duh. I raised four kids. I know when a baby is hungry. Go to sleep. I've got it."

Chloe gives an anemic, concerned grin, then stumbles toward the stairs.

"Chloe," my mom says, stopping her, "your hair looks good."

"Thanks," Chloe answers, half-asleep.

Finn meows louder, and Chloe's eyebrows furrow with concern.

"You know, I was thinking," my mom says, "my boss offered me tickets to the Pacific Symphony on Saturday. Maybe we should go?" There's so much hope in her voice my heart races.

"Do you need me to get the milk?" Chloe says, her voice tight with worry over the kittens' growing distress.

"No, I've got it," my mom says, placing the kittens in the shoebox, all of them now screaming. "What do you think?"

"Yeah, okay," Chloe says absently, her focus entirely on my mom's slow motion rather than on what she is saying, willing my mom to put a little pep in her step.

My mom lights up, a smile on her face as she carries the meowing box to the kitchen. Chloe exhales a sigh of relief and lumbers up the stairs.

I stay with my mom as she nurses each kitten with the eyedropper, soothing and petting the little creatures as tears drip down her cheeks. And I forgive her for tonight, and I hope she forgives herself. Like everyone else, she is stumbling forward, one foot in front of the other, not always in the right direction but staggering on just the same.

I need to remind myself that she doesn't know what Bob did, that she doesn't know what my dad is doing with Vance. She only knows that my dad hates her for not protecting Oz and that he has left, and that Bob loves her and is here—a distorted mortal view.

When she is finished feeding the foursome, she returns to the couch, places the kittens on the couch beside her, wraps her arm protectively around them, and closes her eyes. Finn is a feisty one. She may be the smallest, but that doesn't stop her from insisting on her way. She shoves Brutus (that's what I've named the gray one) out of the way so she can claim the spot nearest to my mom's heart.

65

"Up," my dad orders as he knocks Vance's feet from the couch where he is sprawled out snoring. Vance groans and tries to pull his feet back up, but my dad knocks them away again, this time with enough force to spin Vance off the couch to the floor. "Now."

"Shit, man. Go away."

"We're burning daylight," my dad says.

Vance squints through his swollen eyes at the pitch-black window.

"You've got ten minutes. Breakfast is on the table." My dad hops away on his crutches. On the coffee table is a granola bar and a glass of tap water—prisoner rations.

Vance curls into a ball and closes his eyes.

Exactly ten minutes later my dad is back and knocking Vance on the soles of his feet with his crutch. "Let's go."

"Go where? It's fucking nighttime."

"Actually, it's six in the morning." My dad raps Vance's feet harder until Vance has no choice but to sit up or else continue to have his feet battered. "Time to go find Oz."

Vance cocks his head, concerned my dad has lost his marbles, which I'm wondering myself.

"Body wasn't found," my dad continues. "So we're gonna find it. Now—let's go."

Vance shakes his head, the whole cockamamy idea too wild to comprehend. Oz's body is lost in a tundra that nearly killed both of them only a month ago. There's no way Vance is volunteering to join a brigade consisting of only the two of them—a battalion short on limbs, fingers, and sanity—in search of my brother's decomposing corpse.

My dad sighs through his nose. "It's not a choice, Vance. You see, here's the deal. You screwed up, and your screwup involved my little girl, and there's nothing I care more about than my family. So let's be clear here: I don't give a shit about you. I'm not doing this because I'm a good guy who cares and wants to save you from yourself. If I had it my way, you'd rot in your room. All I care about is Chloe, and right now, Chloe is under the misguided impression that she still loves you."

Vance's face snaps to my dad's, his eyes large. My dad told Vance that Chloe wanted to see him; he said nothing about Chloe still loving him.

I've never been a huge fan of Vance's, but I've always been a huge fan of how much he and Chloe loved each other. My dad wasn't there, so he doesn't know it, but after Vance realized the mistake he'd made, he became desperate to save her, staggering on for nearly two days without rest, his purpose propelling him beyond mortal strength. He's only eighteen. I wish my dad could see that.

My dad frowns at Vance's hope. "So, pain me as it does, Chloe needs to see you so she can get over it. But unfortunately, right now, you're more loser than punk, and that's not going to cut it."

"And if I refuse?" Vance says.

"There's the door. Same door that was there last night. Same door that will be there tonight and tomorrow and the day after that."

Vance turns the choice in his mind, then pushes to his feet. "When do I get to see her?" he says, and my heart swells with how much he still loves my sister.

"When you find Oz."

66

I know I promised not to visit the dreams of those I love anymore, but I can't help it. Mo's having a tough time because of what Natalie told her, and Mo and I have always helped each other out when it comes to Natalie. Even in death, that girl is a royal pain in my rear.

Mo doesn't know what to do with Natalie's confession about Bob trading crackers for Oz's gloves. The exaggerations and lies Natalie has been telling, Mo was willing to let go, knowing Natalie's diarrhea of the mouth would run its course and that everyone would eventually grow tired of it. But in the same way the gloves disturbed Mo as she sat in the camper waiting for rescue, they disturb her now, and she doesn't know what to do with it.

My dad is in Big Bear. Chloe is fragile. And my mom and Bob are thick as thieves. She considers telling her own mom, but Mrs. Kaminski wouldn't want Mo to get involved. She's a practical woman. Oz is dead; what good would come of it?

Mo tries to tell herself this, but her conscience is haunted. Perhaps it's because her own guilt over what happened to Oz weighs on her. She knew something had happened that caused Bob to have the gloves and that caused Oz not to return. She knew it then and did nothing; she knows more now, and it eats at her to do nothing again.

If I were alive, I'd deal with it in the way I always deal with things. I'd tell the world what Bob did, how he sent Oz into the cold and manipulated him out of his gloves. I'd drive through the streets with a megaphone and broadcast it, describing the cowardice and selfishness of all the Golds. And everyone would believe me because I have one of those straightforward personalities that people believe. So if I were alive, that's what I'd do. But Mo isn't me, and calling someone out in public isn't her style, so when she goes to sleep, I sneak into her dream and offer a suggestion that will work for her.

My whisper is simple and disguised as a breath. "Write it. Write the truth."

67

My dad and Vance stand in the awful spot where it all began: the narrow curve in the road where we saw the deer and life changed. Though today the road is clear of snow, and so is the sky, and there is no deer in sight. It doesn't feel dangerous or remarkable, just a bend in a road like a million other bends in a million other roads.

"This will be our base camp," my dad says. From the back of Vance's truck, he pulls out a harness and a long line of rope.

Vance is outfitted to the nines, wearing so many layers his face is beaded with sweat. "We're going down from here?" he says with a glance down the sheer cliff of rock.

"You're going down. I'm out of commission," my dad says with a glance at his braced leg. "You'll rappel down, then work a grid reconnaissance to look for Oz."

Vance shakes his head and looks at my dad like he is nuts. Vance is a boy from suburban Orange County who grew up without a dad. He's never been camping or mountain climbing, and his idea of outdoor adventure is hoofing it to Starbucks because his truck is in the shop.

"Yeah, I don't think so," he says. "Several problems with your plan, Mr. Miller. First, there's no way I'm going down there by myself. Second, I have no fingers to do this rappelling thing. And third, there's no way I'm going down there by myself."

"That's only two problems," my dad says, adjusting the harness. "Rappelling is easy; it's the climbing-back-up part that's hard. You still have most of your fingers, so you should be fine."

"*Should* is not an encouraging word."

"Worst that will happen is you'll fall a few feet."

"Not happening."

My dad sighs. "First things first. You need to learn how to secure an anchor into the mountain. You'll carry rope with you, tie on, rappel down, then do it again until you reach the accident site. Four lengths should get you there."

Vance rolls his eyes like this is never going to happen, but what he doesn't realize is that my dad has that look in his eyes, the one he gets when he is determined. And once my dad gets that look in his eyes, nothing is going to change his mind. So Vance had better pay attention because, whether Vance agrees or not, whether he thinks this is totally nuts or not, after the lesson, he is going down that cliff, even if my dad needs to throw him over the edge to get him there.

68

My mom has taken up running. It's not jogging; that is too gentle a term for what she does. Arms and legs pumping, each day she races through the streets and onto the path that winds beside the golf course, tearing along the asphalt until it's impossible for her to catch hold of another breath; then she stumbles to a stop, wheezing and dizzy, her hands on her thighs as she gasps.

She began the day she returned to our empty home after my funeral, the silence and stillness so haunting her muscles coiled and twitched until she couldn't take it a moment longer and she bolted like a madwoman into the street and kept on going.

On the weekends, she runs in the morning. During the week, she runs after work. All day at her job, she holds herself tight as a Victorian corset, but as soon as she returns home, she ties on her sneakers and explodes onto the street.

Tonight, it is on her stagger home, her head bent to the sidewalk, that she crosses paths with Karen. Karen's back is turned as she stands beside her mailbox leafing through the mail. They notice each other at the same time, when they're nearly upon each other, their faces registering equal surprise before closing into mirrored expressions of scorn.

Karen does not retreat as I expect her to. Instead she pulls her shoulders back and holds her ground.

My mom's chin slides forward as she continues past without a word. "You chose first," hits her from behind. "Maybe I didn't do right by Oz, but you chose first."

My mom stops, her fists balled at her side as she whirls around. "What the hell are you talking about? Oz is dead. Your precious Natalie didn't even catch a cold. Only you, Karen, could somehow twist this around and put it back on me."

"I was protecting *my* family," Karen says. "You made it clear where your loyalties stood when you chose Mo over *my daughter*. So yeah, when the choice came for me to protect *my family* or Oz, I chose us."

My mom squints in confusion, trying to figure out what the hell she's talking about.

"Finn's boots," Karen clarifies. "You gave them to Mo."

My mom's eyes flick back and forth as she processes the words— *Finn's boots*. I can tell she doesn't remember.

I remember, but what I remember most is Mo giving them back.

A pair of ratty, worn-out UGGs saved my mother's life. They probably saved the lives of everyone who lived that day. When I pulled them on that morning, I had no idea I was making such an important decision; neither did my mom when she pulled them off my dead body and gave them to Mo instead of Natalie.

"You're no better than me," Karen continues. "We all made choices that day, but you chose first."

My mom falls back a step as the memory registers. She did. She chose Mo. Her face twists in wonder; then, without a word, she turns and continues on to our house.

When she is safely inside, she slides down the door to sit on the floor, her head resting on her knees as the fingers on her right hand absently clench and unclench, as they do so often these days.

Was the decision as simple as her liking Mo more; or more complicated, based on the platitudes of reassurance she had offered

Mrs. Kaminski; or worse, based on resentment of Karen and her life with Bob?

My mom pushes her legs out straight and stares at her feet, and I know she is thinking of Chloe as she reconsiders her priorities in hindsight: Chloe, Oz, my dad . . . Mo or Natalie? I still don't know who she would choose.

Her eyes slide to a photo on the mantel of her and Karen holding Natalie and me when we were babies, and her shoulders slump. I know by the sadness in her face that she would still choose Mo. No matter how much time she had to decide, the choice would be the same.

I feel bad for my mom and for me. I'd have chosen Mo as well. Not out of spite or because of Mrs. Kaminski, but because of exactly what happened. My mom chose Mo, and when the time came, Mo gave the boots back. Natalie wouldn't have done that.

This does nothing to alleviate the guilt. If Mo had done to me what my mom did to Karen, I'd feel as betrayed as Karen does, a dagger of disloyalty straight through the heart.

The toll of that day grows. Karen and my mom had one of those remarkable friendships—a sisterhood that anyone who knew them believed would persist into old age. And now, over a pair of old boots, it is gone.

69

Mo lies on my bed, her chin propped on her hands. The bed has new sheets and a new comforter.

Chloe lies on her own bed in a similar pose. Both stare at the four fur balls on the floor below them, which stumble around like drunken sailors.

"Are you going to keep them?" Mo says.

"My mom says I can keep one. I'm keeping Finn."

"Is your mom okay with you calling her that?"

Chloe shrugs.

I'm okay with Chloe calling her that. As a matter of fact, I'm honored. Finn is super cute and quite a scrapper.

"I wish I could keep one," Mo says.

"No chance?"

"My dad's super allergic, remember?"

Since the kitten-Chloe rescue four nights ago, Mo has made a habit of spending the afternoons with Chloe. Every day, she comes straight after school. At first I thought it was out of concern for Chloe, but now I know it's more. Mo is lonely.

Mo has always been mature, but since the accident, it's like she has zipped right past everyone her age, as if what happened was some sort of time warp. Adults love to yak about how someday all the petty high school stuff won't matter—what people think, the cliques, the gossip— and it's like Mo has leaped to "someday" in an instant.

"How was formal?" Chloe asks, just to have something to say. Chloe never went to any of the high school dances, the scene and the music way too lame.

"I didn't go," Mo says.

"I thought you asked Robert?"

"I did. But when I was in the hospital, Ally asked him, and since he wasn't sure if I'd be better in time, he said yes."

"That sucks."

"Not really. I wasn't into going anyway."

"Did that boy Finn asked end up going?"

My ears perk up.

"Charlie. Yeah, he went with that tall girl, Cami. You know, the soccer goalie."

My heart plummets, and I wonder bitterly if he draws cartoons of her now instead of me.

"Clover," Mo says. "You know what's been bugging me?"

"Not until you tell me."

Mo smirks. "Natalie."

"Well, there's something that hasn't changed."

Mo smiles again. "So you know how you won't talk about what happened, and I hate to talk about it, and your mom won't talk about it?"

"Yeah."

"Well, that means the only people talking about it are Natalie and her dad, and what they're saying isn't what actually happened."

"So? Let them have their stupid glory."

"I know. That's what I originally thought. But it's bugging me. A lot."

"Why?"

"I don't know. I guess because I need to keep telling myself the truth so it makes sense. It's my way of dealing with it. We crashed. We survived. I run it through in my brain over and over again, every detail, so I can understand it."

"So why do you care what Natalie's saying? I'm sure no one even believes her. After all, it's Natalie."

"Because I'm realizing there are pieces missing. I only know the parts I know, not the whole thing."

Chloe sits up and crosses her legs. "Mo, let it go."

"I can't."

Chloe tenses. "I can't talk about it."

"I know. And I don't need you to. I wrote it all down—well, most of it, the parts I know. And your part I mostly have. After we crashed, you, Vance, and Kyle were piled against the driver's seat."

"Who's Kyle?"

"Kyle was the kid we picked up on the side of the road. His car had broken down."

"I forgot he was even with us. Is he okay?"

"I think so. He's the one who hiked out with your mom to get help."

Chloe shakes her head. "Wow, you're right. We really only know the parts we know."

"Exactly. You were the first one I saw. I opened my eyes, and your mom was stumbling toward you. Your head was cut, and there was a lot of blood . . ."

"I thought Bob helped me?"

"Your mom helped you first. You don't remember?"

Chloe's eyes narrow in on the quilt on her bed as she tries to remember. She bites her lip as her fingers rise to the scar on her forehead, the vaguest recollection of my mom's touch. "Oh," she says.

"Then she realized Finn was up front, so she told Bob to look after you."

Both fall silent, a shared moment of reverence for my death.

"Then, after the initial shock of everything, and after your dad was moved into the back, you and Vance left. Two days later, you were found."

Chloe's jaw twitches. Her story isn't complicated, just horribly, simply awful.

"The parts I'm missing are what caused the accident, why Oz left, and what happened when your mom and Kyle climbed out to get help."

"My mom won't talk about it," Chloe says. "She's even worse about it than me. At least I acknowledge it happened. My mom pretends it didn't, not any of it—the accident, the death of two of her kids. Her way of dealing is to act like Finn and Oz never existed. It's weird, but I'm telling you, she's not going to talk about it. She's in serious denial and has made a superhuman effort to erase all evidence of it."

It's true. After my mom purged my room of all my belongings, she did the same to Oz's room. Then she scoured the house. If she found a sock that was mine, it was discarded; an eraser Oz had used, tossed; a paper clip that was green, thrown in the trash. She no longer buys applesauce or Fruit Roll-Ups, because those were my favorites, or Hershey's syrup or Oreos, because those were Oz's.

Mo rolls onto her back and looks at the ceiling. There are faint outlines of the glow stars she and I pasted above my bed when we were nine. "That's too bad. It's her story I want to hear the most. She was amazing, superhero amazing. I owe her my life. We all do."

"Maybe, but I don't think she sees it that way."

"How can she not?"

Chloe shrugs. "Like you said, none of us know the whole story. We each only know our parts and from our perspective. And I bet the part we don't know about my mom's story is the part that has her racing through the streets like a madwoman and pretending she only ever had two children instead of four and avoiding mirrors like that's where the devil that chases her lives."

70

Chloe had completely forgotten she had agreed to go to the symphony with my mom, but when my mom popped her head through Chloe's door to tell her to get a move on for their big night out, Chloe did a great job pretending she was excited.

In an act of defiance, she chose to wear sunshine yellow for the black-tie event. Her dress is sleeveless with a wide skirt that billows from her tiny waist. Her sandals are silver with jewels of crystals on the straps, her toes still painted blood red. She is breathtaking, and I roar with applause as she and my mom walk toward the concert hall.

For a second, I think she hears me. Her lips curl at the corners, and her hand lifts slightly, a small wave.

Chloe has always been pretty, but suddenly she is exquisite. The scar on her forehead, jagged and pink, glows against her pale skin, drawing stares like flies to fire, eyes lingering before slipping down to discover her missing finger and toes—more enticing clues to her mysterious story—her wounds unabashedly displayed like shiny, curious glittery stones. She is fragile, strong, and utterly fascinating, and hearts quicken as she passes—men and women alike, the women slightly repulsed and the men mesmerized, all of them shifting and maneuvering to get closer, wanting to be near.

Chloe is oblivious. She walks beside my mom, looking at the stars and the people and the architecture.

My mom is nervous, like she is on a first date and wants to do everything right. "Would you like something to drink?" she says when they step inside.

Absently Chloe shakes her head. "This is beautiful," she says, admiring the soaring entrance hall and undulating glass that drapes like waves of water from the ceiling.

"The glass is the clearest in the world," my mom says. "No iron in it, the element that tints most glass green. The architect wanted it to be entirely transparent so the people inside the hall would be part of the facade."

"Wow, that's cool."

It's weird to see how alike they are. Only Chloe would find my mom's extensive knowledge of such minutiae "cool." Aubrey and I would have lost interest the minute we found out the subject matter was glass.

They make their way to their seats, and I watch the concert with them, though I have absolutely no appreciation for it. Violins wail song after song with no words. I inherited my dad's musical gene, which means I don't have one.

Chloe and my mom are lost in it. Their muscles tense with the crescendos and shudder to rest as the tempo slows, as if their pulses are tied to the notes, and again I marvel at their likeness and wonder if my mom was like Chloe when she was young and if Chloe will be like my mom when she gets older. My mom is more athletic and Chloe more sensitive, but the mettle in their blood is the same—an absoluteness of spirit as unique as the copper hair Chloe and I inherited from my dad.

Chloe's eyes well during a sad song, and beside her, my mom smiles, more absorbed at the moment in her daughter's experience than in the music.

After, when they walk from the warmth of the concert hall into the cool night, Chloe shivers.

"Here, take my sweater," my mom says quickly.

"No, thanks," Chloe says, spinning in a pirouette, her dress flaring and her face lifted to the starlit sky, taunting the heavens as the cold prickles her skin. *You tried. You failed. I'm still here.*

Beside the parking structure is a small fountain.

"Penny, please?" Chloe says in a fake English accent, her hands held out like a beggar's.

My mom freezes. Like applesauce and fruit rolls, tossing begged-for pennies into every fountain was my thing, a Finn-ism.

Chloe pretends not to notice my mom's hesitation. Her hands remain cupped in front of her.

Give her a penny, I scream. I'm sick of every memory of me being discarded, avoided, or embalmed in a shrine. I want my mom to smile when asked for a penny and to laugh when she walks through the meat section of the grocery store, remembering the time we baked a ham together with the clear plastic wrapping still on, how we basted it for two hours before noticing it looked strange. I want my dad to smile when he eats chicken wings and watches an Angels game. I want Mo to never pass a dandelion without blowing off the fluff and then running through it to catch the seeds in her hair.

Being dead sucks, but watching them destroy the life I had is worse.

Remember me, I scream. *Celebrate me. Do not box me up and throw me away. Stop avoiding every memory of who I was. I lived, and I do not want to only be recognized for my premature death. That was only the end. Before that was sixteen years of life—good, bad, funny, fun. Finn.*

Numbly my mom reaches into her purse and retrieves not one but two pennies, one for each of them. The coins are held to their lips as they make their wishes (another Finn-ism), and then they toss them into the water.

Way to go, Chloe.

71

My dad is drunk.

It's near midnight, and he's been up since dawn, but my dad rarely sleeps. Despite exhaustion, he lies awake, ignores the pain, and tortures himself with that night, flinching as the accident reverberates in his brain. His arms pull the wheel left to hit the buck instead of avoiding it, his fists clenched so tight his nails draw blood in his palms.

Tonight he drowns the memory with whiskey. He sits on my grandfather's king-size bed, a bottle of Jack Daniel's in his hand, his eyes hooded and his mouth suspended half-open.

Vance sleeps on the couch in the living room, completely done in from five days of searching for my brother. Each day he rappels his skinny butt down the mountain and, using only a compass, a map, and the knowledge my dad has given him, trudges through the woods for hours.

I'm very proud of him and have become his silent cheerleader, coaching from the sidelines and watching out for him, whispering encouragement and applauding his courage as he looks behind every tree and rock in search of my brother.

He's not going to find him. Every inch he canvasses has been canvassed before. Burns was thorough in his search. For a week after the search was called off, he still sent his team to scour the area until it was obvious Oz wasn't going to be found. Wherever my brother's body is, it's long gone from where it was, carried off by animals or the elements or both. The rest of him, who he was, is no longer part of this world. I know it with the same certainty as I know someday I will no longer be here as well. There's impermanence to this state, disquiet that cannot last.

Each afternoon, Vance retraces his steps and climbs back up the cliff to my dad, pride radiating as he tells him how it went. It's hard to believe it's been less than a week since Vance was a puddle of pill-popping self-pity huddled on his bed. His body has regained its strength, his skin glows, and he no longer trembles from withdrawal. Except for his ears, fingers, and hair, he almost looks like he used to.

My dad doesn't even look close to what he used to. He's given up on shaving and looks like a woolly mountain man. His dark rust beard is peppered with gray and grows all the way up his cheeks and down his neck. His once-thick muscles have turned soft, and he's lost at least thirty pounds. But mostly it is his face that's changed—the set of his features and jaw—a transformation on the inside that radiates outward.

Before the accident, my dad was one of those men who are hardy and infinitely capable, the guy people looked to when they needed a tire changed or a couch hauled up a flight of stairs or a car lifted off a toddler. It wasn't so much his size as his confidence: a sureness in his handsome, blunt face that screamed of competence. He no longer looks like that, the vitality he had suddenly missing, as though the muscles in his cheeks have atrophied or gravity has gotten stronger, and looking at him this way makes me horribly sad.

I watch as he takes another swig from the bottle, then mumbles something incoherent.

The way I view alcohol is that it makes you more of whatever you already are. Happy drunks are happy people made happier; nasty drunks, the opposite. My dad is a sad drunk, a grief-stricken, woeful wretch, his eyes glassy and his jaw locked tight as he holds back the tears that threaten to tumble out.

He reaches for the phone, and his fingers struggle with the keys, but finally he manages to dial our number.

My mom and Chloe are at the concert. On the third ring, Mo, who is kitten sitting, picks up. "Miller residence," she says.

Without a word, my dad hangs up, then balls the sheets in his hands and buries his face in the fabric to muffle his cries.

More of what you are, that's what alcohol does. And for someone with a guilty conscience, it transforms you into your worst nightmare: everything you regret and everything you hate about yourself exaggerated, until you want to claw out of your skin or disappear permanently into oblivion.

72

Mo's knuckles are white on the steering wheel as she creeps up the winding road toward Big Bear. She's had her license three months but has never driven farther than two towns away. It's a gray day, the sky threatening rain but holding its load. It's been almost two months since the accident, and the ski season is nearly over. Only a smattering of snow remains along the roads, along with the manmade swaths of white that wind down the mountains, delineating the few ski runs still open.

The temperature gauge on her BMW steadily declines as she rises, dropping from sixty-four at the base to fifty-two when she finally pulls into the sheriff's station just before noon.

"Maureen, it's nice to meet you," Burns says.

The captain looks good. Without thick layers of clothing and worry, he's more youthful than the last time I saw him.

"I'm sorry I didn't stop in to say hello when you were in the hospital," he says.

"I wouldn't have wanted you to. I'm glad all your efforts went into looking for Oz."

"Wish we would have found him. Bothers me that he's still out there. Though I understand Jack Miller and Vance have taken over the search."

Mo's eyes widen in surprise. Chloe told Mo that my dad went to the cabin to recuperate and to get away from my mom. Everyone assumes he went alone. Now Mo knows Vance is with him, a strange duo. And they're looking for Oz, even stranger. The question is what she will do with the information. In true Mo style, her face reveals nothing.

"So I understand you have some questions about that day," Burns says.

"Just about some of the pieces that are missing."

"Can I ask why?"

Mo hesitates, still unsure herself. "History is getting blurred," she says finally. "All of us that were there that day remember it slightly different—not just from different perspectives but with different facts—and I want to get it straight. I'm not sure why, but it's important to me."

"Makes it easier to understand," Burns says, matter of fact. "Helps me when I write a case report for the same reason. Takes the emotion out of it and boils it down to what it really is: usually rotten luck, coincidence, bad decisions, and sometimes lousy people."

Mo nods, relief on her face that he gets it.

"As far as people remembering it different," Burns goes on, "everyone deals with traumatic events in their own way, and sometimes it's not really lying when they tell it different than it was so much as remembering in a way that allows them to live with it a little easier."

"I get that," Mo says. "I do. And I think that's exactly what's going on. But I can't do that. I remember it exactly how it happened, all of it, and I can't just pretend it away or disown the parts I don't like."

"So are you trying to get it straight just for yourself?"

"What do you mean?"

"Or do you want to understand it so the others have to own up to it?"

Mo thinks for a minute before answering, "I don't know. I think it's just for me." She frowns. "Though it does bother me that the people who seem to be distorting things the most also seem to be the ones suffering the least."

"That does seem to be the unfortunate truth," Burns says.

"So I guess that's part of it," Mo goes on, "not so much to make them own up to it as for me to know I have it—a record of what happened so, when I hear the lies, it won't bother me as much." There's determination in her words, a vow to the ghost of her dream that she's going to write it, all of it, and in doing so, somehow it will set her free.

"Then I'll tell you what I can," Burns says.

From a file cabinet beside his desk he pulls out a file more than an inch thick, and he goes through it page by page, covering everything from the first 911 call made by my mom all the way through to the call from the Forest Service that permanently suspended the search for Oz's body five days later.

"Can we go back to before the press conference at the hospital?" Mo says when he finishes. "Tell me again what Bob said about Oz leaving?"

It's the smallest flinch, a twitch of Burns's right cheek muscle, but Mo sees it as well, a tiny tell that Burns also knows this portion of the story doesn't quite add up.

Very deliberately, his words chosen carefully, he recites with exceptional recall what Bob told him. "He said Oz was upset because he was worried about the dog not having enough water, and when it was Karen's turn to take a drink, he hit her and took the water from her to give to the dog." He pauses and, when Mo says nothing, continues, "That's when Bob asked Oz if he wanted to go outside, hoping to calm him down. When they got there, Oz said he needed to find his mom and took off. Bob said this all happened while he was still on top of the camper. He explained that he stayed on top because Oz was upset, and he was worried he might be dangerous. Sound right to you?"

Mo shakes her head. "The first part is kind of right. Oz wanted me to give Bingo water before I gave it to Karen, and then he kind of shoved her with his arm when he took it from her, but he wasn't out of control, and after he got what he wanted, he was fine. I actually thought Bob was being clever when he took Oz outside, that he was distracting him so we could each have some water before they came back. Also, not to be mean, but Oz didn't exactly love his mom all that much, and Oz really loved me, and he really, really loved his dad, so there's no way he would have just left us and took off to look for his mom."

"And did Bob stay on top of the camper like he said?"

"No, that part I'm sure of. Oz helped him back up. I heard Bob ask him for a lift. Also Bob left out the part about trading Oz for his gloves. If Oz was upset and just took off, Bob wouldn't have gotten the gloves."

"He took Oz's gloves?"

"He traded for them. When Bob came back into the camper, he had Oz's gloves. I couldn't figure out how he got them, but the other day, Natalie told me her dad traded Oz two packages of crackers for them."

Burns visibly flinches, and with his reaction, Mo's composure comes undone. Her chin drops to her chest as her head shakes back and forth and tears leak from her eyes. "It's so awful. Oz didn't know what he was doing. I should have gone out with him, or I should have gone and looked for him when he didn't come back with Bob. I knew something was wrong. As soon as I saw the gloves, I knew."

She uses the back of her hand to wipe her nose, and Burns hands her a tissue, then slides the box toward her. "Maureen, listen to me," he says, his voice low as a growl. "First, this is not your fault. If you had gone after Oz, there's a good chance we wouldn't be sitting here having this conversation. Look at me."

She lifts her face and blinks at him through her tears.

"None of this is your fault." His voice rumbles. "Now, I need you to tell me the whole story—every detail from the moment Mrs. Miller left to when you were rescued. Then I need you to tell me the exact conversation you had with Natalie."

"I wrote it down," Mo says, and she pulls a notebook from her shoulder bag and hands it to him.

Mo stares at her hands as Burns scans the pages. Several times she shudders, though the office is warm, a chill running through her as the story replays in her mind as Burns reads it.

Burns's jaw twitches as he reads, his brow seamed over his eyes in a deep V. When he is done, he leans back in his chair, and his fingers form a steeple beneath his nose.

"Maureen," he says, "do you know what negligent homicide is?"

Mo swallows, the words self-explanatory.

"There's a fine line between an accidental death and a death caused by negligence. Do you think Bob purposely encouraged Oz to look for his mom?"

The pause lasts at least five seconds.

"I don't know," she says finally. "I have my suspicions, especially because of the gloves, but the truth is I don't know."

Burns returns Mo's notebook and pulls the case file in front of him. "Was Natalie wearing the gloves when you were rescued?"

"I think so. Karen wore them for a little, but Natalie had them most of the time."

"What color were they?"

"Purple, bright purple," Mo says. "Oz's favorite color."

Burns rifles through the folder until he finds what he is looking for. He pulls out a newspaper article. "Bingo," he says, handing the printout to Mo. The headline reads, **Five Rescued from Crash after Night in the Snow**. The photo below it shows Uncle Bob hobbling from a Forest Service helicopter with his arms slung over two rescue workers. Walking behind him is Natalie. She is almost out of view but visible enough to see a bright-purple glove sticking out from the sleeve of her long down coat.

"Maureen, this is important. Do you think Oz was dangerous?"

Again, Mo takes her time, constructing her answer carefully. "No, but I think Bob and Karen might have thought so. Oz just wanted to make sure Bingo had enough water. He felt responsible for the dog. Everything would have been fine if they had just let me melt enough water for Bingo and then for the rest of us."

"Tell me the order of who you gave the water to."

"Mr. Miller, Oz, Natalie, Karen, but Oz took it—"

"Karen was after Natalie?"

"Yeah, except Oz took it from her."

"But you weren't next, after Natalie?" I feel Burns's anger ignite over this seemingly tiny detail, any doubt he had before about pursuing Bob incinerated.

"Is it important that I wasn't next?" Mo asks.

"It shows a pattern of negligence, a disregard for your welfare."

It shows more than that, but Burns is being polite. Inside he broils, and I know from his expression that he does in fact have a daughter, and at this moment, he is thinking of her.

Mo has begun crying again. I'm not certain if it's the recall of that awful moment or the realization that Bob, a man she's known most of her life, was so cruel.

"It's all so awful," she says through her tears. "I know what Bob did was terrible, but he wouldn't have done any of it except for the situation we were in."

As I watch her cry, I wonder about this, about whether our humanity is determined more by circumstance than conscience, and if any of us if backed into a corner can change. I saw it that day, none of them turning out to be the people they believed themselves to be.

It's different for everyone—some, like my mom and Mo, have more moral fortitude than others—but perhaps in all of us there is a base instinct for self-preservation, a feral nature, that when tested makes us capable of things we never believed ourselves capable of. Not even necessarily selfish. Bob didn't take the gloves for himself. He gave them to Natalie. It was Karen who was terrified of Oz, and Bob sent him away to protect her.

So does that justify what Bob did or merely explain it? Bob didn't set out that day to kill Oz or to neglect Mo. He set out to enjoy a weekend ski trip with his family and friends, and yet, because of him, Oz is dead.

Desperate people do things they wouldn't normally do. Prior to the accident, if you asked Bob or Karen or Vance if they were good people, without hesitation, all three would have said yes, and everyone who knew them would have agreed. All evidence pointed to that conclusion. When they heard a story of cowardice or cruelty, they would have shaken their heads and tsked and thought, *Never, not me,* unaware that at any given moment, all of us are capable of doing what we least expect, them included. It is easy to sit in judgment after the fact. What those who judge don't realize is that, odds are, if they were put in the same situation as Bob or Karen or Vance, that condescending righteousness would freeze its ass off before the sun set.

Oz didn't come back into the camper. Mo didn't go after him. Is this possibly the same? Choosing her own survival instead of risking death to save him?

I don't blame Mo for what she did. I was there, and she was amazing, as brave as any sixteen-year-old girl could be in that situation. But if she is not to blame for her weakness, then is Bob to blame for his? Is my mom to blame for opening her hand when she held Kyle's life in her grip? Vance left the love of his life to freeze to death alone. Karen only looked after Natalie. Natalie did nothing. Bob took Oz's gloves and sent him into the cold. Certainly some seem worse than others, but no one is entirely inculpable.

Mo realizes this as well, and this is why she cries. Nothing is as it was. The pretense of valor, her own and others', has been decimated and the ugly truth of human nature revealed.

"Oz is dead. Bob took his gloves," Burns says, clarifying with stern certainty exactly where the line exists, and specifically who crossed it.

And I lurch back to remembering how unfairly it all turned out. My mom and dad hobble forward, pieces and parts of their lives beyond their dead children permanently gone. Chloe and Vance barely survived, both their lives derailed. Karen lives in a state of manic denial. Natalie lives in a glass house of lies teetering on the edge of a cliff.

Only Bob is unaffected. He sleeps easy, his dreams undisturbed. Each day he goes to his office, jokes with his patients, and flirts with his hygienists. Then he drives his BMW to his home, where his wife dotes on him, the world applauds him as a hero, and my mom is falling in love with him.

He killed my brother.

73

When Mo walks from the sheriff's office to the pizza parlor down the street for lunch, I decide to check on my mom and Chloe.

Chloe isn't home. She's at Aubrey's apartment working on the playlist for the wedding. The concert inspired her, and she is unsuccessfully trying to convince Aubrey how cool it would be to integrate some classical pieces into the mix.

I leave the debate to look in on my mom and groan when I find myself in the backyard looking at her and Bob sitting at the patio table, a bottle of wine and chicken-salad sandwiches between them. The kittens play in the grass, their eyes now open. With their sight, they've gained confidence, and they romp and wrestle and provide endless entertainment.

"They're so frisky," my mom says.

"They're not the only ones," Bob says, rubbing his bare foot against my mom's calf under the table, causing her to giggle and me to cringe.

Thankfully the phone rings, disrupting them. My mom goes inside to answer it, and Bob gets down on the grass to play with the kittens. He taunts Brutus with a long strand of grass, causing the little fur ball to leap and spin and somersault. Finn jumps into the action, tackling Brutus as she swats at the blade. I really like that cat, *Titanic*-size spunk in a dinghy-size package.

Through the glass, I see my mom's shoulders tighten, and I go inside to see what's going on.

She glances over her shoulder at Bob, who is now on all fours growling at Brutus. "That can't be right," she says into the phone. "Mo must be mistaken. He wouldn't have done that."

My mom's laptop is on the counter beside her. She opens it as she continues to listen. "Captain, read me the web address of the article again."

The image appears, the same photo Burns pulled from the file earlier when talking to Mo—Bob, center stage with Natalie behind him. My mom stares, her eyes fixed on the purple spot of Natalie's hand. Her brow pinches, and then the receiver drops from her hand, and she stumbles to lean against the counter.

"Everything okay?" Bob says, appearing behind her, his arms wrapping around her shoulders.

She steps away, breaking his hold. "You took his gloves?" she stammers as she turns to face him, her eyes sliding back to the spot of purple on the screen.

Bob follows her gaze, and the grin drops from his face as his Adam's apple lodges in his throat. "He gave them to me," he says.

Like mercury in a thermometer, color rises in my mom's face. "Go," she says through clenched teeth.

"Ann . . ."

"Now," she growls, her hands balling into fists.

"Ann, he gave them to me. I swear. He said he was going to look for you, and he handed me his gloves. I don't know why he did it, but he did. Then he took off before I could stop him."

He reaches for her, and she stumbles out of his reach.

"Out!" she orders. She knows, just as I know, just as Mo knows, that Oz never gave anything to anyone ever. *Mine* was his favorite word, his temperament and sharing mentality that of a two-year-old.

Bob stands his ground, his eyes skittering side to side as he searches for a plausible explanation.

I see my mom reach for the bottle of wine on the counter, her hand wrapping around the heavy glass.

"Ann . . . ," he starts.

As if her name is a trigger, the bottle rises and swings down, and Bob stumbles back as his arm lifts to defend himself. The glass shatters against his forearm, red wine exploding everywhere. She raises the bloody weapon again, and Bob spins and flees.

Before the door closes, my mom has slumped to the ground, her body convulsing with sobs as she realizes what she has done.

74

Tentatively, Mo drives through the gusting gray weather. The temperature now hovers at forty-eight, and the storm clouds have closed ranks to darken the early afternoon to an eerie dusk. The wind slaps the car with irregular bursts and slams, causing Mo's shoulders to hitch up around her ears and her speed to slow to a crawl, and by the time she pulls into the parking lot of Snow Summit Ski Resort, she's a wreck. She puts the car in park and rests her head against her hands on the steering wheel.

Her boots are Sorel hiking boots designed to withstand the cold of Mount Everest, and her jacket is a North Face parka guaranteed to insulate against temperatures as low as twenty below. Before she steps from the car, she pulls on ear warmers, a hat, and Gore-Tex gloves. In her trunk are granola bars, a case of water, and a massive first aid kit.

The lady at the lift-ticket window directs her to chairlift three.

Kyle sees her before she sees him, as if her presence has triggered an alarm in his brain and has caused him to look up and scan around to find her. His head tilts with surprise, and a smile fills his face. He taps the shoulder of the other lift operator and says something that causes the girl to look at Mo; she nods and gives Kyle an encouraging shove in Mo's direction.

He hurries past the snowboarders and skiers waiting in the lift line to get to Mo, who is cautiously trudging up the snowy slope.

"Hi," he says brightly.

Zap, like static electricity: Mo lifts her face, and their eyes meet, causing a shock, a jolt that hurts, then tingles, then makes you want to rub your feet on the carpet so you can feel it again.

"Wow," he says. "It's you."

And I witness something I've never witnessed before—Mo flustered and shy. "Hi," she manages.

He takes her by the elbow. "Come on. Let's go inside where it's warm."

If he looked closer, he would see Mo is sweating, beads of dew on her temples and her cheeks flushed with heat. She is seriously over-dressed for the spring weather, but Kyle doesn't see that. Like déjà vu, his brain is unable to leap forward from the last time he saw her, and his heart races with leftover concern.

Once they are inside the lodge, he relaxes. "Can I get you a hot chocolate?"

Good move, Kyle. Mo loves chocolate.

She nods, and he practically runs to the counter.

I forgot how good looking he is. He pulls off his hat, revealing mussed honeycomb hair to his ears that is lighter than I remember. His eyes seem lighter as well, sage with sparks of bronze.

Mo takes a seat near the window, her gaze fixed on the snow outside.

"What are you doing here?" Kyle says as he slides into the seat across from her and sets the hot chocolate in front of her. I notice and Mo notices that he didn't get a hot chocolate for himself, and my guess is his budget only allows for one hot chocolate a day.

Mo explains her mission.

"Oh," he says, his mouth puckering slightly around the word.

"Are you okay with talking about it?" she asks.

Kyle is silent a moment, his eyes on the table between them. "I don't know. I haven't really talked about it to anyone."

"Not even your girlfriend?"

"We broke up a few days after the whole thing."

"What about your family?"

He shrugs. "I didn't want to worry them. It was that guy Bob who gave the interview, and I don't think he knew my name, so the news never mentioned me. I don't think, other than the rescuers, anyone even knew I was involved."

Mo's eyes grow wide. "So no one who knows you knows what happened?"

Kyle gives a thin smile. "Probably better that way."

Mo thinks about this, and I watch as her expression changes from shock to agreement. "I think you might be right. It's kind of awful, people knowing." She takes a sip of her hot chocolate. "I mean, everyone's real nice and concerned, but they don't really get it."

"Yeah, well," Kyle says, "it's kind of hard to describe."

Mo nods and wraps her hands around her cup as she watches the steam rising from it. "It's like, people, they think it was this great big adventure, and it's like they're all excited to hear about it." She shudders.

"Too many action movies," Kyle says. "Nothing too great or exciting about kids dying or people losing fingers and toes."

The color drains from Mo's face.

"Sorry," Kyle says quickly. "I'm so sorry."

"No," Mo says. "It's okay. It's why I came here. I want to hear it, all of it." Her eyes are moist and her skin white as the snow outside.

"Are you sure?" Kyle asks, concern lining his face.

She nods and lifts her face so her eyes are fully on his. "I need to know I'm not crazy," she says, and my heart breaks a little as I realize how much she has been struggling, all of this too much and with no one to talk to about it.

"You're not," Kyle says, clearly distressed and out of his depth, unfamiliar with having a beautiful girl ask him to recount the most awful thing in the world, especially knowing it will undoubtedly upset her, which is the last thing in the world he wants to do.

"So I need to know what happened," she says, "all of it." Her nose pinches, and she closes her eyes. With a deep breath, she opens them, settles her gaze on his, and says, "Then I need you to tell me it won't happen again."

Kyle reaches over the table and wraps his hands over hers and then, with a deep breath of his own, begins, "My car broke down as I was driving from my apartment to my job . . ."

It takes him nearly an hour to tell the story. His hands hold hers the entire time, and Mo listens with her eyes fixed on the table between them. At several points she shivers, and at others, tears leak from her eyes. Each time, Kyle stops, and I watch as his nose opens and closes with his rapid breaths, his desperation to soothe her and somehow make this easier pulsing off him.

Minutes pass as she works her way through it, and then bravely she nods for him to go on.

The only lie he tells is an omission. He leaves out the part about him slipping over the ledge and my mom letting go. I watch his expression as he does it: the smallest wince at the memory before he moves past it.

"And then I was taken to the emergency room," he says. "And now I'm here with you." She looks up, and he gives a thin, crooked smile. Then his hands slide farther around hers to envelop them completely, and he adds, "And it will never happen again."

"Thank you," she says.

"You're welcome." He releases her hands and leans back.

Mo slumps in her seat, exhausted. "How did you know which way to walk?" she says.

"Mrs. Miller," he says. "She was amazing. I still don't know how she did it, but somehow she knew which way we needed to go. When I think back on it, I wonder how we did it, made it out of there. I mean, we had no food, no water, and it was freezing. We had no idea if we were going the right way, and we kept hitting dead ends. I remember thinking it was impossible, but then I'd look back at Mrs. Miller, and I'd think if she could keep going, so could I. And . . ." He stops, leans back, shakes his head, and smiles.

"And what?"

He huff laughs through his nose. "And I just kept thinking about you and those ridiculous boots you were wearing."

"My boots?"

He smiles a wide, toothless grin. "Yep. Like you were off to a concert or something, with that shiny leather and the heels."

Mo blushes. "I'll have you know those were Prada boots."

"Yeah, well, anyways, that's what I kept thinking about. How ridiculous they were, and how cold your feet must have been, and so I knew I couldn't stop, that no matter what, I had to keep going."

My whole nonbody lights up, Fourth of July fireworks going off everywhere. Mo feels it as well. What girl wouldn't? The guy hiked through a blizzard to save her, propelled by his concern for her freezing feet in her ridiculous boots.

Mo lifts one of her Sorels. "Better?"

"Much. Very sexy."

Mo throws her napkin at him, and he bats it away with a sweet laugh that is very becoming. Everything he does now is very becoming. He could blow his nose, and I would think it was sexy.

"So now that you've gotten what you came for," Kyle says, "are you done with me?"

"I would be," Mo says, "except you're lying."

Kyle squints and tilts his head.

"What happened that you're not telling me?"

"I told you everything," Kyle says, squirming with a conscience that doesn't allow him to lie often or easily, making me like him even more.

"You told me *almost* everything," Mo corrects. "Something happened that Mrs. Miller is having a tough time with."

"She lost two of her kids."

"That's not it. Something happened that has nothing to do with Finn or Oz. I thanked her for what she did, and she freaked out. I thought she was going to slap me. And you're a terrible liar. So what happened?"

"It was nothing," Kyle says.

"Not to her."

"I'm telling you, it was no big deal."

She frowns at him, and he runs his hand through his hair, leans forward, leans back, then sets his mouth in a firm line. "It was nothing," he repeats, then adds, "some things . . . they're not . . . it's not worth talking about. We all did what we had to that day," and the harshness of his words destroys her. Her head shakes, and her chin drops to her chest as fresh tears fall from her eyes.

"I'm sorry," he says, his voice pitching high with instant regret. "I didn't mean to upset you."

"It's not you," she manages. "It's all of it. I hate it. I hate what that day did to us. And I thought I could do this"—her eyes slide to the snow through the window—"but being here and remembering . . ."

Kyle reaches over and takes her hands again. Then he brings them to his lips and blows warm breath on her fingertips.

She lifts her teary face to his. "Are you going to do that every time I remember?"

"Every time," he answers.

"You don't even know me," Mo says. But even she knows the words are wrong. More was revealed in that single tragic night than most people reveal in a lifetime.

75

My mom runs until she cannot catch a breath, then stumbles to a stop and bends over, gasping for air. It's late afternoon, and she is alone. Beyond the golf course, homes sparkle with life: families with husbands and wives and children, doing all the wonderful things that families with husbands and wives and children do.

The tremor begins as a small hiccup that causes her shoulders to jerk. Then, like a ripple, the spasm grows, turning my mom's body liquid, the bones melting as she sinks to the cold, hard sidewalk.

A man with a dog, midfifties and fit like a marathoner, jogs over the rise, sees my mom, and quickens his pace. "You okay?" he asks when he reaches her.

"How do I get past it?" she mumbles, not necessarily to him. Hate. Hurt. Guilt. And grief. So much of it that I feel its thickness and its weight, like she is drowning and can't breathe.

"A single step at a time," the man says, speaking from some profound experience of his own and with deep understanding, making me wonder if all pain might be the same regardless of its origin. "You're still here," he goes on. "So there's not really a choice. An inch, a foot, not necessarily in the right direction, but onward nonetheless."

My mom shudders a deep breath, looks up at him.

"Until eventually," he says, "the present becomes the past, and you are somewhere else altogether, hopefully in a better place than you are today."

My mom bends her head again and nods, and the man straightens and continues on. And I am so grateful I send a prayer to God to witness this man's kindness and to grace him in some way. And as I watch him jog away, I think that in some ways this perspective is not so bad and that, sometimes, humans surprise you.

76

Kyle walks Mo to her car in the parking lot. A single fat drop of rain hits her cheek, and she looks up at the dark sky. Another hits her forehead, then another, and Kyle grabs her by the elbow and guides her quickly to her BMW. He takes the keys from her fumbling hands, clicks open the locks, and nearly pushes her into the passenger seat before hustling around to the driver's side to climb in beside her.

Her whole body shakes, and he wraps her in his arms. "Shhh," he soothes, "it's just rain." Still holding her with his right arm, he turns on the ignition and the heat with his left, then rewraps her in a full embrace until her shivering stops.

With a deep breath to suck in her emotions, she pushes away. "I'm pathetic," she says.

"You're amazing," he answers, his face reverent as he brushes a wet tendril from her face and tucks it behind her ear. "I can't believe you came here. It was incredibly brave."

"Or stupid," she says. "I should have known I'd be a mess."

And then it happens . . . like it couldn't not happen . . . like what she said was something else entirely, something seductive or romantic. Kyle leans in and kisses her, not smooshing, lip-smashing kind of kissing, but soft and gentle, his lips barely grazing hers as her eyes close and his mouth molds to hers. Then his arms are around her, and they are melting against each other.

The rain patters on the roof, but Mo pays it no mind, her body warm and protected and oblivious to everything except for Kyle kissing her. It's amazing and grand and beautiful, and I cheer and cheer and cheer, every bit of me happy and jealous as I watch and pretend I am her, all our girlhood dreams realized in the front seat of her car in the rain at the base of a snow-covered mountain.

Her right hand slides from his neck to the zipper of his coat, and he puts his hand on hers to stop her. "Not here," he whispers, and with the confidence of a white knight, he straightens in his seat, fastens his seat belt, glances over to make sure she has fastened hers, and pulls from the parking lot and onto the road.

He drives to the Timberline Inn, and I watch, stunned, as Mo says nothing to protest the incredible boldness of it all. He parks in front of the lobby and hurries around to open the door.

My nerves are jumping. This is crazy. Mo's not *that* kind of girl. She won't even kiss a boy unless he's taken her on at least three dates. Or, I should say, Mo didn't *used to be* that kind of girl.

Really, Mo? You hardly know this guy. But another part of me is still cheering. Because I get it. You only live once, and no one has any idea how long that once is going to be, so grab on tight and hold on for the ride and don't worry about it and don't look back.

Go, Mo, go! Live it, love it, do it. Do it!

77

"I told you, I was carrying my glass of wine from the bar toward a table where one of my patients was having dinner, and I slipped," Bob says. "The glass broke, and I cut myself. It's no big deal."

Karen looks unconvinced, but she knows the lie is probably better than the truth, so she lets it go.

They are in the emergency room, waiting for the nurse to return with instructions and supplies for keeping the twelve stitches in Bob's forearm clean.

Karen looks awful. She's never been a great beauty, but pristine grooming and diligent upkeep have always kept her attractive. Since the accident, though, her attentiveness has slackened, and tonight she looks downright disheveled. Her hair is unkempt, and streaks of gray show at the roots. Her face is makeup-less, and her eyes are bruised. Her body has gone soft, and so has her posture, as though distress has devoured her muscles.

Karen's phone rings. She pulls it from her purse and looks at the caller ID, and despite the sign posted on the wall that prohibits cell phone use, she answers it. "Hi, baby, everything okay? . . . Captain Burns? From Big Bear? . . . He was at the house? . . . Baby, calm down."

I move to where Natalie is to see her huddled in her bedroom closet with her phone, the clippings she collected from the accident spread out in front of her, the picture of her with the gloves front and center. She is crying and rocking back and forth on her heels.

"Mom, what if he was here to arrest Dad?"

"Arrest Dad? For what?" Karen says, clearly mystified as to what Natalie is talking about.

Natalie says nothing as her rocking intensifies.

"Honey, don't worry about it," Karen says. "I'm sure it's nothing. He probably just has some follow-up questions. I made a pan of lasagna. It's in the fridge. Heat it for two minutes in the microwave, and make sure you cover it with a paper towel."

Natalie hangs up and, for a long minute, stares at the clippings, her eyes frozen on an article from a local paper that shows a headshot of Mo, and I know she is wondering if Mo betrayed her. She presses the heels of her palms to her eyes as if trying to blot it away, to erase what she did, but I think even Natalie knows some things cannot be undone.

I return to the hospital as Karen says to Bob, "Babe, are you sure you're okay? You don't look so good."

She's right. Bob's skin is ashen, and he looks like he might be sick. "I'm fine. What the hell is taking the nurse so long?"

"Natalie says Captain Burns came to the house and that he wants to talk to us. What do you think that could be about? Do you think maybe he's going to reopen the search for Oz and he thinks maybe we can help? I'd like to help. We could organize another press conference. What do you think about that? Maybe even get a caravan together, call our friends and neighbors, go up and help look for him. I could organize it, set up a Facebook page, call the local papers to run an article about it. It's awful that they never found him. What do you think?"

"I think Oz is dead is what I think," Bob hisses. "He's dead. Gone. What happened, happened, and it's over. And no, I don't think you should organize another one of your fucking crusades to try and find him. Where the fuck is the nurse?"

Karen falls away from him, then stumbles through the curtain to find the nurse. She nearly crashes into Captain Burns, who is walking toward their room.

"Mrs. Gold," Burns says, "just the person I was coming to see."

78

My mom throws back the covers and paces through the house. Ten minutes later, she is in the kitchen, a cup of coffee and her laptop in front of her. She finds the news stream from the press conference at the hospital and watches Bob's performance—his lies, then his genuine plea for help.

She perches on the edge of her stool, her attention rapt on Bob, then narrowed beyond him to Natalie in the background. She does not cry or rage. Expressionless, she watches as the hand not holding her coffee absently opens and closes, and I realize she is wondering the same thing I wondered about earlier. How much is Bob to blame for his weakness and his betrayal, and is what he did any less forgivable than what she did?

It's strange how I know these are her thoughts. I do not read minds or have psychic powers, but this perspective does give me heightened awareness that allows me to see things I never saw when I was alive. When I was alive, I never really looked at my family. We existed around each other in our own worlds, like those screen saver balls that intermittently touch before ricocheting and bouncing off each other, affecting each other's momentum but never really paying attention to one another. Now, if I look hard enough and long enough, I see it all. The cast of my mom's eyes, the curve of her shoulders, the intensity with which she watches Bob on the screen, the softening when she looks at

Natalie. Manifested in small, almost imperceptible details is everything she does not say: her hurt and disappointment, her guilt and regret. When she looks at Bob, she does not hate him, but I feel the hate she feels for herself for thinking she loved him and the immense burden she bears because of his betrayal.

I realize now that my mom has an astounding talent for concealing her thoughts and disclosing nothing with either her expression or her words. It makes her a fantastic lawyer, but it is also what makes her seem like a bitch. Only now, when I really see her, do I realize how mistaken that perception is.

A soft knock on the patio door startles her. It's three in the morning. She looks through the glass to see Bob. He wears jeans and an old USC sweatshirt that is too tight around the middle, from twenty years of either his belly growing or the sweatshirt shrinking or both. His face is flush from alcohol, and his hair is wild and sticking out in all directions, his forearm wrapped in gauze.

It doesn't surprise me that he is awake. Like my dad, he rarely sleeps, and after what happened today, I doubt he will sleep for days. Karen spilled her guts to Burns before Bob walked from the room and saw them. Burns stood before Bob reached them, tipped an imaginary hat, pivoted, and walked away, leaving Bob staring after him and wondering what Karen had said and what was to come.

With a deep sigh, my mom opens the door.

"Ann—" he starts, but she cuts him off.

"Sit," she says. "I'll get you some coffee."

He slumps on a stool, and she takes her time getting a mug from the cabinet, filling it with coffee, and adding cream the way he likes it. It's quiet. Night noises come through the window—crickets, the tide, wind chimes from the house next door.

My mom places the mug in front of him, then takes the stool beside him and curls her feet beneath her. Her toenails are a freshly pedicured pale shade of pink, and I watch him notice them and then look away.

Her right hand rests on the counter beside her own steaming mug, and as she looks at the steam rising from it, I know she is thinking of Oz and gloves and fingers and warmth.

Bob lifts his eyes to look at her. "What Burns is saying isn't right," he says, his head shaking with either denial or disbelief.

"What part does he have wrong?" she says, her tone cool and law-yerly, and I try to decipher it. There's no anger, but is it possible there is ulterior motive? Does she want Bob to confess so she can then use it against him, or does she honestly want to hear his side?

"I didn't . . . I wouldn't . . . the only reason it happened was the accident."

"You took his gloves," she says flatly.

"He gave them to me. You know me, Ann."

"Do I?"

He startles. "Of course you do. You know me better than anyone."

But my mom knows now, as I know now, that none of us really know each other. We don't even really know ourselves. She looks at him for a long minute, her face revealing nothing, and finally she says, "Bob, you should go. Go home to Karen and Natalie."

"But . . . ," he stammers, his bloodshot eyes looking up at her. "But what about us?"

She stands and steps close to him, her hips brushing his knees. Then she takes his hand and twines his fingers through hers, and I watch as relief floods his face. "There is no us," she says plainly. "There's you. There's me. There's Karen, Natalie, Chloe. But if nothing else was proved that day, it's that there is no us."

Bob's head bobs between his shoulders. "Ann, please, I can't lose you. He gave them to me, I swear."

She offers a kind, sympathetic smile, gives his hand an encourag-ing squeeze. "We both know the truth," she says. Then she pulls her hand from his, closes the screen of her laptop, pivots, and walks away, leaving him alone.

I watch as he stumbles to his feet, out the door, and back to his miserable life. *He deserves this,* I remind myself. But somehow I can't entirely convince myself, my love for Oz not equaling my hate for Bob. Because in the end, nothing is absolute. Bob is not all bad, and when he was with my mom, he was mostly good. He loves her and is a better person when he is with her, and had she been there, he wouldn't have done what he did.

My mom only knew the better Bob, the one who stood beside her in the blizzard and used his bare hands to pack the windshield with snow, who helped pull people from the camper, and who tended to Chloe and Jack. The Bob who stayed at her side during the rescue mission and who championed the search for Oz. Until this afternoon, when she received the call from Burns, Bob had been a good man, not pretending, but actually good because she made him that way.

I watch him staggering down the street and tell myself again that he deserves this, but instead, I find myself hoping Karen is waiting for him, that he will manage to get some sleep, and that in the morning he'll figure out a way to get his life back.

79

It's daybreak. Through the window, the granite peaks of the mountain lighten to pale gold as Mo and Kyle sleep curled together. Mo yawns awake and rolls to face him, a naughty, knowing smile on her face.

His eyes flutter open, then startle with pleasant surprise when he sees her. He pecks her on her nose. "Good morning."

"Morning," she says, then purrs and wriggles closer as if it is the most natural thing in the world and as if they've been together forever. He wraps his arms around her and brushes a kiss across her hair, inhaling through his nose as he does, and I pretend to inhale with him. Mo always smells like expensive shampoo, and her breath is high pitched and sweet, even when she hasn't brushed.

I miss being able to smell. It's like a dimension is missing, as if I am viewing the world in black and white rather than color. I don't know what Kyle smells like. I try to imagine it and decide he is odorless, and I'm impressed. It's very difficult for a man to not smell.

This is the new game I play, remembering or making up smell. It almost works. I can look at the ocean and remember the salt and the taste of brine or see a toddler and think of the baby smell that only exists on the very young. I hope wherever I'm going there is taste and smell.

"It's strange," Mo says.

"Hmm?" he says, breathing her in again.

"This feels so right, like I've known you forever. But I actually know nothing about you, and you know nothing about me."

His fingers caress her back. "Yeah, I thought about that a lot after the accident. How strange it was to have shared such an intense experience with people I didn't know and who I never saw again. I thought about you all a lot—mostly you, but also Oz's mom and dad. Is his dad okay? I didn't think he was going to make it."

"He did, barely. He wouldn't have if we'd had to stay out there another night." She pulls away so she can look at him. "Which reminds me, I never thanked you for what you did. After all, you did save my life."

He gives a toothless smirk, the left side of his mouth higher than the right. "I'd say you thanked me pretty well last night, but if you want to thank me again . . ." His eyebrows arch in invitation.

"Mmm," she says and then, with amazing assertiveness, rolls on top of him so she is straddling his legs. The sheet falls away to pool around her nakedness, and I blush wildly, though Mo seems entirely at ease.

Kyle sits up partway, wraps his hand around the back of Mo's head, and pulls her into a kiss, and zap, like being struck by a bolt of lightning, I am jolted away.

I startle and look around to find myself in my room at home, Chloe on the bed across from me. For a moment I'm confused, until the reason I'm no longer with Mo rises like the sun along with an uneasy feeling in my stomach.

Suddenly I know why I am here. Lingering. Just as suddenly I know now, with certainty, that someday soon I will be gone, the two epiphanies colliding in my brain to make me dizzy. A future beyond this one exists, the revelation almost as startling as my death. The thought of leaving those I will be leaving is still as horrifying as it was the moment my life ended, but its inevitability can no longer be denied. I feel it. The bright light of death, a persistent glow and warmth just out of reach. It has been there since the day I died, but until this moment, I have paid it no mind, distracted by the world from which I came and the people who remain.

I look at Chloe, her earbuds plugged in and her foot tapping to the beat, and then I close my eyes and focus on the distant glow. I feel the gentle tug between the two, between this world and the next. It does not scare me. Quite the opposite. Whether it is heaven or merely peace, I know what waits is better than where I am, and my heart quickens with the thought of it.

I return my thoughts to the present, and my pulse resumes its steady pace. *Chloe, my mom, my dad*—the three precious threads that remain. And I realize this state I am in is not hell or some sort of purgatory. I am not here as punishment for my sins. But rather, I remain to assure peace in my future. My life was violently ripped away and the lives of those I love torn apart. I had no time to prepare or to say goodbye, and I was not ready to leave. *Rest in peace* is not merely an epitaph for a tombstone; it is the best we can hope for in death.

It's not that Mo has left me, but rather, her world has suddenly shifted, moved forward in a new and unexpected way, and while I will always hold a place in her heart, with her newfound feelings for Kyle so large and overwhelming, I no longer occupy space.

It is the same with Charlie, my teammates, and my friends. Like a wave receding, I have dissolved into a memory, exactly as I should be. I can still visit, but unlike before, I am no longer a constant presence in their minds that draws me to them, the volition now entirely my own.

While slightly stunned, I am not sad. There is lightness in my liberation, like a burden lifting. Mo is happy, really happy, and because of that she is no longer consumed with everything that was lost, the future suddenly brighter than the shadow of that awful day.

Closing my eyes, I send a prayer of love and gratitude to the best friend a girl could have. *You are the most remarkable dung beetle in the world,* I say with a smile. The two of us have used the compliment for years, ever since we discovered that the insects are the strongest animals on the planet. *I wish I could be here to see all the things you are going to do.* I stop and think about it, trying to wrangle a vision of what her future might hold, but I cannot see it; too many possibilities exist. So instead I say, *Soar, Mo, reach for the stars or the moon or another universe altogether, and shine so bright you blind everyone around you, and though I am gone, carry me with you, but only as lightness and never as weight . . .*

I stop, feeling Chloe looking my way, my pulse suspended as I watch her tilt her head, the thinnest smile on her lips. She looks away and returns to scrawling in her notebook.

A day, a month, a year—I cannot know, but when the time comes, I will be ready.

80

Two hours after Bob left, my mom was dressed and on her way to Big Bear.

She lets herself into the cabin, silent as a burglar. "Jack?" she calls.

Vance lurches awake, falls off the couch, stumbles to his feet, grabs a carved deer statue from the table, and raises it over his head to slam it down on the intruder.

My mom flicks on the light, sees Vance charging, and screams.

"Mrs. Miller?" he says, the antlers of the statue stopping an inch from impaling her skull.

My mom screams again. She doesn't recognize him.

My dad charge-hobbles on his crutches from the bedroom. "Ann?"

My mom's eyes dart from Vance to my dad and back again. "Vance?"

"Yeah, it's me," Vance says. I don't blame her for not recognizing him. He's dressed in nothing but boxers, his hair is gold from the sun, and he's not supposed to be here.

My mom's eyes slide to his fingers as he sets down the statue, then take in his damaged ears. When he turns back to her, she pulls him into an embrace that is shocking, her arms wrapping around his waist and her head nestling against his bare chest. Awkwardly he wraps his hands around her.

She pulls away, sniffs back her tears, and brings her hand to his cheek. "I'm so glad you're okay," she says.

Numbly he nods.

"Ann, what are you doing here?" my dad says, his voice going for gruff but laced with excitement. He straightens the glee immediately and says, "You need to leave. I told you I need time to think."

"No," she says, marching forward and planting herself in front of him.

My dad straightens as much as he can on his crutches. He wears dirty sweats and a ratty T-shirt. Laundry is not exactly high on his or Vance's priority list.

My mom's jaw slides forward, her chin twitching with emotion. "No," she says again. "You don't get to kick me to the curb."

"Ann, I need—"

"No. We . . . WE!" she hisses, pointing back and forth between them. "*We* are in this together. I didn't ditch you on that mountain, and you don't get to ditch me now."

"It's not about that."

"It's all about that. That day. That horrible, horrible day. Finn died. Oz died. You were right: I shouldn't have left Oz with Bob."

"Why are you here?" my dad roars, the implication of her words like a cattle prod. "What did that bastard do?"

"He screwed up," my mom says, not intimidated in the least by his bluster. "Just like I screwed up and you screwed up." She thumbs her hand at Vance. "And he screwed up. And Chloe screwed up. We all screwed up, and you don't get to blame me or ditch me because of it."

My dad's eyes narrow. He looks like a rabid grizzly. His hair is long and wild, sticking out in all directions, and his eyes are red and puffy from alcohol and lack of sleep.

My mom is beautiful. The running has toned her muscles to youth, and her hair has grown long and is tied loosely back from her face, showing off her high cheeks and large eyes. She looks like Chloe, and despite my dad's angry squint, his eyes roam over her.

My mom takes a deep breath to rein in her emotions and, in a quaky voice, continues, "We. It's always been we. That's how we managed to make it this far, and you don't get to quit on us now."

"What did he do?" my dad seethes, still stuck on Bob, and I'm thankful Bob is two hundred miles away.

My mom ignores him. "That day, do you know what kept me going?"

My dad's nose flares with his huffs.

"You," my mom says. "You and the stupid fortune cookie philosophy you're always doling out to the girls. *Every journey begins with a single step. Clear your mind of can't. Fear is what stops you; courage is what keeps you going.*"

My dad's eyes slide to the window, his anger blindsided by larger emotion that is difficult to define. Through the glass, the glowing dawn cuts a shimmering crystal ribbon across the patches of icy snow that remain.

"I shouldn't have left Oz," my mom continues. "I know it now." She stops suddenly, and a small gasp escapes as her fingers rise to her lips.

"That's not true," she mumbles more to herself than to my dad—a revelation. "I did know." Her eyes track back and forth. "It's why I didn't say goodbye." She stumbles back a step and catches herself against the couch. "I knew, but I went anyway."

"Ann, what the hell are you talking about?" my dad says, his attention and irritation returning.

My mom lifts her face to look at him. "I chose," she says. "Like giving the boots to Mo instead of Natalie." Her hand opens and closes, and she doesn't say it, but she is thinking of Kyle.

My dad shakes his head in confusion and annoyance.

"I chose," she repeats. "I knew I couldn't take Oz with me, and I knew he wasn't safe if I left, but I left anyway."

And you saved everyone else, I cry, but it is unheard.

My dad closes his eyes, his accusations confirmed, and I watch as the last thread of my parents' marriage ignites. But perhaps silk doesn't burn, because Vance steps in and says, "And you saved everyone else. And Mr. Miller, no offense, but you're off your rocker." He turns to my mom. "He is, you know, off his rocker."

My mom tries for a smile but doesn't quite make it.

"I mean, seriously, dude, do you have any idea how amazing it is what Mrs. Miller did? I'm real sorry about Oz, but you seriously can't blame her for leaving him. It was leave him behind and climb out of there, or everyone was going to die. You, me, Chloe, everyone. Seriously, you need to get over yourself."

My dad glares at him.

Vance ignores it and, instead, steps in front of my mom, eager anxiousness on his face. "How's Chloe?" he says, causing my dad to forget his anger for a second to look worriedly at my mom as well, his concern for the living momentarily overshadowing his regret for the dead.

My mom raises her hand to Vance's cheek, and her eyes well up. She's so incredibly glad to see him alive and in front of her. "Come see for yourselves," she says. "The Sunday after next is Easter. I'm cooking a ham." She looks at my dad. "I'd like you both to be there."

My dad says nothing, but I feel his harrumph.

She frowns at him. "Dinner's at six. Don't be late. And shave your beard. You look like an old goat."

My mom spins away, and Vance walks her to the door. Only I see my dad stroke his bearded neck, a thin smile playing on his face.

"Chloe is okay with me coming?" Vance says, hope making his voice tight.

My mom touches Vance's cheek again. "She'll be as relieved as I am to see how well you're doing."

And I feel it, her words making him believe. His chest fills up, and his shoulders straighten. My breath knots in the back of my throat, and I can't believe how much I'm rooting for him.

As soon as the door closes, my dad says, "We're not going."

Vance spins to face him.

"Oz is still out there, and until we find him, we're not leaving."

81

An hour after my mom leaves, Captain Burns calls my dad. Twenty minutes after that, Burns is on the couch in the cabin explaining his suspicions about Bob.

Vance sits in the rocking chair across from them, listening.

As Burns talks, my dad's forearms tense, the muscles in his shoulders bunch, his expression tightens, and his eyes turn dark. Like a lion, he sits coiled, ready to pounce.

"Jack, let me handle this," Burns says, sensing my dad's desire to storm from the house and back to Laguna Beach to rip Bob apart.

My dad's jaw twitches.

"Think about it," Burns goes on. "If you do something stupid like confront him or, worse, assault him, you hurt our chances for conviction, and you end up in a legal mess of your own."

My dad's face is red, so hot I think it might burst into flames, but he manages a nod. As much as he'd love to tear Bob limb from limb, he knows Burns is right. He also knows a felony conviction for negligent homicide will destroy Bob far worse than a beating ever could.

Burns's interview with Karen at the hospital muddled things more than it clarified them. Like Natalie's, Karen's memory of what happened is spotty and distorted. Concerning Oz, she remembered only that he was there and then he wasn't. Yes, he might have hit her, but she wasn't sure. She remembered being cold and scared. She didn't recall being scared of Oz, but she might have been. She told Burns that she tries not to think about it, and when she does, she gets a stomachache. She kept asking him if they were done.

Vance sits frozen in his chair as Burns tells what happened as he understands it from Mo and Karen. He doesn't embellish or editorialize but delivers the facts straight and without emotion, making the story far more horrible to hear: Oz wanted water for the dog, and because of that, Bob manipulated him into walking into the blizzard to look for his mom, but before sending him on the suicide mission, he finagled away Oz's gloves for two packages of crackers.

"Do you remember any of this?" Burns asks my dad when he is done.

My dad shakes his head. "I remember asking Oz to take care of Bingo. Oz was good if he had a purpose. He would have taken the responsibility very seriously."

"How seriously?"

"What do you mean?"

"I mean, was Oz dangerous?"

"He was thirteen," my dad says.

"But he was big for his age, yes?"

"Bob's forty-five and a man. Oz wasn't *that* big."

"Bob was hurt, his ankle severely sprained."

My dad stands suddenly, drawing himself up to his full height. "My leg is broken—you think I couldn't control a thirteen-year-old?"

Burns remains sitting. "Sit down, Jack. I'm not excusing what Bob did, just trying to understand it."

My dad's fists are balled at his sides. "Bob took Oz's gloves and sent him to his death. What more is there to understand? My son was thirteen. Thirteen!"

Burns nods, yet he repeats his question. "Was he dangerous?"

My dad shakes his head and slumps back to his seat. "Oz was just protecting Bingo like I asked him to. All Bob needed to do was distract him."

"Because otherwise, what would happen?"

Vance speaks up for the first time. "Because otherwise Oz would have gotten upset. Oz wasn't your typical thirteen-year-old. Oz was big and really strong, and when he got mad, it was hard to calm him down." Vance's hands are clenched on his knees, his head shaking as if trying to clear whatever's in it. "And what happened . . . what Bob did . . . it's not like he was sitting here like the two of you and thinking rationally, telling himself, I just need to distract Oz and everything will be fine. It's freezing, and you're freaked out, and you're thinking, *Shit, I'm going to die, we're all going to die, both of us. I can't save us. I can't save her and me. I can only hope to save myself*—but then the next minute, you change your mind, but it's too late, because when you turn back, the snow has already swallowed up the decision, and you can't change it . . ." He stops, his breath coming in big gulps and his shoulders quaking. Then his eyes wander around the room until they find my dad and Burns looking at him. "I bet Bob wishes he would have done it different, but sometimes, you just make the wrong damn choice."

82

The kittens are old enough to drink on their own, so today Chloe and Finn will say goodbye to Brutus and his sisters, whom Chloe has aptly named Lindsay and Britney for their continual poor decision-making. The two kittens each have used up at least three of their nine lives.

Finn meows up a storm as her brother and sisters are taken from the crate and put into a cardboard box. Chloe sniffles a little as she carries them to the car.

She sniffles even more when she carries them into the shelter.

The boy who greets her is not much older than she is. His hair is dreadlocked, long, and the color of old wheat, his eyes sharp and dark as onyx. Tall and thin, he wears leather sandals, two dozen colorful woven bracelets, and a T-shirt that says MY KARMA RAN OVER MY DOGMA.

"What do we have here?" he says as Chloe sets the box on the counter.

She lifts the lid, waving her deformity around like a flag and pretending not to care, challenging the kid to react. The boy barely glances at her stubby pinky.

"Oh, look how young." He strokes Britney, then lifts her up. She twists awkwardly, nearly squirreling out of the boy's hands and using up another of her lives. "Shhh," he soothes, and amazingly, she does. The kid is a cat whisperer, or something like that. Britney nudges his hand with her nose, then licks his palm.

"You nursed them?" he says.

"How'd you know?"

"Kittens this young don't normally take to humans so quickly." He looks away from Britney and straight at Chloe and gives a crooked grin. "Impressive."

"Thanks," she says, a blush rising in her cheeks.

"You want a job?"

"Excuse me?"

"Well, obviously you like animals enough to save three kittens, and obviously you're good with them and had the time to take care of them, and it's Monday and you're not in school, and we need help during the week. So are you looking for a job?"

"I'm not a dropout," she defends.

Technically this is true. Chloe has until the end of summer to complete her coursework and take her exams, though she has yet to crack open a book.

The kid shrugs. "Don't care if you are or aren't, just stating the facts. It's the middle of the day on a Monday, and now that you're done helping out these little guys, you probably have some time on your hands."

Chloe's brows slash over her eyes, miffed at his presumption that she has no life, and I watch as a grin spreads across his face and as his eyebrows arch, baiting her to tell him he has it wrong, and amazingly, her anger vanishes into a giggle.

He's positively charming.

I look closer at him. He's kind of cute, or was at one time, or could be again if he got a haircut and shaved the tufts of brown fuzz on his face that stick out like mold spores on his cheeks and chin. He has a nice profile, with a long greek nose and high cheekbones. He's one of those people you don't realize is good looking until suddenly you do.

Take the job, I cheer, encouraging her. Chloe is bored, intermittently depressed, and constantly lonely, and those damn pills are still in the lining of her suitcase.

"How much does it pay?" she says.

"It's volunteer."

"Nothing?"

"A little thought and a little kindness are often worth more than a great deal of money."

"You're quoting John Ruskin to get me to work for slave wages?" Chloe says.

"You're right—that was horrible. You're obviously far too smart to work here," he says, his eyes widening with respect that Chloe recognized the quote and its author.

I have no idea who John Ruskin is, but it doesn't surprise me that Chloe does. My sister is freakishly smart, and her memory one that snatches bits and pieces of information and doesn't let go. School has never held much interest for her, but she knows more than just about anyone.

Brutus is not happy. He screams at the top of his wee kitten lungs. Chloe pulls him from the box and strokes him, causing Lindsay to get upset at being left alone. Chloe picks her up as well, holding her in her other hand. Using her chin, she pets each of them in turn.

"Well, I guess we're done here," the boy says. He sets Britney back in the box, and she starts to cry. Chloe's hands are full. The boy turns and starts for the door. "Go ahead and leave them, and I'll get to them when I'm done cleaning the cages."

"They're hungry," Chloe protests.

"Yep," he says. "Formula's in the fridge." He nods toward the minifridge in the corner. "Microwave's beside it." Then, without a glance back, he continues on. Only I see his lips curl into a grin of triumph when he hears the door to the fridge open and Chloe's muttered swears.

83

It's Easter, and Vance and my dad are faced off in the kitchen, both of them looking so slovenly I realize why God created women. A man without a woman is a disoriented and pathetic creature. Bags and boxes of half-eaten food along with dishes and silverware and clothes are piled everywhere, as though cabinets and drawers have no purpose. Both have been living in the same three sets of clothes for over a month, and the one trip they made to the Laundromat resulted in everything that was white turning dishwater gray.

"I'm going, and you should go too," Vance says, with attitude that reminds me of the old, cocky him. "I need to see Chloe. You want to stay here and feel sorry for yourself, that's your business. Give me the keys."

"Go to hell."

"I'm sure that's where I'm headed, but I'm not there yet. Now give me the keys, before I come over there and take them."

"You think you can take me," my dad guffaws. "Even with one leg, I can kick your skinny butt from here to next Sunday."

"Is that a challenge, old man?"

"That's a fact. Come on. Give it a try. I've got a little pent-up energy I wouldn't mind working out on your sorry, ungrateful ass."

"Ungrateful? What the hell do I have to be grateful to you for?"

"Stop your yapping and put up or shut up." My dad pulls the keys from his pocket and dangles them in front of him.

"How about we make it interesting," Vance says. "If I get the keys from you, you have to come with me."

"And when you don't get them?"

"If I don't get them, I stay," Vance says, his voice getting caught with the thought of not seeing Chloe.

"That's stupid. If you don't get the keys, you're staying anyway."

"No. I could hitchhike back," he says. "But, the deal is, if you win, I'll stay until I finish the search for Oz."

My dad considers this. "Fine, you're on."

Shoving the keys in his pocket, he drops one of his crutches and awkwardly assumes a fighting stance, though his leg brace and crutch make it look more like a rehabilitation exercise.

Vance huffs through his nose and circles, trying to figure out the best angle of attack. He's definitely not a fighter. His hands are balled, but the thumbs are sticking up, and I feel bad that he never had a dad around to teach him how to make a proper fist.

His attack shocks me and surprises my dad. Arms out like he's lunging for a tennis ball, he dives and rolls, smashing into my dad's good leg and sending him crashing to the floor.

My dad spins onto his back like a turtle, his damaged leg held up and his crutch whipping around wildly. He looks utterly ridiculous. They both do.

Vance scrambles away from the slashing weapon, then grabs hold of it and wrenches it from my dad's grip. My dad, still on his back, holds his fists in front of him. Vance pops to his feet and circles again. My dad follows, spinning himself on his back with his good leg.

When Vance leaps, my dad lands a solid wallop to his jaw, and Vance's head snaps back, and before Vance can regain his senses, my dad has him in a choke hold.

As my dad strangles him, Vance wriggles his fingers into my dad's pocket, trying to get the keys. His face is red and his eyes bulge, but he continues to dig, and just as his air is about to run out, that's when I see it: the slight relenting in my dad's face along with the slightest shift of his hips to make it easier for Vance to pull the keys free.

My dad wants to go. He wants to *have to* go home for Easter.

I cheer and cheer and cheer.

84

Vance calls my mom from the restroom of the gas station where he and my dad stop to get gas to tell her they are coming, and my mom nearly drops the phone with her surprise.

The things I see now that I'm dead astonish me. My mom is like a schoolgirl. She does a pirouette, claps her hands together, then runs to her room and changes her clothes three times, settling on a tight sweater and a loose skirt that stops above her knees. She pushes up her boobs and pulls the cowl neck down, and I giggle.

She returns to the kitchen, and I watch as she mashes garlic and cloves into the potatoes, then slices pears for the apple-pear salad. My phantom mouth salivates, and my imaginary stomach rumbles.

She pulls the ham from the oven to add the carrots, and I imagine its smell, the delicious scent of the plum-and-ginger glaze. My mom laughs, the basting brush suspended over the ham, and then she laughs harder, and I know she is thinking of me and our plastic-covered ham. I watch as the dish of glaze sloshes with her fit, and I laugh with her, both of us cracking up until she manages to paint the ham and put it back in the oven.

When she is done, she goes to the living room. She fusses with the pillows and combs her hair with her fingers. She sits and then stands, looks out the window, returns to the couch. She's skittish as a newborn colt, and it makes me smile.

The door opens, and she leaps up, her mouth unsure how to position itself. She tries for an expression that's glad but not too glad, still slightly upset, perhaps a little pouty—a lame attempt not to reveal how giddy and thrilled she actually is.

"Hi, Mom," Aubrey says, walking in carrying a pie. Ben is behind her with a bouquet of lilies and a garment bag slung over his arm. "What's wrong?" Aubrey says to the screwed-up expression frozen on my mom's face.

"Nothing," my mom says, straightening the grimace and kissing each of them.

Chloe bounds down the stairs carrying Finn the Mighty, her new name, earned after she chewed through her box in the kitchen while Chloe was at the shelter and managed to scale the steps in search of Chloe and her brother and sisters.

"Ohhh," Aubrey coos to the kitten. "Can I hold her?" She takes the little cat in her arms. "Mom says you're working at the shelter?"

Chloe shrugs, but pride radiates on her face. She's been there every day this week, arriving when they open in the morning and not leaving until late in the evening. She'd probably stay all night if they'd let her. The last two days, she's brought Finn the Mighty with her to keep Brutus company, since Britney and Lindsay were adopted.

The door opens again, and this time my mom doesn't have time to pose or worry about her smile. My dad gusts in like a burst of wind and is immediately engulfed in hugs and handshakes from Aubrey, Chloe, and Ben.

My mom stands back, a real smile filling her face and her eyes glassy at the sight of our family together. The moment, however, is short lived because behind my dad is Vance, so tentative at stepping over the threshold that I wish I could give him a nudge. Chloe spots him, and her eyes grow wide. Then an identical smile to my mom's spreads across her face, and she leaps past my dad to hug him, burying her face against his collarbone. His arms wrap around her, his damaged hands splayed across her back. Fortunately Vance's eyes are closed, so he doesn't see Aubrey and Ben suppress their gasps.

Chloe pulls away, grabs his hand, not noticing the deformity at all, and pulls him back out the front door, not ready to share him.

My mom steps up to my dad, her arms rising to hug him but stopping, unsure. My dad is also uncertain. He wants to be bristly and tries to put on a scowl, but his eyes betray him, running over my mom from head to toe and causing my mom to blush. My mom chose her outfit well. His eyes slide to the sweater and her pushed-up boobs, and even I feel his pulse quicken. Aubrey and Ben scoot past them and into the kitchen, Bingo tight on Ben's heels and Aubrey still holding Finn the Mighty, who is meowing up a storm.

My mom pats my dad on his freshly shaved cheek. "Much better," she says.

I'm proud of him. Not only did he shave off his mountain man beard, but he and Vance stopped at a convenience store and picked up new T-shirts. He almost looks like himself.

Anyone who doesn't believe in chemistry is wrong. And anyone who settles for less sells themselves short. The air is absolutely electrified, pheromones flying everywhere. Now there's a great word—*pheromones*. The very sound of it makes you want to kiss someone.

"I'm glad you came," she says.

Kiss her, kiss her, I encourage.

And he does. He wraps his hand around the back of her head, and his mouth comes down on hers, his pheromones defeating all the other stuff between them. *Yay, pheromones!*

When he releases her, he says, "I only came back for the cooking."

Her hand shoots out and grabs his crotch, shocking me. "Liar," she says, causing him to kiss her again, this time harder, almost violent. She melts against him, her lips succumbing to his as they open to let him in.

"Mom, I think the ham is done," Aubrey yells from the kitchen, causing them to break apart. My dad winks, and my mom winks back. The whole exchange lasts less than a minute, a flicker of the heat and romance they once had, but it is grand.

My mom walks to the kitchen, her smile so wide I think her cheeks must hurt, and happy as I am for her, I am also scared. Pheromones can only put off the inevitable for so long. My dad is not who he was. Beneath the almost normal appearance, dark anger brews. Bob is two doors away, and a need for retaliation that borders on insanity lingers.

85

Chloe and Vance sit on the beach looking at the ocean. Their shoes are beside them, their bare feet dug into the sand. She examines his fingers, then shows him hers. They compare notes and agree that Vance's surgeon was a hack who botched the job pretty badly.

He brings her damaged hand to his lips and brushes a kiss across her skin. "I'm sorry," he says, his eyes glassy. "I tried to go back for you."

She swallows, then stands and holds out her hands to him to pull him up. She doesn't want to talk about it. She wraps her arm around his waist, and he drapes his across her shoulder. She tells him about the kittens and the shelter, and he tells her about looking for Oz and putting up with my dad.

"I'm surprised you two didn't kill each other," she says, her eyes sliding to the bruise on his cheek from this morning's scuffle.

"Came close," Vance says. "Your dad is crazy. Did you know that? Fucking nuts."

"Runs in the family," Chloe says, grinning up at him.

They walk at the edge of the water, the tide washing over their feet—Chloe's seven toes, Vance's ten.

"Silk socks," he says, knowing Chloe is wondering about this. "The doctor said the socks I was wearing were made of a silk weave, and that's what saved my toes."

"Bet you didn't realize what an important decision you were making when you bought those socks."

"Nope. No idea."

He stops, turns to face her, and rests his hands on her shoulders. "I'd have given them to you," he says. "If I would have known that the socks would have saved your toes, I would have given them to you."

He wants to believe this, and perhaps he does. And I believe that if the accident happened today, he would be telling the truth. He would give her his socks. But today he is different than he was on that day. I was a witness. On that day, when the time came, he wanted to live.

Chloe knows it too. With a weak smile, she turns to continue down the beach. She walks with her head down, and he walks beside her, his shoulders stooped and his focus on the sand. Chloe takes his hand again, then bends down to pick up a tiny piece of white sea glass. She puts it in her pocket. When she gets home, she will put it in the glass jar we keep on our shared dresser, a lifetime collection from our walks on the beach.

"You're amazing," Vance says, looking at their hands twined together. It's not a compliment so much as a statement. She forgives him for the unforgivable, and it's almost too much to bear.

~

They arrive back at the house just as the ham hits the table.

"I thought we were going to have to send out a search party," Aubrey says as they walk in, causing everyone except Ben to freeze at her choice of words.

Aubrey is completely oblivious or does an amazing job pretending to be. "Can you believe our wedding is in five weeks?" she says, and again, miraculously, her normalcy resets the balance.

The six of them have a surprisingly great time during dinner, and I love it and hate it. I want to be there having a great time too.

When they're almost done with dessert, Aubrey says, "Hey, Chloe, I brought the dress for you to try on."

Chloe half grins, half groans, like she's unsure how to react. "Snarky teenager" doesn't quite fit anymore.

"What's this?" my mom asks.

"Chloe has agreed to be my maid of honor," Aubrey says.

My mom claps her hands together and yelps with excitement, her eyes getting moist. "And you're going to wear the bridesmaid dress?" she says, as if this is too much to hope for. "Will you try it on? Please."

"Now?" Chloe says, her skin growing pink.

My mom looks like a kid at Christmas who's just unwrapped a bike she's been wanting for a year. Her hands are still clasped in front of her, and she's nearly jumping up and down in her chair.

"Fine," Chloe says, "torture me on Easter. Cruel and unusual punishment, Aubrey, bringing that dress, knowing everyone was going to be here. I'll get you back for this." She stomps off to grab the dress beside the door.

"I'll help you," my dad says as she carries it up the stairs. "Payback's my specialty, and we do have a wedding to liven up."

He winks at Chloe, and I want to cry. Practical jokes and pranks were *our* thing. Oz and I were his partners in crime. We were already plotting a carefully wrought plan for the wedding that would make the event truly memorable, and now he's conspiring with Chloe. Being dead sucks. I'm stuck here watching while everyone else is doing all the things I want to be doing and all the things I was going to do.

"Don't ruin my wedding," Aubrey says, half-scared my dad is going to mess up her day, half-hopeful that his plan will add a bit of levity to what is looking to be a very boring event.

"Chloe and I are just going to have a little fun," my dad taunts.

I ache, hating that I will never concoct a plan with my dad to prank my sister's wedding, or eat my mom's ham, or sit with my family at the dinner table again. It's so unfair.

Chloe walks down the stairs in the dress, her Doc Martens peeking out from beneath the lime taffeta that swims around her in a cloud of great green pouf, a grimace of pain on her face.

The sound when she walks is like crumpling paper. My dad keeps his poker face, but my mom's laughter can't be contained, and she bursts into giggles, wine spitting from her lips. Aubrey laughs, too, a small giggle that erupts into side-stitching hysterics that spread like a virus to all of them until my mom is swearing she's going to pee her pants.

Chloe plays up the moment, pulling Vance from his chair and waltzing with him across the room. Aubrey and Ben join in, Ben swinging Aubrey around as they pretend to bounce off the billows of green tulle. Bingo jumps around and yips like a pup. My dad sits with his braced leg extended out from the table, grinning ear to ear as he admires it all. My mom's eyes slide to look at him, and he feels it and turns her way. She quickly looks away, but his eyes linger, more than pheromones. I see it: the love of a lifetime, his one and only.

Aubrey and Ben volunteer to do the dishes, and together they go into the kitchen.

Chloe disappears with Vance to the backyard.

My mom and dad settle on the couch, my dad's leg propped on the coffee table.

"Jack," my mom starts, but his lips on hers stop her. "Not tonight," he says. "Tonight is good and normal, and I just want it to last."

"And tomorrow? Will you still be here tomorrow?"

"Tomorrow I'll be here, and we'll figure it out then."

My mom rests her head against his shoulder, and my dad closes his eyes, and I wonder if it could stay this simple.

~

Aubrey dries her hands on the dish towel, refolds it, and hangs it on the oven door before saying, "Do you think there's a heaven?"

Ben shakes his head and wraps his arms around her. He's so much more affectionate than I thought. When they're alone, he can't keep his hands or lips off Aubrey. He's always hugging and kissing her and telling her he loves her, marveling that he has the right to do so, like he can't believe she's really his.

I like him very much from this perspective.

"When you die, you die," he says.

"That's sad," she says, relaxing against him as he kisses her hair.

"More sad than existing in a world apart from everyone you left behind?"

Aubrey thinks about this. "It's just the other's so permanent." Of everyone I love who remains, I feel as if Aubrey feels me the least, our connection severed almost instantly after I died. But it does not mean she doesn't think of me. Tonight she misses me, and she misses Oz. "My brother loved holidays," she says into Ben's shirt.

"I remember," Ben says. "I've never seen anyone so excited about Christmas in my life."

Aubrey smiles and nods. Oz had his very own Santa suit, and he started his quest for gifts as early as Halloween. He loved the decorations, the food, the customs, but mostly he loved that our family was together so much. He said it all the time. *Christmas is coming. It means Aubrey will be home, and Mom won't have to work.*

"He's at peace," Ben says, and I watch as his eyes drift to the night sky through the window as if imagining it. "Finn too."

Aubrey looks into the blackness with him, then returns her gaze to his and paints a smile on her face. "Five weeks," she says. "I can't believe it."

He lifts her off her feet and swings her around. "Yep. In five weeks, you're all mine." Setting her down, he backs her against the sink, and his fingers thread through her hair as he kisses her.

I can't believe I didn't like this guy.

~

"Should I stay?" Vance asks, more prayer than optimism in his voice. "Or should I go back to Big Bear?"

Chloe touches his cheek and gives a sad smile. In her eyes is the wish that things had turned out differently, along with the hard truth that Vance's greatest loss that day was not his fingers. "I'm so glad you're okay," she says.

"I wish I could do it over," he mumbles.

"I don't," Chloe says. "I wish it never happened."

"Well, yeah, but if it did happen, I wish I could do my part different."

Silence sits between them.

"What now?" she says. "When fall comes, will you go to UC Santa Barbara?"

He shakes his head. "School's not my thing. I want to finish looking for Oz. We're almost done with the grid, and I want to finish it."

"And then?"

"Then I don't know. Maybe I'll stay there for a while. There's lots of work, and I like it in the mountains."

"No more tennis?" she asks sadly.

He holds up his wounded hands, then drops them to his lap. "Truth is I was second rate. It's not like I was ever going to be good enough to turn pro."

"You were good," she says.

He shrugs. "Past tense. What's weird is how much I don't miss it, like this weight of expectation is gone. Living with your dad, it's been good for me. He's a fuckup like me."

Chloe's face darkens.

"Not in a bad way," Vance goes on quickly. "But in the way that he didn't go to college, bummed around awhile, didn't follow a clear path, but somehow still did it right, still ended up with your mom and having a family. That's why I said I wish I could do it over. Not because I want the accident to happen again—I would never want that. But because I know I'd do better, be more like your dad."

Chloe's eyes well up, and so do mine. My dad didn't set out to save Vance, but he saved him just the same.

~

It's a good night, one that ends with Chloe and Finn the Mighty sleeping peacefully in the room beside my parents' bedroom and my dad lying in the same bed as my mom, his fingers touching hers.

86

Laguna Beach is a small town, a place that still has a Main Street with cute little shops and an annual parade. It's a community where families live for generations. My dad's family has been in Laguna Beach since the early 1900s, and my mom's parents moved here before she was born. Everyone knows everyone, and like in all small towns, news spreads quickly. Two local newspapers, an online news stream, and a glossy magazine do a thorough job of covering all the local happenings.

The online news stream reported the story first, blasting it over the internet on Tuesday afternoon, an hour after Bob posted bail. The headline read: **Local Dentist Arrested for Negligent Homicide of 13-Year-Old Boy.**

On Thursday, both newspapers featured the story on their front pages, and that afternoon, the phone rang at our house, and my dad was asked to do an interview for the glossy magazine. He declined.

It's Thursday evening, and I decide to pop in on Bob and Karen to see how they are handling their new celebrity.

They are not handling it well.

Bob sits on the couch in a drunken stupor, a glass of scotch in his hand and his eyes fixed on the newspapers strewn on the coffee table in front of him. Judging by the liquor remaining in the bottle beside him and the glassiness of his eyes, he's been there awhile.

Karen and Natalie are in the kitchen. Karen looks at least ten years older than she did a week ago, twenty years older than she did before the accident. Her clothes are rumpled, her hair unbrushed, her eyes swollen and red. Natalie looks like she always does, dazed as she sits at the counter eating low-fat rocky road ice cream.

Shockingly, there are dirty dishes in the sink, and the counters are spotted with spills and stains. Karen sits beside Natalie, staring out the french doors that lead to the backyard. The phone rings, startling her, and I watch as she squeezes her eyes shut and covers her ears to block out its noxious blare.

Natalie lifts her face to look at it, then looks at her mother, a shadow of guilt crossing her face before the look of vacancy returns. System overload, I think as I watch her; she's unable to cope with everything that is happening.

The answering machine picks up on the fourth ring, and a perky voice introduces itself as a reporter from the *Orange County Register*. Karen listens intently, her body rigid as she waits for it to end, and when the woman hangs up, she stands and walks stiffly into the living room.

"Can I get you anything?" she asks Bob.

Bob looks up, his face riddled with such confusion and despair it causes my breath to hitch with pity. "How?" he says as his eyes slide from Karen back to the life-destroying vilification in front of him.

Both papers report that the trial is scheduled for late September, though it doesn't look like it will come to that. The district attorney has already offered a reduced sentence for a guilty plea: six months' probation and no prison time. Bob's lawyer is urging Bob to take the offer. Despite it meaning a felony conviction and the virtual destruction of Bob's dental practice, he thinks it is his best option. The lawyer does not believe Bob will prevail against Mo and my family in court, and if he loses, he could face up to ten years in prison.

Karen looks at the carpet at her feet. "They're wrong," she says. "You didn't do what they're saying." But her voice wavers, confirming what a terrible witness she would make.

Bob turns to her, and his voice edged with hate, he says, "I did it for you."

Through the archway, Natalie jolts with his words. Oz is dead. She wore his gloves. Then she told Mo what her dad did. She begins to rock on her stool, and her eyes take on a faraway stare, conscience a terrible thing to discover when you're sixteen and have lived all those years never having recognized it.

Karen glances back, sees her rocking, and turns back to Bob, her face distraught with stress and worry. "I think it might be best," she says, "if Natalie and I go to San Diego for a while . . . you know, to stay with my parents . . . just for a bit, maybe until after the trial . . . they're wrong . . . I know they're wrong . . . but until this whole thing blows over . . ."

"Get out!" Bob roars, sending her racing from the room, the scotch bottle smashing against the wall behind her.

87

Chloe is at the shelter. She practically lives there these days—leaving home at dawn and not returning until the sun goes down. A purpose, the animals, and Eric, the boy who gave her the job, have turned out to be an irresistible combination.

At the moment, Eric is giving a surly German shepherd a bath. The shepherd, who Eric named Hannibal on account of his psycho personality, was brought in a week ago by animal control. He was found half-starved and collarless in a gully beside Laguna Canyon Road. The chances of him being claimed or adopted are slim, but the shelter gives each animal a month before they put it down. In order to be tended to, the dog needs to be sedated and muzzled, and even with those precautions, Chloe gives the animal a wide berth.

As Chloe walks by, Eric's head comes up. Hannibal, sensing something even in his drugged sleep, grumbles. Eric ignores the rumbling and waves his gloved hand at her. It's completely uncool, making it incredibly cool. I love this guy. Today he wears a T-shirt that says I HAVE THE BODY OF A GOD beneath a drawing of Buddha, which is hilarious, considering he looks like Gumby.

Chloe blushes as her hand barely lifts from her thigh to give a small wave back. This is how it's been with them, tentative on her part and certain on his—a growing friendship, undeniable chemistry, and wary reluctance. Chloe's scars are less than three months old, and her wounds on the inside are far worse than those that can be seen. Eric senses this and is endearingly gentle, but it doesn't stop his face from lighting up when she walks past or his eyes from lingering as she continues on.

Chloe makes a show of not caring, but it's an act. Today she wears ripped black jeans, a faded Metallica T-shirt, and worn-out Converse sneakers. Only I know she spent nearly an hour working on her hair to shape it into just-rolled-out-of-bed cute and rubbed Vaseline into her lips to make them shine.

She sits at the front desk, inputting this week's ledger into the computer. She hears Eric throwing down a bag of food and his boots on the concrete growing closer, and her posture straightens. Her head stays bowed as he walks through the door, but I feel her pulse quicken.

He hardly slows as he walks past but manages to swipe the pencil from her ear. When she whirls, he tosses it to land in the spine of the ledger, then continues on, humming something to himself. And it seems like nothing, but it is definitely something. Chloe goes back to her numbers, reading the same column three times, a silly grin on her face.

88

Five days have passed since Easter, and things are precariously calm, as if all of us are holding our breaths.

My dad has begun physical therapy again and is attacking his rehabilitation with a vengeance. His therapist, an ancient woman, thick as a stump, shows little mercy as she tortures his leg into compliance. Unlike with the home health nurse from before, there is zero flirt factor with this woman, which makes my dad grumble and causes me to grin.

Each morning, after she leaves, my dad goes to the garage to lift weights, and then he hobbles around the neighborhood until his leg trembles with exhaustion. His determination is spurred by both desire to regain his strength and desire to return to work, to reclaim the life he once had, not just before the accident but before he needed to give up one love for another.

When Oz was three, my dad quit his job as a yacht captain, a decision of necessity when it became clear Oz was too much for a sitter to handle. Before my dad met my mom, he had been a lot of things—a river-raft guide, a ranger, a silver miner—but he'd found his calling on the ocean. Like it once did for me, salt water runs in his veins.

He used to tell me how it's the last frontier, the only part of the earth not entirely known. His eyes would shine as he talked about how little is understood about its deepest depths, that two-thirds of ocean species still remain undiscovered, and that all the technology in the world still can't predict a squall. He loved it—the adventure, the camaraderie of the crew, the unbridled freedom—and when he was forced to give it up, something went quiet in him. He missed it so much you could feel it. Every time we were at the beach, his eyes would squint at the horizon, and he would lick his lips. If he heard about a storm in some distant ocean, his jaw would flex and his muscles would tense, eager to jump into action.

My dad says goodbye to his therapist, then goes to the garage and loads the weights onto the bench press.

The garage is a shrine of sorts, a place untouched by my mom's giant eraser. Bits and pieces of Oz and me are everywhere, stacked on the racks and hanging from the rafters, bats and mitts and old uniforms and bicycles and boogie boards and tennis rackets and golf clubs—a million memories collecting dust as my dad grunts and sweats and pushes himself to his limit.

Between sets, his eyes roam the remnants as he forces himself to remember us and refuses to let us go, a self-flagellation worthy of a saint or a devil. And as I watch, I wonder if my mom wasn't right to throw it all away. This place is like quicksand, and each time my dad is here, it pulls him down, drowns him, and stops him from moving on.

The back corner is particularly awful. My softball bag and glove from my last game are still kicked in the corner. And my jersey, number nine, the same number my dad wore and his father wore, sits balled on top. I decide, looking at it—its color growing dingy and a layer of dust making it grimy—and then looking at him—beaten, angry, and miserable—that if I could, I would incinerate every last scrap of it with heat so blazing that not even a speck of ash would remain.

When my dad finishes destroying himself physically and emotionally, he stumbles into the house. I'm curious why today he doesn't go for his walk, and I realize, when I join him in the kitchen, it's because the Angels have a day game.

The Angels are our team—my dad, Oz, and me—and the three of us had a very specific pregame routine, mostly for Oz's benefit, who loved rituals and believed in superstition. Before every game we held hands, closed our eyes, and chanted, "May the Force be with the Angels," repeating it and repeating it until we were shouting with religious fervor. We only ate chicken wings and celery sticks with Hidden Valley ranch dressing, and we were required to each eat nine of each— one wing and one piece of celery before each inning. Oz was in charge of the clicker, and none of us were allowed to touch it during the game, or it was sure to jinx the outcome.

The house is empty. Perhaps this is why he does it. With great deliberateness and care, my dad prepares the chicken wings and celery. He talks to Oz as he pours the ranch dressing into a bowl. "Just the way you like it, buddy," he says. Bingo lifts his head with great interest. "Angels against the Giants. It's going to be a tough one."

I watch as he sets the food—nine wings and nine celery sticks—on a plate. Just one plate. Carrying it to the couch, he turns on the television, and I take my spot beside him, imagining the smell and taste of the chicken wings and feeling very sorry for myself.

It happens in the eighth inning. Albert Pujols hits a homer to drive in two runs and tie the game, and my dad's fist punches the air in victory. For a miraculous moment, he forgot about us, and my heart both celebrates and seizes at the breakthrough. My dad yanks his fist down as a flash of guilt crosses his face, causing my own guilt to rage. *No!* I cry. *Be happy.*

And maybe God is listening because in the next inning, with two outs, Kole Calhoun rips a double off the wall, and again my dad can't help but feel alive and applauds with the audience. He leans forward, and I lean in with him as Mike Trout steps to the plate. I can't think of another player I'd want more at the dish.

"Come on, Trout," my dad says.

It's a three-balls, two-strikes count.

Please don't walk him.

The delivery.

The ball is outside and low.

Trout swings and connects, a blooper between first and second.

Calhoun takes off, pumping it around the bases.

Joe Panik goes back as Andrew McCutchen runs in from right field.

Panik dives and doesn't get there, and the ball falls inches from his glove.

McCutchen hurls it home, but the throw is too late.

The chicken wings and celery sticks are gone. Our mojo worked. The Angels won.

"We did it, Oz," my dad says with another fist pump just as the door opens and my mom walks through.

Bingo leaps up as my dad turns to look at her.

My mom scans the scene, taking in the empty plate on the coffee table and the clicker set beside where Oz used to sit, and her eyes slide to my dad's.

"I'm going for a run," she says, walking past, her jaw tight, and my dad lowers his fist, and desperately I wish she would have walked in one minute later.

By the time she comes down in her running clothes, my dad is gone. He is in the garage talking to my jersey and telling me about the game. My mom glances at the door and hears him mumbling, and with a heavy sigh, she sets off, sprinting through the streets until she can't catch a breath.

An hour later, she stumbles home to find my dad in the kitchen washing the dishes he used to make his chicken wings.

"They're gone," my mom says.

He doesn't turn, and only the tightness of his shoulders betrays that he heard her.

"You need to get past it," she continues. "If you insist on dredging it up constantly, then it will never be behind us."

The glass dish he's washing squeaks as he presses too hard with the sponge.

My mom inhales deeply, then sighs. "If you want me to clean out the garage, I will."

He whirls, causing water to slosh from the sink. His eyes dark, he says, "Stay out of there. They're gone but not forgotten, and I don't need to *get past it*. Unlike you, I can't just forget them. I won't forget them, and they will never be *behind me*."

My mom pivots and marches away, her hands balled at her sides, and I tremble. Five days. That's how long they made it before it all fell apart again.

89

It's Sunday. The shelter is closed to the public, and no one is there except Chloe, Eric, and the animals. They go about their business of cleaning the cages and tending to the animals, both pretending that them being alone together is no big deal.

Halfway through the morning, Chloe makes her move. She will probably claim it was Eric who moved first, but it was definitely her. Eric sets a crate against the wall, and she walks toward him, a mischievous grin on her face.

"What?" he says.

With a lack of inhibition that awes me, she backs him against the crate, causing him to sit down, and then she steps between his legs and kisses him. He does not seem like a boy with much experience, and at first he looks a bit frozen and shocked. Fortunately, he is a quick learner, and his arms wrap around her waist to pull her to him. He is a man starved and now confronted with a feast, and his mouth opens to devour hers.

"Slowly," she says with a giggle as she pulls away, and then she smiles coyly. "We have all day." My heart nearly pounds out of my chest. I had no idea my sister was so sexy.

She lifts her T-shirt over her head, revealing an indigo-blue bra so dark her skin glows against it, and despite her admonition, Eric ravages her again, first with his eyes and then with his lips, causing her to laugh out in delight.

With surprising strength, he stands, lifting her with him. And with her legs wrapped around his hips and their mouths attached, he carries her to the cot beside the stacks of dog food. He pulls off her sneakers and then her socks. She tenses as her toes are revealed, but Eric doesn't notice. He sees her wounds but pays them no mind, his attention already moving back up her body and his mouth back to her lips.

90

It had been a week since my mom and dad fought: seven nights that my mom had slept in Aubrey's old room instead of her own. But last night my mom decided she'd had enough. Dressed in pj shorts and a thin T-shirt that showed her nipples, she walked from Aubrey's room to her own, stopped at the threshold to smooth her hair, and stepped inside.

This morning, they wake in each other's arms.

My mom rolls toward my dad, and sensing her eyes, he blinks in the morning as a smile creases his face. As I watch them, I imagine them when they first met and how amazing they must have been, the kind of couple who turned heads and stirred hearts, bold and uncompromising—Scott-and-Zelda kind of wonderful.

When I was young, I witnessed it, their amazingness—their over-the-moon attraction to each other, their energy and passion. At night, Chloe and I would hear them through our wall: laughter, muffled moans, the creaking of their bed. We would pinch our noses and cover our mouths to stop our giggles. In the morning, my mom would bound down the stairs in my dad's sweatshirt and a pair of his boxers, and he would smile, leer at her legs, and lift and lower his eyebrows. And my mom would tease, "Daddy's in an awfully good mood this morning." As she passed him, his hand would trail across her behind. "A very, very good mood," he would answer, and my mom would blush.

As we got older, our sleep was interrupted less, until over time, the disruptions ceased altogether.

It's been years since I've heard them. But last night, as I sat on my old bed beside Chloe, the walls echoed with the sounds of that long-ago passion. Chloe rolled her eyes, then put on her headphones to drown them out, a smile on her face.

This morning they bask in the afterglow, worn out and wholly in love. My mom lies with her head on my dad's shoulder as her fingers comb the hair on his chest.

Across from them, on the dresser, is a photo of our family: our annual Christmas portrait. As always, we are dressed in matching outfits, all of us in jeans and black tops, the six of us seated on a large rock in front of the ocean.

"Ann?" my dad says.

"Hmmm?"

"Can I tell you something?"

Her hand stops combing the ringlets as she tenses, knowing by the tightness of my dad's voice that his next words will likely break the spell.

My dad's jaw is locked forward and his stare fixed on the photo. He closes his eyes and says, "Sometimes I'm relieved he's gone."

He squeezes his eyes tight at the awfulness of the confession as my mom says, "Shhh." She wraps her arm around him and lifts her face to kiss away the tear that has escaped from his eye. "It doesn't lessen your love. It's just who he was."

And she's right. Because the thing about a boy like Oz is no matter how much you love him, you also hate what he does to your life, the way he sucks the energy from it and uses up all the air, so relentless and demanding it's like sometimes you can't breathe. None of us admitted it when he was alive, but we all felt it.

My dad trembles with his guilt and his grief, emotions he's held inside since waking in the hospital to discover the awful truth, and my mom continues to hold him, his confession one only she can understand and forgive.

91

Finn the Mighty is at the shelter with Chloe, though today is the last day Chloe will bring her along. Brutus was adopted this morning, so Finn the Mighty no longer has playmates, and she detests being locked in a kennel with no friends.

She roars and roars her unhappiness until finally Chloe relents and lets her out of her cage. Finn runs in circles around the office, tumbling over herself and having all sorts of fun chasing a lint ball that blows and twirls just out of reach. Chloe sits at the desk, reviewing the charts of their new charges and making notes for the night crew.

The lint ball drifts, bounces up, then floats out the dutch door that leads to the dog kennels, and I watch in horror as Finn leaps after it with just enough force to crack open the door. Chloe doesn't notice, her attention tight on her work.

The kitten coils and pounces, just missing the elusive piece of fuzz and sending it whirling down the path and straight into the kennel of Hannibal, the German shepherd. Finn bounds after it, easily slithering between the posts.

Growl.

Shriek.

Finn's fur bristles, poufing her to twice her size, though she is still no larger than a softball. Hannibal bares his teeth, and the other dogs, now aware, bark wildly.

In the next second Chloe is there, her hand on the gate.

"Don't," Eric yells, racing in from the yard.

Chloe glances at him, and I watch as something dangerous crosses her face. Then she opens the door and steps inside.

She scoops Finn the Mighty into her arms and whirls to face the shepherd, her eyes narrowing as if challenging the beast, and the dog crouches as his hackles lift.

A bucket crashes beside him, causing the dog to turn. "Over here, Lecter," Eric says as he charges into the kennel. He circles away from Chloe, and Hannibal shifts and snarls.

"Chloe, go," Eric hisses, then waves his hands in front of Hannibal to keep the dog's attention. "That's right. Come on, big boy, you want a piece of this?" He wiggles his fingers in invitation.

Chloe runs with Finn the Mighty out the gate and swings it open wide, keeping herself and the kitten behind it so it is a shield. Hannibal's eyes dart from Eric to his chance at freedom, the shelter yard glowing through the open door at the end of the kennels, and mercifully he chooses freedom, racing through the open gate and straight for the outdoors.

Chloe charges after him and slams the door shut behind him, then races back to the kennel.

Eric sinks to his knees. "Shit," he says as he bends over his thighs and sucks in air.

In one hand, Chloe still holds Finn. With the other, she helps Eric to his feet. When he is standing, she reaches around his head and pulls his forehead down to touch hers. "Thank you," she says.

He pulls away, his face dark, and he lifts her chin so she is looking at him. "Don't do that again," he says.

"Say thank you?"

"Test me."

Chloe tries to step back defiantly, but he doesn't let her. His arm holds her tight as his eyes sear into hers. "I'll jump in every time," he says. "But I might not always be so lucky. So don't do that again."

She lowers her eyes and nods, then lets him pull her into his arms.

~

Chloe leaves the shelter, drops Finn the Mighty at the house, then drives downtown. She gets a caramel frappé from Starbucks and carries it toward the beach.

The town is mostly unchanged, yet I notice the differences. There's a new sandwich shop where Angelino's Pizzeria used to be, and the Hurley Surf Shop is now an art gallery. The swim trunks displayed in the windows of the stores are a little shorter this year than last, and the bikinis are trending toward neon pinks and blues. Life goes on.

Chloe passes the ice cream shop, and I imagine the smell of fresh-baked waffle cones and the taste of mint ice cream. A teenager holding a chocolate-dipped banana notices Chloe's deformed hand and stares. Chloe waves at him, causing the boy to blush crimson and hurry away.

It's as beautiful a day as a day can be. Full spring clouds that make you think of popcorn float across the sky, the sun twinkles off the water, and a warm breeze whispers with the promise of summer. On the ocean a dozen sailboats race south, and on the beach hundreds of tourists slathered in sunscreen lounge on towels and play in the waves.

Chloe walks across the boardwalk, sits on the sand, squints out at the waves, then lifts her face to the sun, letting the brightness and heat soak into her skin.

And that's when I feel it: the letting go, the bond between us weakening as she gently releases me, a thin smile on her face and a single tear leaking from her eye as she brings her fingers to her lips to blow me a kiss goodbye.

92

She stands just outside the front door, looking distinctly uncomfortable, her eyes on the ground as she shifts foot to foot, her cashmere sweater set and herringbone slacks belonging to another time and place.

"Joyce?" my mom says as she looks at Mrs. Kaminski curiously.

In Mo's mom's hands is a manila envelope, the kind with Bubble Wrap on the inside. And the way she grips it makes me believe it is important, and I wonder what is inside.

"Would you like to come in?" my mom says, opening the door wider.

Mrs. Kaminski shakes her head as her clutch tightens, causing the package to bend. "I didn't realize," she says as her eyes flick around like a bird, avoiding my mom's, the words so low my mom needs to lean in to hear them.

My mom straightens and tilts her head, and Mrs. Kaminski pushes the envelope toward her. My mom doesn't take it. Instead she steps back, leaving the hoodoo suspended awkwardly between them.

"In the hospital," Mrs. Kaminski goes on. "They asked what I wanted them to do with the clothes Maureen was brought in with."

I watch as my mom stiffens, but Mrs. Kaminski doesn't notice, her attention solely on delivering her burden. "I wasn't paying attention," she says. "And I didn't realize," she repeats.

The envelope is too small to hold any clothes, no bigger than letter size and barely thicker than a finger.

"So I told them to get rid of them," she says. "To throw them away." Her voice cracks, and I realize she is close to tears. "I didn't want anything from those awful days anywhere near Maureen again."

My mom's arms are now folded in front of her, her features dark, and I feel her fierce desire for Mrs. Kaminski to leave.

A tear escapes from Mrs. Kaminski's left eye to roll down her cheek. She reaches up with the hand not holding the envelope and wipes it away. "I only just found this," she says as she extends the envelope another inch, her eyes still looking everywhere but where my mom is. "My husband, he brought it home from the hospital. It was in his office . . ." Her voice trails off, and her arm trembles.

After a long second, when it is clear my mom is not going to take it, Mrs. Kaminski pulls it back and opens the flap. She pulls out a single sheet of paper along with my cell phone, and I watch as my mom recoils, her eyes seizing on the navy cover and the phosphorescent lettering that says, *We are all worms. But I do believe I am a glowworm.*

The phone case was a gift from Aubrey from her senior trip to London. The quote is by Winston Churchill. She said it made her think of me, which might have been one of the nicest things anyone's ever said to me. I loved that case and quoted that line all the time.

My mom shakes her head against it, but Mrs. Kaminski's eyes are on the paper as she reads out loud, "Inventory of items disposed of for patient Maureen Kaminski." She takes a deep breath to rein in her emotions, then continues. "Brown leather boots. Black tights. Denim jeans. Red sweater. Maroon Laguna Beach High School soccer sweatshirt. Navy parka with hood. Gray sweatpants. Black socks. Striped wool socks."

She stops, sniffles, wipes away another tear, then forces her eyes to my mom's, though only for a second, the reflection of looking at a mother who lost what she was so terrified of losing too much to bear.

"Until I found this," she says, the words wavering, "I didn't realize what you had done."

My mom's jaw slides forward, and I'm worried she might slam the door in Mrs. Kaminski's face. But she doesn't. Instead she remains remarkably still as Mrs. Kaminski finishes her unintentional lashing. "I'm sorry I didn't realize it sooner and that it has taken me this long to acknowledge it." She slides the sheet of paper and phone back in the envelope and reaches past my mom to set it on the table beside the door. Her eyes drop as she steps back. "Thank you," she mutters, the words completely inadequate for what she feels. My mom forces a stiff nod, and Mrs. Kaminski turns.

The door closes behind her, and a second later, something crashes against it. She looks back, her chin quaking as she realizes it was the sound of the package being hurled against the wood.

93

My dad watches from the shadows of the kitchen as my mom races up the stairs and closes their bedroom door behind her.

His expression is dark, and I watch as he walks to the entry and retrieves the envelope. He carries it to the kitchen, pulls out the phone, and tries to activate it, but the battery is dead.

He plugs it in, and as he waits for it to charge, he looks at the sheet of paper. His eyes run over the words, and I watch as their meaning registers, his expression changing from curiosity to shame as he realizes what my mom went through while he was unconscious.

Setting the sheet down, he picks up my phone and powers it on. The screen saver shot is of me hanging from the mouth of the enormous lion statue in front of the San Diego Zoo. He was the one who hoisted me up and then darted back to snap the photo as I dangled. Security ran out and yelled at me to get down, and my dad, Oz, and I hurried away, laughing hysterically, the photo priceless.

He smiles and glances again at the sheet, reading the lines carefully, and I know he is considering each article of clothing, deciphering which belonged to me and which were Mo's.

He returns to the phone, opens my photos, and scrolls through them, hundreds and hundreds of images from my remarkable life. Mountains and forests and rivers. The ocean and the beach. Parks and sports fields and the thousand other places I've been. Family and friends and teammates. Laughter, love, and fun—so much it is impossible to be sad when you look at them.

When he hears my mom walk from their room, he powers down the phone, stashes it in his pocket, then crumples the envelope and paper and buries them deep in the trash.

She sticks her head through the door. "I'm going into work for a bit," she says, her eyes not meeting his and betraying the lie.

He pretends not to notice.

I do not know where she is going, but it is not to work. My guess is she will go someplace where it is crowded and noisy, someplace where she can sit and pretend she is a part of it, where she can forget who she is and pretend she is the person she used to believe she was.

My dad stands and takes a step toward her, but she steps back.

"Okay," he says. "I'll take care of dinner."

She nods and shuffles away, and as my dad watches her go, his muscles twitch. As soon as her car pulls from the driveway, he walks to the garage.

He starts with the sports equipment, unceremoniously throwing everything that belonged to Oz and me in the back of his truck. I wince when he tosses my skateboard onto the pile and need to stop from crying when he grabs my surfboard from its rack.

"Time to get this mess cleared out," he says to Bingo, who follows him around, sniffing at each item and thumping his tail as he remembers our scent.

It's amazing how much people talk to their pets when no one else is around. Chloe talks nonstop to Finn the Mighty, my mom and dad both talk to Bingo, and Eric yaps all his secrets to whatever animal he happens to be taking care of.

"I should get you a dog tuxedo for the wedding," he says. "If I need to wear a monkey suit, so should you."

He stops for a minute to wipe the sweat from his brow, thinks of something, touches his pocket where my phone is, then forces his hand away.

"Ah, hell, if it makes Aubrey happy," he says, "I'll wear the damn tuxedo." He grabs Oz's collection of Nerf footballs and throws them into the truck. "Bet they end up pregnant quick. Aubrey's not a patient one. Poor Ben—he has no idea what he's in for."

Tennis racket. Golf clubs. Bicycle.

"You know we're gonna be watching the kid," he says. "We'll need to get a crib, a changing table, one of those swing things. For being so small, babies take up a hell of a lot of space."

I smile as I listen, understanding that this is how it needs to be for him, a task—a responsibility and an obligation to do what needs to be done to protect those who remain, spurred on by that thin sheet of paper and what it revealed. I feel his resolve and his blinding love, his willingness to do anything for Aubrey, including letting us go.

"Chloe's got herself another damn boyfriend," he says. "Hope he's better than the last one." He hesitates. "Ah, hell, Vance wasn't all that bad. Damn kid had balls—I'll give him that."

Bingo tilts his head and thumps his tail on the ground.

Only when he reaches for my jersey does he hesitate, his grip tightening around the satin before he forces his fingers open to release it on top of the heap.

I drive with him to the thrift store and watch as he dumps the load into the donation bin, each item like a weight lifting, until finally the last remnant is tossed away, and I am free. Released like a balloon into the sky, the brightness so close I feel it, warm and magnetic as I float above him, watching as he climbs back in his truck to drive back to the single thread that remains.

94

Aubrey is a radiant bride, and Ben beams beside her. They kneel for the benediction, and tears stream from my eyes—hysterical laughter buckling my stomach and causing me to cry. The audience snickers with me. Aubrey, Ben, and the ancient priest have no idea what's so amusing and look around, baffled.

In the front pew, Mrs. Kinsell elbows her husband to do something, though there's really nothing for him to do. Written on the soles of Ben's shoes, which face the two hundred witnesses of this blessed event, in bright-pink nail polish are the words *Help Me.*

Chloe, who stands beside Aubrey wearing her ridiculous green taffeta dress, looks over her shoulder and gives my dad a wink. Payback. They did it, pulled off the ultimate wedding prank.

Aside from the moment of humor, the ceremony goes off without a hitch, and Aubrey ends up hitched to the person she's meant to be hitched to. I cheer and applaud and dance and sing.

The reception is at the Ritz a few miles from our house. My mom and dad beam as the couple is introduced. Twenty-four years ago, their own wedding was a simple justice of the peace affair that my dad likes to say "cost me a hundred bucks and a lifetime of freedom." Then he always adds with a smirk and a wink, "And I might even have paid two hundred had I known the lot of you were going to be thrown into the deal."

My mom looks exquisite. The emerald-green silk dress she wears is embroidered with silver and pink roses and is cut three inches above her knees, showing off her runner's legs. Her hair is piled loosely on her head and held in place with a small jeweled clip. Gold tendrils frame her face, and a choker of pearls circles her neck. She bends down to adjust a ribbon on the edge of a table, causing her skirt to pull tight across her rump, and from across the room, the heat of my dad's stare causes her to lift her head. He gives a full-wattage grin that causes her to blush.

Mo and Kyle are here and are inseparable—hands, fingers, lips, shoulders, hips, something literally always touching. She looks so good and he looks so good and they look so good together I want to applaud. And since no one can hear me, that is what I do. I whoop and holler and dance and clap my hands. *You, Maureen Kaminski, are beautiful, and you, Kyle Hannigan, are gorgeous, and I now pronounce you king and queen of stunningness.*

Chloe brought Eric, and my dad took to him like a bear to honey. Perhaps it's because Eric is so different from Vance, but I think mostly it's because Chloe is so different with Eric. She's still abjectly devoted like she was with Vance, but Eric is not the least bit needy or possessive, and Chloe seems to be the best version of herself when she is with him, confident and carefree and goofy and fun. Her copper hair glints wildly as she dances, her smile lighting up the room as the music she chose adds the perfect accompaniment to the night.

At one point, breathless and sweating, Eric leads her outside to the patio for some air. She looks out at the ocean and then turns to him and says, "You never asked me."

"Asked what?"

"About the accident." She holds up her half-pinky hand as if to make the point.

He takes hold of it and kisses the stub. "Do you want to tell me?"

Chloe tilts her head, thinking about it. "Not really, but I'm curious why you never asked."

"It wouldn't change anything. I would still love you."

Her smile spreads. "But aren't you curious?"

"In the beginning, maybe a little, but then, not really."

"What if I wanted to tell you?"

"Then I would listen."

"But you don't want me to tell you?"

His eyes hold hers, his face etched with the promise of the strong man he will grow to be. "Truthfully, no."

"Why?"

"Because I love you." He sighs through his nose. "You see, that's the problem. I love you, so if you want to tell me, I will listen, but at the same time, I know the story is going to be awful, really awful, and so I know I would be supposed to feel bad, but the truth is inside I wouldn't be feeling nearly bad enough because a selfish part of me would be grateful it happened."

Chloe stiffens.

"See how terrible that is?" he says. "So I'd rather look forward, not back, and just be grateful that God or Buddha or whoever the hell runs the universe spared you and brought you into my life."

He opens his mouth to say more, but he can't because Chloe's lips are on his, and I wonder if he's right, if some strange karmic destiny is at work. Oz and I were lost, but Chloe and my mom and my dad were spared and their fates altered. I don't know if I believe it was providence, but looking at Chloe and Eric standing on the balcony beneath the stars, wholly in love, I know for all that was lost that day, something also was gained.

Chloe pulls away, a perplexed look on her face.

"Something else on your mind?" Eric says.

"Why do you love me?"

He laughs. Eric has a great laugh, a deep, rolling rumble. "You're kidding, right?"

She shakes her head and glares at him, not thinking her question funny in the least.

"I think it's the way you glare at me when you're mad."

She punches him in the chest. "I mean it. Be serious."

He pulls her close, his eyes still smirking with humor. "It was your mouth that caught my attention first."

"My mouth?"

"Yep. When you first came in with the kittens, it was your mouth I noticed, the way it skewed to the left. You acted all tough and certain, but your mouth gave you away."

She pulls him into another kiss, then pulls away. "You still like my mouth?"

"Yep. I must say, I'm a very good judge of mouths at first glance. But that's not why I fell in love with you; that's only what I noticed first. It was your eyes that put me over the top, the way you roll them when anyone says anything nice to you, like when I tell you you're beautiful."

Chloe rolls her eyes.

"Exactly," Eric says. "They're a strange color, mostly green, but when you're happy or . . . you know . . . in the moment"—he thrusts his hips just slightly, causing me to grimace—"they're soft gray."

Chloe blushes.

"But really, who knows why any of us fall in love?" He lifts her hands to his lips, then lowers them to hold them against his heart. "All I know for certain is that my heart pounds harder when you walk in a room or when you look at me or when you smile."

Vance was with Chloe for over a year, and in all that time I doubt he ever said anything like that. Karmic destiny or just random fate, I have no idea—the only things definite are my gratitude that the two of them found each other and my certainty that they were meant to be.

I leave them lip locked on the patio and return inside to the party, where Chloe's playlist has everyone on their feet dancing up a storm. Everyone except my dad, who is still out of dancing commission, and my mom, who is short a partner.

Mo, who is boogying to the beat of Madonna's "Into the Groove" with Kyle, notices my mom on the sidelines and whispers something in Kyle's ear that sends him her way.

Earlier in the evening, in the receiving line, my mom and Kyle said hello. It was awkward and brief, my mom's eyes darting around, Kyle unsure of his place.

"Would you like to dance?" he says, his right hand extended in invitation.

My mom's eyes grow wide as she looks at the outstretched palm, and I feel her heart begin to race.

He continues to hold it in front of her, unflinching, an easy smile on his face.

No cold, no hunger, no thirst.

He wears a tuxedo. She wears a gown.

Chloe is not lost in the snow with Vance. My dad is not injured and bleeding. No one is waiting for her to save them.

His hand is bare, and so is hers.

Her fingers tremble as she reaches out, and that is when I feel it: the last golden thread dissolving as his hand wraps around hers and he helps her to her feet.

With the same athleticism that saved them, they glide across the dance floor, and I watch as the world lightens and the edges begin to glow, my mom and Kyle in the center, dancing in the brightness, until all that remains is light.

AUTHOR'S NOTE

Dear reader:

This story was inspired by an event that happened when I was eight years old. At the time, I was living in upstate New York. It was winter, and my dad and his best friend, "Uncle Bob," decided to take my older brother, me, and Uncle Bob's two boys for a hike in the Adirondacks. When we left that morning, the weather was crisp and clear, but somewhere near the top of the trail, the temperature dropped abruptly, the sky opened, and we found ourselves caught in a torrential, freezing blizzard.

My dad and Uncle Bob were worried we wouldn't make it down. We weren't dressed for that kind of cold, and we were hours from the base. Using a rock, Uncle Bob broke the window of an abandoned hunting cabin to get us out of the storm.

My dad volunteered to run down for help, leaving my brother Jeff and me to wait with Uncle Bob and his boys. My recollection of the hours we spent waiting for help to arrive is somewhat vague except for my visceral memory of the cold: my body shivering uncontrollably and my mind unable to think straight.

The four of us kids sat on a wooden bench that stretched the length of the small cabin, and Uncle Bob knelt on the floor in front of us. I remember his boys being scared and crying and Uncle Bob talking a lot, telling them it was going to be okay and that "Uncle Jerry" would be back soon. As he soothed their fear, he moved back and forth between them, removing their gloves and boots and rubbing each of their hands and feet in turn.

Jeff and I sat beside them, silent. I took my cue from my brother. He didn't complain, so neither did I. Perhaps this is why Uncle Bob never thought to rub our fingers and toes. Perhaps he didn't realize we, too, were suffering.

It's a generous view, one that as an adult with children of my own I have a hard time accepting. Had the situation been reversed, my dad never would have ignored Uncle Bob's sons. He might even have tended to them more than he did his own kids, knowing how scared they would have been being there without their parents.

Near dusk, a rescue jeep arrived, and we were shuttled down the mountain to waiting paramedics. Uncle Bob's boys were fine—cold and exhausted, hungry and thirsty, but otherwise unharmed. I was diagnosed with frostnip on my fingers, which it turned out was not so bad. It hurt as my hands were warmed back to life, but as soon as the circulation was restored, I was fine. Jeff, on the other hand, had first-degree frostbite. His gloves needed to be cut from his fingers, and the skin beneath was chafed, white, and blistered. It was horrible to see, and I remember thinking how much it must have hurt, the damage so much worse than my own.

No one, including my parents, ever asked Jeff or me what happened in the cabin or questioned why we were injured and Uncle Bob's boys were not, and Uncle Bob and Aunt Karen continued to be my parents' best friends.

This past winter, I went skiing with my two children, and as we rode the chairlift, my memory of that day returned. I was struck by how callous and uncaring Uncle Bob, a man I'd known my whole life and who I believed loved us, had been and also how unashamed he was after. I remember him laughing with the sheriff, like the whole thing was this great big adventure that had fortunately turned out okay. I think he even viewed himself as sort of a hero, boasting about how he'd broken the window and about his smart thinking to lead us to the cabin in the first place. When he got home, he probably told Karen about rubbing their sons' hands and feet and about how he'd consoled them and never let them get scared.

I looked at my own children beside me, and a shudder ran down my spine as I thought about all the times I had entrusted them to other people in the same way my dad had entrusted us to Uncle Bob, counting on the same naive presumption that a tacit agreement existed for my children to be cared for equally to their own. Amusement parks, the beach, the mall, vacations nearby and afar—each time assuming my kids would be looked after and that they would be in good hands.

This book is about a catastrophe, but the real story takes place after the catalyst, in the aftermath of the calamity, when the ramifications of the choices each of the survivors made come back to haunt them. I've always believed regret is the most difficult emotion to live with, but in order to have regret, you need to have a conscience: an interesting paradox that allows the worst of us to suffer the least in the aftermath of wrongdoing.

I chose to tell the story from the viewpoint of Finn in order to have a fly-on-the-wall perspective that allowed honest insight into the characters, even when they believed they were alone. Writing the story through Finn's eyes turned out to be a gift. Though she is not me, in many ways I wish I were more like her. Rarely do you get to write a character so pure in spirit. She holds a special place in my heart, and I hope you enjoyed reading her story as much as I enjoyed telling it.

Sincerely,
Suzanne

ACKNOWLEDGMENTS

Enormous thanks to the following people, without whom this book would not have been possible:

Kevan Lyon, my agent, who kept the faith and offered invaluable guidance.

Alicia Clancy, my editor, for "getting it" and providing insight and feedback that elevated the story to the next level.

My family, for simply being them and believing in pipe dreams and miracles.

My brother Jeff, for that long-forgotten day in the mountain and his bravery, and my dad, who heroically ran down the mountain for help.

The entire team at Lake Union, including Riam Griswold, Bill Siever, and Nicole Pomeroy, for turning a humble manuscript into the beautiful finished work it became.

Sally Eastwood, for reading it first. Halle and Cary, for reading it second. Lisa Hughes Anderson and my art sisters—Amy Eidt Jackson, Helen Pollins-Jones, Cindy Fletcher, Lauren Howell, Nancy Deline, Lisa Mansour, Jacquie Broadfoot, April Brian, and Sharon Hardy—for the mystical magic of our circle that continues to go round.

DISCUSSION QUESTIONS

1. Do you have children? If so, how often have you entrusted them to someone else? Have you ever considered the possibility of something catastrophic happening and, if that person were faced with the dire choice, whether your children would be taken care of? How about the reverse: Would you look after a friend's child as much as your own in the face of disaster? How much do you think we should trust someone else to look after our children?

2. Consider Ann as a mother. Do you think she was a good mother? How about at the start of the story? Do you think she was too harsh when Finn got in the fender bender? How do you feel about her relationship with Oz? Do you sympathize with her?

3. Chloe followed Vance into the storm, and when she couldn't go on, he left her. How do you feel about his abandonment? Do you sympathize with his decision? If the choice was both of them dying or him leaving her so he had a chance to live, does it make sense that he did what he did? Do you think he would make a different choice if placed in a similar situation now?

4. Ann gave Finn's boots to Mo instead of Natalie. Why do you think she made that choice? How would you feel if

your best friend did what Ann did—chose someone else's child over yours?

5. Kyle fell, and Ann made the split-second decision to release the scarf that held him so she wouldn't be pulled over the edge. How do you feel about the choice she made? What if he had died—would you feel differently?

6. How do you feel about Oz and the effect he had on the family? Jack admitted to sometimes feeling relieved that he was gone. Does that lessen your opinion of Jack? Consider where the Miller family might be had the accident not happened. Do you think something was saved that day as well as lost?

7. How do you feel about Kyle being a part of the accident? No one even bothered to ask him if he was okay. How much obligation do we have to a stranger?

8. After the accident, Bob was eager to help. He stepped up to do the news conference and was Ann's rock throughout the recovery. How do you feel about Bob? In your opinion, did he cross a criminal line? If so, where was that line: Sending Oz to look for Ann? Negotiating him out of his gloves for two packages of saltines? Sending Burns in the wrong direction to look for Oz to cover up his lie? How do you feel about him taking credit for Mo's survival ideas (closing up the camper with snow and melting the water)? Does it matter who got the credit? Do you think the way the story ended for Bob was just, or do you feel sorry for him, or do you think he deserved worse? Does it affect your opinion to know he did what he did to protect his wife and daughter?

9. Finn died, and the story was narrated from her omniscient view. Do you think your perception of the characters was altered because of her fly-on-the-wall perspective? If you

instead read the story from the characters' points of view, how might your opinion of them have changed (e.g., Bob had good reason to be terrified of Oz, and you felt his fear; you understood Vance's thinking in the moment he left Chloe, his belief that the only chance for either of them was for him to get help)?

10. Would you want to witness your own funeral? How about having a view of those you've left behind after you are gone?

11. The story deals a lot with death and how people cope with loss. Ann's approach was to purge the house of all remnants of Finn and Oz. Jack's was the opposite: he constantly tortured himself with their memory so as not to forget. How would you deal with such a loss? Finn didn't want the people she loved to be sad every time they thought of her. How do you think we should honor the dead? Do you think perhaps we should be happy when we think of them rather than sad?

12. Do you believe our humanity is determined more by circumstance than conscience, that if we are backed into a corner, our behavior will change? Do you think that in all of us there exists a base survival instinct of self-preservation that makes us capable of things we never believed ourselves capable of? Bob didn't set out that day to kill Oz or to neglect Mo. He set out to enjoy a weekend ski trip with his family and friends, and yet, because of him, Oz is dead. Oz didn't come back into the camper, and Mo didn't go after him. Is this the same as what Bob did? And if she is not to blame for her weakness, then is Bob to blame for his? Is Ann to blame for opening her hand when she held Kyle's life in her grip? Vance left the love of his life to freeze to death alone. Karen only looked

after Natalie. Natalie did nothing. Bob took Oz's gloves and sent him into the cold. Are people to be blamed for their cowardice or for being selfish because they are scared? Are we born with our strength? If so, should we condemn those who don't have it?

13. Are some lives worth more than others? If you had to choose between saving Mo or saving Oz, would the choice be a coin toss, or would other factors weigh in to the decision? How about Mo or Natalie? How about Kyle, a complete stranger, or Oz?

14. Have you ever been in a near-death situation? If so, are you proud of how you dealt with it, or do you have regrets?

15. After reading this story, do you feel differently about death, mourning, or the precious threads that tie you to this earth?

16. Who was your favorite character? Why?

17. Movie time: Who would you like to see play each part?

ABOUT THE AUTHOR

Photo © 2015 April Brian

Suzanne Redfearn is the award-winning author of three novels: *Hush Little Baby*, *No Ordinary Life*, and *In an Instant*. In addition to being an author, she's also an architect specializing in residential and commercial design. She lives in Laguna Beach, California, where she and her husband own two restaurants: Lumberyard and Slice Pizza and Beer. You can find her at her website, www.SuzanneRedfearn.com, on Facebook at SuzanneRedfearnAuthor, or on Twitter @SuzanneRedfearn.